Letters

for

Scarlet

a novel

Julie C. Gardner

velvet morning
press

Published by Velvet Morning Press

Copyright © 2016 by Julie C. Gardner

ISBN-13: 978-0692578728
ISBN-10: 0692578722

Cover design by Ellen Meyer and Vicki Lesage
Author photo by Ana Brandt Photography

Discover more from
JULIE C. GARDNER

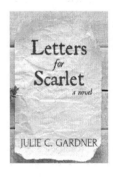  

For new releases, deals and a free ecopy
of *Running with Pencils*, sign up here:
http://bit.ly/runningwithpencils

To Bill and Jack and Karly
I love you more than all the words

Fall

Corie

I've always liked my nickname and the fact that those who are close to me have an easier time of it, subtracting a syllable from more formal introductions. *Corinna* is a mouthful, but *Corie* is simple, the way things should be when people are friends. Tuck digs even deeper, calling me *Core*, a single word that can be either a noun or a verb. Both imply a goal. Something central. Intimate. Four letters that unite this pair of opposites.

He's all action and go, go, go. I'm content with stillness, the noun of our relationship. Tucker is black hair and lashes like warm silk. I'm blond curls and eyes so icy-blue my sister said I was adopted from a wolf pack. She chanted *See-Through See-Through*, and I hated being pale. So thin. Practically transparent. Then one day Tuck Slater suggested I was *translucent in a good way*, and I began to count the number of times his skin chose my skin, to memorize the way his bones fit my bones.

That was a decade ago when we attended Conejo High, before I landed a job teaching literature instead of writing it. Parking in the faculty lot was uncomfortable at first. So was using everyone's first names.

Hey, John! Not Mr. Pickett.

Good morning, Bev! It still feels strange to call Mrs. Fox by her nickname.

What remains uncomfortable now is wondering what they

see when they greet me in the halls: Corinna the student, the John Keats wannabe, the one from "the terrible tragedy"; or Ms. Harper, the English teacher who scribbles in journals on her lunch breaks.

Today I've barely settled on a couch in the corner of our lounge when the new assistant principal strides toward me, skinny and fresh-faced, a bag of microwaved popcorn steaming in his hands. His cheeks shine with the hope of someone starting his career, and the sleeves of his oxford are rolled up at the wrists.

"Ms. Harper." He nods at me.

"Hello, Mr. Callaghan."

He's wearing glasses of the Clark Kent variety, and his dark hair spikes upward like a head full of licorice. "That smells good." He indicates the frozen meal in my lap. "Chicken parmesan?"

"I think so," I say. "I just grab whatever my husband puts in the freezer." I shove a forkful of mozzarella into my mouth, but after I chew and swallow, he's still studying me, eyes round and quizzical.

"Mr. Harper does the grocery shopping?" he asks.

"Slater," I say. "Mr. Slater. Harper is my maiden name."

"Ah. Progressive choice."

I shake my head. "It's less *progress* and more *I hate going to the market*. Tucker—that's my husband—he's great, but he hates to cook. So he buys the groceries, and I make the food. You could say we take on each other's bigger hate. So to speak." I inhale a chunk of chicken to stop myself from rambling, and Mr. Callaghan smiles at me.

"Sounds equitable," he says. "But I was referring to the fact that you use your maiden name."

"Oh!" I cough on the chicken chunk, and my forehead warms to the point of sweating. "No," I manage to say. "You see, Harper was the name on my credential, and then my dad died, and I decided to stay a Harper. For him. Not that he would have expected me to. I just thought it was the right thing to do. And easier too."

So much for not rambling.

Mr. Callaghan sets down his bag of popcorn and takes a

seat on the opposite end of the couch. He smells like aftershave and hot butter. "I'm sorry about your father."

"It's been a while, but thanks." I picture my dad's kind face, his strong hands. I drop my chin, and my hair is a drape of white-blond curls along my neck.

"Anyway." Mr. Callaghan exhales as if he might clear the awkwardness in one gust. "I came over here for a reason." His voice is softer now but still deep. I lift my head to hear him better and catch Stella Womack and Bart Kominski grinning at me from across the room.

Great.

"I wanted to compliment you on your lesson yesterday," says Mr. Callaghan.

"I got a copy of your evaluation this morning," I tell him. "You were very generous."

"It's not easy to act natural when you're being observed. But your class? It was a pleasure."

"Thanks again, Mr. Callaghan."

"Please," he says. "Call me Henry. We've been working together for a month. I think it's time."

"Has it been only a month?" I ask. "This school year's really dragging." I paste on a smile in case he doesn't have a sense of humor. Henry nudges his glasses higher on his nose.

"I hope you don't mind if I call you Corinna," he says. Behind him Bart and Stella wave and blow kisses.

"Nope," I say. Then I set down my fork and pick up the pencil next to my journal. "But I'd better get back to writing. No rest for the weary."

"No rest for anyone on this couch." His small laugh is reassuring. Henry Callaghan likes to joke. "It should be against the law," he says. "Or at least a health code violation."

"That's funny," I tell him. *A little*, I think.

"It's true," he tells me back. "I'll leave you to your work, then."

I look up at him. "My what?"

"Work," he says again. "I see you writing in that journal every day. Concentrating. Serious. I figure it must be pretty important."

My forehead grows even warmer, and I worry I might

blush. "No one ever calls my writing work. Not even Tuck."

"Then let me be the first."

"Do I have a choice?" My smile is crooked. "After all, you are the boss."

"So I am," he says. "But don't forget. It's Henry."

He pushes himself up off the couch and collects his bag of popcorn. When he stands, I notice his pants could use a decent ironing. Then, as Henry Callaghan walks across the lunchroom and out the door, I watch him go from under lowered lashes.

৩৽৶

For my afternoon classes I write these instructions on the board:

- *Read the poem at your desk.*

- *On the paper below the poem, share what you think the poet implies about IDENTITY.*

- *After five minutes, pass your poem to the left and repeat the process.*

When the bell rings, the students amble into the room in packs and take their seats.

"How much do we have to write?" they ask.

"There's no minimum or maximum," I say. "Just tell me how you feel."

"I feel tired," says Greer Larson. "I need caffeine."

"Trust your instincts," I suggest. "Trust yourself."

"What if my instincts are telling me to go to Starbucks?"

I shake my head. "You have five minutes per poem. Starting now." I check the wall clock and make a mental note of when to tell my students to stop trusting themselves and pass what they have written to the left. I'm collecting the papers from my sixth period class when I begin to feel the ache. It is dull. Familiar. Regular as the tide. A hand slides to my stomach as the kids stack their work in the wire bin next to my computer.

I tell them, "Don't forget to check out your copy of *Inferno* from the library by Friday," although it has been written on the white board for a week. As they exit the classroom, I ask

Troy Solomon to shut the door behind him. A stump of a boy with ferocious acne, Troy waves at me from the hallway.

"See ya, Ms. Harper."

Another cramp tugs at me, emptying my insides without permission. I listen for the click of the door latch and fumble in my purse for a tampon and liner.

After dinner Tuck washes dishes while I remain in the dining room with a folder of student essays. I mark them with purple ink instead of red and try to write at least one positive comment for each critique. Sometimes the writing is so bad I'm stuck with *Good choice of college-ruled paper* or *Thanks for removing the raggedy edges from the left side of the page.*

Greer Larson's character analysis of Sydney Carton seems especially awful, but the truth is, I am harboring a negative attitude like a fugitive in an attic. Since leaving school today, I've cradled it, this lump of sadness swaddled in my arms. The failure leaves room for nothing else. It's all I see now, what I look for.

Tucker enters the room so quietly I do not notice him at first. Since my sister and her children moved in with us, Tuck and I have taken to creeping around on tiptoes. But tonight the kids are with their father, and Bets won't be back from her night shift until morning. Tuck clears his throat, and I look up. He has changed out of his work clothes into gray sweatpants and my favorite of his T-shirts. The cotton is faded red, frayed by frequent washings. From ten feet away my husband smells like Tide.

"Almost done in here?" he asks.

"Never," I tell him. "Ever."

"Give 'em all As and take me to bed." He grins, and I imagine I could fit my whole thumb in his dimple.

"I wish. Didn't you bring any work home from your trip?"

"Just a suitcase." He takes the pen from me and sets it on the table. "Come on, Core. These kids won't spontaneously combust if they don't get their essays back tomorrow."

"No," I admit. "They won't." I study my empty hand and

remind myself that Tuck doesn't mean to minimize my career. He values teachers and me in particular. But the way his words erase my goals—even in jest—leaves me feeling hollow. Unimportant. Less than.

Act full, Corie. You have so much already.

"I missed you this week," I tell him.

"Don't you always miss me?"

"Hmm," I say by way of agreement. He pulls out the chair next to me, and I push my gradebook away. I can make room for him. I will.

"I forgot to ask how your evaluation went with the new guy. What's his name? Calloway?"

"Callaghan. Henry Callaghan." I picture his spiked hair and wrinkled pants, hear him calling the words in my journal *work*. "He's on the young side. Not much older than I am." My lips are dry, and they crack on a smile. Tuck shifts in his seat and appraises me.

"He any good?"

I consider the question. "I have no idea," I say.

Tucker prompts me with a tilt of his head. "Come on. What does your gut tell you?"

"Stella and Bart haven't organized a lunchtime protest against him yet. I guess that qualifies as good." Before Tuck can push any deeper, a cramp cuts through the center of me, and a grimace replaces my smile.

"Hey, hey," he says. "You all right?"

"Yep," I tell him, although I'm not.

"Headache?"

"No," I say. "Unfortunately, it's not a headache."

"Oh." Tuck studies my face for the answer he already knows. "I'm sorry, Core."

"I'm sorry too."

He stands and puts a hand on my shoulder. "Guess I'll shower and unpack."

"I'll finish up here soon," I say. "Promise." When he leaves, I stuff the essays in my book bag and grab some Advil from the lidless container above the refrigerator. Throwing away the childproof tops is a habit Tuck hasn't broken.

They're a pain in the ass, and we don't have kids.

Yet, I tell him. *Not yet.*

Filling a glass with water, I swallow three tablets. Then, once I hear the shower running, I pluck my cell phone from its charger. Almost a year has passed since I tried the number, and I enter it quickly before losing my nerve. Eleanor Hinden never answers anyway. Each time, I get her answering machine with the same old message Scarlet and I recorded more than a decade ago. I like to listen and hang up without saying a word. I'm simply being kind, making sure Scarlet's mother is all right. Still, I don't tell Tuck about the calls. He would claim they're motivated by something else entirely.

Tonight the phone rings four times, and I await our giggled greeting. Scarlet's voice with my bright laughter in the background. A bridge across ten long years. Instead, there is a hiccup followed by the robotic sounds of the default message: *No one is available to take your call; please leave your name and number at the beep, and someone will get back to you as soon as possible.*

Truth settles in the pit of me, a friendship replaced by the programmed lines of a stranger. Scarlet has finally left me.

Forever.

Scarlet

She expected to be tired. Perhaps even exhausted. But emptied as a chrysalis? That came as a surprise. If she hadn't been so damn hungry, she would have fallen asleep while proofreading the motion. Her stomach growled, demanding another bagel. Fortunately Gavin liked her body lush. Full-breasted. Hour-glassy. Scarlet blew a strand of mahogany hair out of her mouth, then licked her lips.

At lunch she remained at her desk checking voicemail, a half-empty carton of beef broccoli in her lap. First up was Izzy Garcia wondering when Scarlet would be back in yoga class. *Wondering that myself,* she thought, erasing Izzy's message. The next call came from Mama, but before Scarlet could play it, she was interrupted by a text from Gavin.

Dinner. You. Yum.

She pictured him now. The untamed thatch of carroty hair. Lids heavy over bottle-green eyes. This was like him, offering a few quick words to connect, to let her know he was thinking of her. Their offices were in separate wings after all, their days overly full. Time rushed by in brief increments. Billable minutes. *Productivity.* But from the moment they had become a couple, long before she agreed to move in with him, Gavin would anticipate her needs. Physical. Emotional. Even when she didn't want the attention. Especially when she didn't. While she squirmed, uncomfortable with his easy affection, Gavin would draw closer to her both figuratively and literally. Each time, the man kept trying until she caved.

Yes, I know you love me, she'd say. *But why? You could have anyone.*

"That's the point," he liked to tell her. "I love a challenge, and you are the very best one."

A challenge. The best. Perfect words to crack her shell. Right now she needed strength, though. To lean on logic, not her heart. Most of all, Scarlet needed to believe she'd be OK. Her finger hovered over the message from Mama still waiting to be heard. *Not yet,* she decided, shoving her phone into her purse. *It isn't time.* Besides. Young attorneys at Olson, Brickman & Steinway were not supposed to deal with personal issues at work.

They also weren't supposed to close their eyes and take a nap.

⚮

For Gavin's sake Scarlet tried to be lively at dinner, nodding through his update on the morning's discovery, picking at cubes of beets in The Cellar's enormous Cobb. She nibbled a slice of avocado. Coaxed her lips into an upswing. But when she frowned at the lemon slice in her water glass and scooped it with a spoon, Gavin stopped her.

"We can ask for a drink without lemon," he said.

"No, it's fine. But if I wanted lemonade, I would've ordered some." She deposited the sliver of fruit onto a saucer next to a cup of bleu cheese dressing. "Why do restaurants serve this lemon-water hybrid that doesn't taste like either one?"

"Maybe they think it's refreshing."

Her eyes, both the color and shape of toasted almonds, blinked at Gavin. "Maybe they're wrong."

When their stiff-haired waiter Esteban brought him a second martini, Gavin shot Scarlet a grin across the table. "Drinking for two," he said.

"Enjoy it, sir," gushed Esteban. Then he turned his attention to Scarlet whose skin had drained of color. "And how is everything tasting?" he asked. "Do we require anything else?"

"Esteban," answered Gavin gamely, "we require a fresh glass of water with no lemon. For the lady." The waiter glanced around the restaurant as if he had been caught failing a test.

"Whatever," he grumbled. His fine-dining pretense collapsed as he stalked across the restaurant and disappeared behind the kitchen's double doors.

Scarlet leaned over her salad bowl. "I told you I was fine."

"I know what you told me. I was improvising based on how you look."

"How do I look?"

Gavin took a long sip of his drink and smiled. "More beautiful than ever," he said. Then he tucked into his meal, a hunk of salmon gleaming on a bed of wild rice.

"Oh," said Scarlet as a wave of nausea ambushed her.

"Want a bite?" Gavin extended his fork across the table, but the smell of garlic and rosemary made her gag.

"No!" she blurted out. He dropped his fork, a clatter on the plate.

Get a grip, she told herself. *You love salmon. You love garlic and rosemary. For God's sake, you love Gavin.* Still, she fought the urge to knock his second martini into his lap.

"I'm sorry," she told him.

"Sorry that you don't want to try my fish?" He smiled again. "You are forgiven."

"Gavin, don't."

His shoulders sank, and he leaned back in his chair. "What do you want me to say, then? You cut me off whenever I try to talk seriously about the… our… future. Now you don't want me to make jokes. Tell me, Scarlet. Please. What *am* I allowed to discuss?"

"I don't know."

"Well. We're obviously free to apologize, so I'll say sorry too. Sorry that I'm making you unhappy tonight." She shook her head, bit her lip. "And whether or not you want to hear this," he continued, "you should know I fully support whatever you decide to do about our… situation."

"Our *situation*?" she repeated in a whisper.

"I can't call it *our baby*. Not until I know what you're planning to do." Gavin's eyes were wet at the edges. "I'm on board with the whole woman's right-to-choose thing. I am. But I can't pretend to be indifferent about your decision."

"My decision."

"Yes," he said. "Yours."

Blood rushed to her cheeks, thickened her tongue. This was far too big for her to handle on her own. "Gav," she began, then she spotted Esteban hurrying toward them with a glass of clear water and a dish of maraschino cherries, lemon slices and wedges of lime.

"In case you change your mind," said the waiter, baring two rows of teeth. "A woman's prerogative, no?"

"That's right," said Gavin. He sucked an olive from the bottom of his martini glass, and Esteban shifted his weight.

"Did we save room for dessert?" the waiter asked. Scarlet shook her head again.

"It seems the lady is saying 'no,'" Gavin said. "And what the lady wants, the lady gets. Or doesn't get. Either way."

"Gav." She brought the tips of her fingers to her lips. "If you'd like—"

"It's fine, Scar. Really. A woman's prerogative, no?" He turned to Esteban. "When you get the chance, would you please wrap up the rest of our meal?"

"As you wish." The waiter produced the bill from a pocket in his apron and began to gather their plates. "I'll just grab a couple of take-out boxes for you and be right back."

Scarlet opened her mouth to ask Gavin if he, in fact, would like to split some cheesecake, but instead she began coughing until she threw up on Esteban's rubber-soled loafers. The horrified waiter gaped, eyes tracing the spittle from her lips down to the puddle at his feet.

Gavin handed him a credit card and cleared his throat.

"Esteban, my friend," he said, "I don't suppose we'll need those take-out boxes after all."

ふくく

The next morning Scarlet awoke so green and shaky, she

feared Clara would inquire about her health and raise
suspicions among their curious coworkers. Perhaps it was the
volume of Clara's voice or the intermittent accent she'd
nurtured since her family moved here from London. Maybe
the associates at Olson Brickman were especially prone to
gossip. Whatever the reason, Clara's words were famous for
circumnavigating the office, and Scarlet planned to forestall
any rumors.

"Bloody hell!" squawked Clara. She shook her head, and
her sleek bob, a few shades lighter than Scarlet's mahogany,
brushed her chin. She wore red lipstick, a skin-tight pencil
skirt and four-inch heels that would have been scandalous
were it not for the tailored blouse she had paired with them.
"How long have you been up the duff?"

"Shhh!" Scarlet grabbed Clara's arm and dragged her into
an empty conference room. The smell of leather assaulted her
nose, and Scarlet steadied herself against a high-backed chair.

"Hey now," Clara said. "Take it easy."

"I'm trying to, believe me. But Patricia and Alice have
been eyeing me all week, and being pregnant isn't exactly a
career catalyst these days."

"Exactly when was it, ever?"

"Good point." Scarlet collapsed into the seat. "Will you
promise to keep this between us?"

"It's your business, isn't it? You know you can trust me."
Of course Scarlet knew, had known for almost ten years, since
they'd lived together in the dorms at Berkeley. "I take it your
condition wasn't planned?" Clara asked.

"God no!"

"Then what happened? I need details."

Scarlet took a breath, lifted an eyebrow. "I didn't think
you of all people would be in need of a refresher. But the
penis goes in the vagina—"

"Right, then." Clara folded her arms, stuck out her chin.
"I see pregnancy hasn't killed your razor-sharp sense of
humor."

For the first time in days Scarlet hazarded a smile. Her
friend still found her funny, a small consolation. When the two
of them first met, Scarlet had all but forgotten how to laugh,

and it was Clara who had brought her back to life. The Clara Broxton Cyclone blew onto campus armed with two trunks of clothes and a dirty mind. But it was her warm heart and stone-cold loyalty that finally knocked down Scarlet's walls.

"So tell me." Clara leaned her petite frame against the conference table. "What was Gavin's reaction when he found out he was going to be a papa?"

"I didn't use those words. Not precisely."

Clara smirked. "I didn't expect you to call him *papa*. I meant how is the charming Mr. Newstedt taking the news about becoming a daddy?"

She considered Clara's question. How *was* Gavin handling the pregnancy? He had promised to remain neutral, said he wouldn't attempt to sway her decision. Yet she would catch him peeking at her stomach as she undressed, and he was quick to bring her water or a snack at the end of a long workday. When she pointed out any special treatment, he would say, *Can't a gentleman spoil his lady?* Then he'd cover her legs with a blanket.

Scarlet decided to let herself be spoiled.

"Gav's playing it close to the vest," she told Clara. "He says he'll support whatever I decide to do. But I think he's already half in love with the idea of being a father." Scarlet inhaled deeply, heart thrumming in her chest. "God, Clare. I don't want to hurt him."

"No, I'd imagine not." Clara's steady gaze unnerved her. There were few things Scarlet had managed to hide from her friend for very long. "So, what *are* you planning to do?"

"I have no idea," she said. "I do know I'm totally unprepared to handle a baby. Especially on my own."

Clara frowned. "But you're not alone, are you? I mean, you're pretty well stuck with me. And you've already got Gavin. And he's—well—he's Gavin, isn't he? The man adores you, and I can't imagine you being pregnant changes anything. Except perhaps to make him love you more. For heaven's sake, you are having his baby."

Scarlet's jaw felt suddenly loose, as if it had come unhinged and might crack off entirely. "But what if I'm not?"

"Not what?" asked Clara. "Having it?" Scarlet pressed her

fingertips to her eyelids, and Clara sucked in a breath. "Oh, shitshitshit," she muttered, bending over Scarlet.

"I'm not going to cry," she told Clara, surrendering to the fold of her friend's arms. But Clara's neat shelf of hair smelled of cantaloupe shampoo, and Scarlet stiffened, recoiling at the scent.

"Are you quite all right?" Clara asked. "Let me pour you some coffee."

"I'm off caffeine these days. I thought you'd have caught on by now."

"You've given up coffee?" Clara narrowed her eyes and examined Scarlet's face. "You do realize you're keeping this baby, don't you? Oh, Scarlet. You so are."

"Honestly, I can't see much beyond five minutes from now. But I could use some plain hot water if you wouldn't mind getting me some."

Clara nodded.

"With lemon?" asked Scarlet.

"Brilliant. I'll be right back."

"Not here," she said. "I'll meet you in the courtyard."

ஓ∾ல

Scarlet was slouched on a concrete bench just outside their building when Clara approached with a cup of hot water and several lemon wedges. "Until now, I despised lemon water," Scarlet said. "But I guess all the normal is being leeched from me."

Clara took a seat beside her. "I have to admit you do look awful."

Scarlet squeezed lemon juice into her cup. "That's shocking because I feel absolutely fabulous." She lifted the Styrofoam to her cheek, and the heat sent a shiver up her spine.

Clara inched closer to her. "We're going to figure this out together," she said. "After all, I'm the smartest person I know. Besides you, of course. When you're not being stupid."

Scarlet sighed. "I didn't want to get you involved, Clare. Especially before I've decided what to… and if I…" Rather than finish the thought, she sipped her hot lemony water.

"Don't be ridiculous," Clara said. "You've rescued me from my own messes too many times to count. Just accept it: There's no way you're getting rid of me."

"All right then. If you insist."

Clara studied Scarlet's pale face. "Have you been very sick?"

"I've been in denial. Which is sort of the same thing."

"I can't imagine what your mother's got to say about all this," said Clara. "From what you've told me, Eleanor's bad on a good day. I don't suppose she's suddenly become supportive."

Scarlet's body went rigid, and she set her cup down on the bench. "Mama doesn't know yet. But she'll figure out something's up when I go home for Thanksgiving. She'll take one look at these breasts of mine and—"

"So don't," said Clara. "Go home, I mean. You were just there in August."

"But I promised I'd come back for the holidays if she behaved."

"She didn't though, did she?"

"Barely." Scarlet's face was grim. "Can you picture the dinner conversation? *No, Mama. I'm not engaged to Gavin yet. But I've got great news! You're going to be a grandmother. Please pass the cranberry sauce.*"

"With any luck, you'll have a miscarriage by then."

"Jesus, Clare! And you ask if I'm sick!"

"Was that sick? I was aiming for practical." She nudged Scarlet with her elbow. "Come on now. I was only kidding. Trying to cheer you up."

Scarlet nudged her back. "Thanks, but there's nothing anyone can do to make me feel better now."

Clara took Scarlet's hand. "Stay here, then. Have Thanksgiving at my place instead of Eleanor's."

"I don't know."

"It's the only solution, really. Whoever said 'there's no place like home' was completely cracked."

"That's from *The Wizard of Oz.* After Dorothy's house blew away in a tornado."

"Right," Clara said. "Poor girl."

"Hardly." Scarlet's laugh sounded more like a moan. "Dorothy didn't have a mother, remember? God, Clare. How lucky could she be?"

Corie

The alarm clock on Tuck's nightstand wails, and I fling myself across the bed to smack it silent. Stumbling to the bathroom, I splash cold water on my face and assess the damage done since last night's shower. Not bad but not good yet. So I finger-scrunch my bedhead curls, swipe mascara on pale lashes. Then, while I'm brushing my teeth, I smell the bacon.

Ma is here.

Through a crack in the door, I spy a blur of blond rearranging pillows against our headboard: My mother in pleated slacks, her real estate agent's badge pinned to a trim blazer. She is hustling as usual. Brisk and efficient. Laura Harper always rushes like she's late.

"Hmmph, mmmph." Toothpaste drips down my chin, and I return to the sink to rinse my mouth. When I emerge from the bathroom, I find my mother fluffing the cloud of our duvet.

"Thanks, but you don't have to do that, Ma."

Over her shoulder she says, "I made pancakes!"

"Pancakes *and* bacon? That's a lot of breakfast for a Tuesday."

She turns and perches at the foot of my bed. "Just trying to put some meat on those skinny bones of yours."

"Bones can't be skinny," I say. "And I've got plenty of meat."

"Is your husband aware of that?"

I meet her gaze. "Did you pull your ponytail too tight this morning?"

"No." She sniffs. "As a matter of fact I didn't."

I suppress a twinge of guilt for teasing her about the trick she claims will keep her from the Botox. "Sorry, Ma," I tell her.

"You didn't mention Tucker would be gone overnight again," she says.

"Like I said, sorry."

"I appreciate knowing if he's going to be here, that's all. Last week I thought he was away, and when I let myself in, I found him sitting at the kitchen table in his underpants."

"It's his kitchen."

"So it is," she says. "But until your sister's off the graveyard shift, somebody has to show up at the crack of dawn to help out with the kids."

I take a breath, remind myself I'm glad Bets moved in with us. The arrangement is temporary and kind. What *good family* does. And with our niece and nephew living here, it's almost like Tuck and I have children of our own.

"Believe me, Ma," I say. "We all appreciate the fact that you're the *somebody* who helps. But please. No more comments about Tuck's job. I'm begging you."

"It's just… I don't know how he can stand it." She unfurls a shred of tissue from her sleeve as if by magic. "All that blood." She dabs at her nose. "Day in. Day out. And through the night, even. So much time spent in hospitals instead of at home."

"Thanks for not commenting," I say. Ma's eyes remain steady above her Kleenex, my sarcasm beading off her like water on duck feathers. "At least Tuck enjoys what he does," I add. "Not everyone can say that."

"I like my job."

"See? Then you get it. He sells spine implants. You sell houses. You're practically in the same line of business."

"I never thought of it like that." Ma shrugs, and her magic tissue disappears. "We're just a couple of salespeople, aren't we?"

"Exactly." I nod. "Exactly."

Gathering clean socks and underwear from the dresser, I move to the closet and select black pants and a thin wool sweater. From behind me my mother appears and squats in a pile of shoes. After a minute of fussing she hands me boots, tall leather ones with a buckle across the zipper. "Wear these today," she says. "That new principal of yours might be young, but he won't think you're administrative material if you show up in sneakers."

I could tell her that Mr. Callaghan is only an *assistant* principal with no say in my position. Or that by October, most teachers at Conejo High have abandoned formality for the comfort of jeans and T-shirts. There's also this truth: I have no desire to be any sort of school administrator. Ever. But I keep my mouth shut. Let Ma embrace a professional goal she can understand. My becoming a *writer-of-some-kind, someday* is really kind of vague. Or so my mother's told me more than once.

I take the boots from her and slip them on.

"That's the ticket, Corie! Now you're acting like a winner!"

Ma claps twice to urge me along before bustling downstairs to feed the kids. By the time I finish dressing and join her in the kitchen, the three of them have eaten all the pancakes.

Campbell, who just turned nine, hops up first. "Wella wants to watch TV!"

"Cam does too!" she howls. She is six years old and feisty. Hands on hips. A practiced glare.

I pretend to weigh the options, a finger to my lips. "I think you two can squeeze in some screen time before I take you to school." At this, Cam and Wella offer up a collaborative whoop and tumble over each other racing toward the den.

"Not so loud," Ma warns them both. "Your mother is still sleeping."

"OK!" Cam shouts from the hall.

Ma sighs. "He needs to practice being quiet."

"We all do," I tell my mother. "We all do."

After rummaging in the refrigerator, I decide on a carton of blueberry yogurt while Ma heads to the sink with the breakfast dishes. She scrapes syrup from the plates as the sink fills with hot soapy water. From the den comes the sound of laughter.

"They're growing up to be such great kids," Ma says. "Even though…" Her sentence tapers off, but I finish it in my head.

"I wish I could make them stay young forever," I tell her.

"If you had children of your own," she says, "you would realize you can't *make* them do anything." She shuts off the faucet and spins around. "Oh, Corie. I didn't mean—"

"Believe me, Ma," I interrupt. "No one wants me pregnant more than I do. And Tuck, of course."

"Of course." We are both silent for a moment.

"Can you pick the kids up from school?" I ask. "I've got an errand to run after work."

Ma nods.

"Tuck should be home by five o'clock."

Her lips bend like a pretzel. "Don't mind me, Corie. You know I've got a big old mouth."

I'm tempted to tell her if she stopped making that face, she probably wouldn't need Botox. Instead I tell her, "Ma, I'm OK. Really."

ॐ᭜

It's five-thirty by the time I slip through the front door, a pink-striped lingerie bag swinging at my side. This month's purchase is white and lacy. Sexy but still virginal. I cannot wait for Tuck to see me in it.

"I'm home," I call out, and my husband ambles around the corner in low-slung jeans and a vintage T-shirt.

"Sorry I'm late." I hold up the pink bag. "Purchasing inspiration for later."

"I do like to be inspired." He crosses the room to wrap his arms around me. His black hair is damp, and a scruff of chin nuzzles my neck.

"You smell good," I say. "Did you just shower?"

"Mmm hmm. Cleaning up for my lady."

Over his hunched shoulder I see our picnic basket on the floor. I step back, and he releases me. "What's the basket all about?"

"It's about your love of sandwiches."

"Roast beef on sourdough?"

Tuck smiles. "Naturally." His dark eyes cut to our coffee table where my sister's keys are puddled in an abalone dish.

"Bets hasn't left yet?" I move to the sofa, set down my bag.

"She's resting up before her night shift. Hence the picnic. I figured this way, we could still be together. But, you know. Somewhere else."

"What about Cam and Wella?"

"I told the kids to beat it."

"Be serious."

"Seriously? Your mother offered to take them out for pizza and a movie. I heard her say something like 'Aunt Corie and Uncle Tucker could *really* use the alone time.'" We lock eyes, and I picture the shake of Ma's head filling in the blanks of her opinion. "It was a good idea in theory." He pauses. "But that was before."

"Forget about Bets." I saunter toward him, lift a brow. "I'm not above a little romance in the flatbed of your truck. Park over by the Chumash preserve, and I'm all yours. Just like old times."

"Core." He stops me, a hand on my elbow. "I appreciate your... flexibility." After a beat he adds, "But something came up."

My stomach twists in all too familiar knots. "What is it?"

"You know I'd rather be with you than Dr. Kahn, right?"

"But."

"She added on a case at Memorial."

"Oh, Tuck, no. You have to drive to LA? Now?"

Instead of answering me he sighs. We've both heard my mother tell homebuyers that Conejo Springs is *just a frog's leap* from downtown. "Twenty miles of rolling hills," she says. "And the chaparral is beautiful." But in traffic it can take more than an hour.

"They're setting up the operating room," Tuck says, "then bringing in the patient. I'm not sure how long I've got. I'll keep calling in until they're ready for me."

"But you're flying to Portland in the morning," I remind him. "Until Friday."

"All the more reason to squeeze in some fun while we can."

"Fun." I clear my throat to dislodge the lump. "Right."

"Come on, Core." He runs a finger along the ridge of my ear. "I miss you already. Don't make me feel worse."

"Fine." I try to smile. I feel like a mannequin with a plastic face. "But there'd better be wine in this girl's future."

"I've got a bottle chilling in the fridge as we speak. I'm so prepared I could've been a Boy Scout."

I laugh, despite myself. "You were a Boy Scout."

Tuck grins. "I'll be right back." He heads to the kitchen while I grab a couple of blankets in case we have time to visit the flatbed. Then he returns with the cold Chardonnay, a wine opener and a pair of red solo cups. "I almost forgot." He sets our supplies beside the basket. "There's another surprise in here."

"Is it *two* bottles of wine?"

"It's a letter," he tells me. "Your mother left it for you. Said it was delivered to her mailbox today. The envelope looks kind of old." Tuck lifts the lid of the basket. "It says DO NOT OPEN but it's covered in hearts and peace signs. Addressed to Miss Corinna Marie Harper."

Corinna Marie.

I suck in a breath as if ten years might dissolve upon my lips.

Exhale, Corie. Now.

"Can I see the letter? Please?"

"I think that can be arranged." Tuck digs below a stack of beverage napkins and slides a thick envelope from under the picnic supplies. Holding it out to me, he says, "Just promise you'll model whatever you've got inside that pink bag when I come home Friday."

I nod and take the letter from him. The flap peels away in jagged tears revealing a stack of triple-folded pages.

"Oh," I say. "Oh."

"You all right?" he asks. "Core?" But I hardly hear his question.

I'm far too busy visiting a ghost.

Dear Corie,

It's weird writing to Future You, but Mr. Roosevelt swears this ten-year-letter assignment will get easier if we keep putting words down one after the other—like in those stream-of-consciousness exercises from the James Joyce unit. I guess I'll take his word for it.

(Mr. Roosevelt, not James Joyce!)

I kind of admire Mr. Roosevelt's attempt to "fight the good fight" against technology, especially since he's not even that ancient. He says there is something noble and elegant about a hand-written letter—that the scratch of pencil or the whisper of a pen is more inspiring than keyboard clicks.

I wouldn't say this out loud—I mean, who wants to admit being old-fashioned to your friends? But I agree with him. After all, Neil Gaiman and Jhumpa Lahiri write their books out longhand, and they are as modern and talented as any other novelists. So if a legal pad and pencil works for them, it works for me. (I wonder if they digress as much as I do?)

Anyway, if this experiment has worked, you are twenty-eight years OLD and reading what I, your eighteen-year-old self, am hoping will be true ten years from now. So in no particular order, here goes:

- *I hope I've finally got my own car so I don't have to drive Dad's Dragon Wagon*
- *and that I've got my own apartment so I don't have to share a bathroom with Bets*
- *and that I'm well on my way to being a successful writer*
- *and I hope hope hope that Scarlet has forgiven me.*

You and Tuck are telling her tonight. About each other. About Berkeley. The whole truth. Finally. Which is why you are feeling a bit sick right now, afraid she won't understand. It's not that you don't love her; it's that you and Tuck are IN love with each other. Going away to school with Scarlet would have been good. No, it would have been great! But you and Tuck simply have to be together even if it means breaking a promise. (Side note: Admitting that I'm in love with Tucker Slater in actual words gives me goose bumps. I wish he was in Mr. Roosevelt's class so he could write his own letter too.)

Anyway, you have already reached your most important goal (Tuck!), and I'm sure ten years has been more than enough time for you to achieve that second goal. So tell me:

Do you love love love being a mom? And do you always respect your children's privacy unlike your own mother? (I wrote that last part in case you're reading this, Ma, even though I specifically wrote DO NOT OPEN on the envelope. You're so busted! Just kidding. I love you, Ma. Mostly.)

Well, that's pretty much it, which is good because I'm running out of time.

So for now I'll say "Goodbye." And I guess I'm also saying "Hello." Which is pretty mind-blowing if you think about it. It's like two realities existing at the same time: I'm writing this now, but you are also reading this now. I think it's what we writers call a paradox. Kind of like life.

Still and always,
Corinna Marie Harper (Slater)

P.S. Mr. Roosevelt, if you're reading this, you're right. It did get easier.
P.P.S. Scarlet Hinden thinks you're hot. No joke.

Scarlet

A pink sky filled the window, day breaking over steep streets. Outside, rows of houses huddled together like frosted cupcakes. From the bedroom, a rustle of sheets. Gavin is restless in his sleep.

Please don't wake up. Not yet. In socked feet she padded to the kitchen.

The coffeemaker gurgled through its brew cycle, and the scent of dark roast filled the air. She would have liked a cup, could have used the liquid heat. October mornings were chilly near the bay. Instead she moved up the thermostat and belted her bathrobe before retrieving the *San Francisco Chronicle* from the mat.

Their mat. Why was this so hard for her to remember?

They'd been dating only four weeks when he first asked her to move in with him, and she had made him wait six months before agreeing.

At first, Gavin's stiff couches and stainless appliances had screamed "Bachelor Pad!" to her. She added paisley throw pillows. A pair of ceramic lamps. Even a houseplant she had managed to keep alive. And yet she could not escape the nagging fear that this 900-square-foot space was not her home. That once she made it hers, he would decide to leave. Taking off without warning was what men did, wasn't it?

No. Not Gavin.

This was her issue—not his. She knew that. What she

didn't know was how to make it stop.

Sliding the plastic off the newspaper, Scarlet centered *The Chronicle* on the table—their table—in front of Gavin's chair. Then she found her phone and curled up on the cushion of the window seat to make the call. *Better to dial quickly and not think too much.* When she thought too much, she always got cold feet.

"Hey, Mama," she said when Eleanor answered. "Did I wake you?"

Scarlet spoke quietly, hoping Gavin wouldn't hear the conversation and that her mother wouldn't detect her false enthusiasm.

Eleanor's reply came to her in waves.

"Scarlet? Is that you? What a surprise."

Really? Mama shouldn't have been surprised. For ten years Scarlet had labored to piece together what remained of her broken family. Making phone calls every Sunday. Taking weekend trips back home. But as Eleanor grew more hostile, Scarlet's visits became less frequent. Neither one could stand the memories. A revival of shared pain.

"Come 'ere," Mama would slur from one corner of the couch. Scarlet would move to her side and sit. Not too close, though. *Keep your distance.*

"You look tired," her mother would say, her breath so hot and sour.

"Can I get you something, Mama?"

She would frown. "You've done enough."

Later, when Eleanor slept, Scarlet would explore her childhood home, ignoring the smell of dirty scalp and linens that needed changing. Room by room, she traveled slowly, collecting empty bottles, wiping counters. That done, she'd touch her mother's gray forehead, a cool palm on papery skin. *I'm sorry,* she would whisper. *Mama. Please forgive me.*

Eleanor wheezed now into the phone. "Scarlet? What's wrong?"

"Nothing," she said.

"But it's Tuesday."

Scarlet gulped, and the taste of metal coated her mouth. "I had time this morning, and you're usually up early."

"You all right, then?"

"I think so. I'm not sure."

This admission preceded a series of pops like someone tapping on a microphone. Scarlet couldn't hear her mother's chopped response. "Did I lose you?" she asked.

"I didn't go anywhere," Eleanor said. "I never do."

Scarlet studied her mother's speech for telltale signs she'd been drinking, but all she heard were rhythmic pauses, a side-effect of the oxygen tank. On the table beside Mama would sit an empty ashtray which she kept close as a reminder of something else she was denied.

"So, Mama," Scarlet said. "What have you heard from Dr. Shapiro lately?"

"Thankfully, nothing." Pause. Breathe. "His news is never good so I stopped taking it."

"What do you mean you 'stopped taking it'?"

"Maybe I should've said 'I stopped going. Period.'"

"To the doctor?"

"Yes," her mother told her. "That man doesn't know anything."

"But he does." Scarlet's pulse quickened in preparation for a battle. "It's his job to help you."

"He doesn't give a crap about me," she said. Pause. Breathe. "No one does."

"That's not true."

"What kind of bullshit—" Scarlet's mother started coughing, and they both went silent, waiting each other out, like Gary Cooper in the classic western *High Noon*. It was Eleanor's favorite movie, and when Scarlet was young, the two of them used to watch the old videotape together, curled like conch shells under Mama's bedspread. Those were the days before Sam left them, back when Eleanor worked only one job. After that, her mother wasn't available much and definitely not for movie-watching.

From Eleanor, there now came a long rattling exhale, and Scarlet picked up the severed thread of their conversation. "So how is everything else there?"

"Like I keep telling. I'm good. So you can stop picking at me."

"I don't want to fight, Mama."

"Then why did you call me on a day that isn't Sunday?"

Scarlet gritted her teeth. Hard. She could have predicted this turn in their call. Once the formalities gave way to real concern, Mama typically grew combative. Paranoid, even. *What's that old saying about doing the same thing over and over but being surprised when the outcome does not change?* This time Scarlet refused to take the bait. She had other issues on her mind. A question to ask while her mother sounded sober.

"The truth is, I was thinking about you," Scarlet said. "But I was also wondering about something."

"What's that?"

Although her arms were wrapped most of the way around her waist, Scarlet felt vulnerable and cold. "Do you still regret having me, Mama?"

Eleanor coughed again, a gunshot in Scarlet's ear. "What the hell kind of question is that? I gave you everything I could, worked my fingers to the bone to put food on the table. A roof over our heads. But that wasn't enough for you, was it? No, you wanted a fancy job and a fancy apartment. A fancy boyfriend. You never even bothered to bring that boy home to meet me. Like I'm some kind of embarrassment. Like my life's nothing but shit. And if it is, well, you made it that way. You and those friends of yours."

"Your life isn't shit, Mama. And no one is to blame." The lie escaped her lips. She hoped it sounded honest.

"You all turned out just fine, didn't you? You and Corie and that Tucker. Always took care of yourselves and to hell with anybody else."

Scarlet closed her eyes. She had survived. She'd escaped. But the guilt still festered, a vulture picking her bones. "I'm sorry, Mama."

"Oh, yeah? If no one's to blame, what're you sorry for?"

Between them another stretch of silence. Scarlet pictured her mother's rickety body cloaked in the same stale housecoat she wore to burn her good black dress. Mama told Scarlet that night she wouldn't need the dress any more. *The next funeral I attend will be my own.*

"I shouldn't have asked," Scarlet said. "I know things

were hard for you. After."

"Things are hard for everyone."

"Yes, but—"

"I don't need my daughter's pity."

"No," said Scarlet. "Of course not."

"So you can quit calling me on an off day to dump on me."

"You're right, Mama."

"Can I assume we're done here?"

Scarlet tested the weight of her mother's question, words balanced on a tightrope.

Are we done?

Sometimes Scarlet wanted to be. But she kept wishing there might be more to their relationship than constant standoffs. That she could—one way or another—preserve what was left of her diminished family. Stars flashed across the insides of her lids. *How could she bring a child into a world when Eleanor was her role model, a mother who would always resent her?*

Dread sank over Scarlet, a lead quilt covering a skeleton. If only she could crawl once more into her childhood, under the covers of her mother's bed, the TV winking, a steady companion in the dark. "No, Mama. There's nothing else. I'll call you again on Sunday."

"You don't have to," her mother said. "You met your weekly quota."

"I don't keep score."

"That's true, isn't it?" Pause. Breathe. "Guess I do it enough for the both of us." The fight was already draining from her voice, each syllable leaking slowly. The spigot of Eleanor's rage could flow so fiercely then twist down to a trickle.

"Don't hang up yet." Scarlet licked the desert of her mouth in one wet circle. "I also wanted to tell you I'm pregnant." In the beat that followed, she heard what sounded like a twig snapping on the other end of the call. "Are you there, Mama? Say something. Please."

"I'm here."

"That's it, then," said Scarlet. "I just thought you should know."

"About what?"

Caught off guard by the question, Scarlet stumbled over her reply. "The baby," she said. "My baby."

"You're not keeping it, are you?"

Scarlet looked out the window, her eyes darting left to right. A spindle-legged pigeon hopped across the ledge below her and dipped its beak to peck at nothing. Spots on a concrete sill. "Yes," she said. "I think I am."

"Then I've raised a fool," said her mother.

The line between them disconnected.

Leaning toward the window, Scarlet pressed her forehead against the glass. With one swift twitch the bird lunged into the sky, its wings flapping madly before it disappeared.

"Goodbye, Mama," said Scarlet to no one but herself.

Dear Scarlet,

I realize you will never read this letter, and that makes writing to you easier. I've been thinking about you more than usual, and I had to get these words out before I end up choking on them all. I keep a lot inside of me, and I don't have you to listen. I realize that's my own fault, and I understand if I'm not forgiven; but maybe someday you'll see your way toward not hating me so much.

Did you get your ten-year letter from Mr. Roosevelt? Until Tuck handed me that envelope, I had completely forgotten about the assignment. But since I read those words from the past, I've been prompted by a desire (more like a need) to say a few things to you. Some old. Some new. All of them true. For what it's worth.

Do you remember the day things started up between us? Of course you do. The whole eighth grade was stuck in the gym because of some stupid spring thunderstorm, and after they showed us that documentary about the exploding blimp, everyone walked around shouting "Scarlet Hindenberg! Oh, the humanity!" I know you won't forget that. Not ever.

It was actually Bets who came to your rescue, offering you a ride home when you were walking in the rain. She pulled over and told you to get in. Then she insisted on driving you after school every day. My sister wouldn't take no for an answer, and eventually you gave in. She might be the only person in the world more stubborn than you.

It took a while for you to trust us. To trust yourself. To find your voice. But once we got you going, you never stopped. Oh, you had big plans for that summer. I never told anyone, not even Tuck, that we sneaked duct tape from my dad's work bench. Or that you used it to cover your mouth, thick strips across both lips. It was a stupid game we played, trying to make your starvation bearable. We talked to each other with only our hands. Held weigh-ins every day. And when you showed up the first day of high school, no one would shut up about how gorgeous you were.

As if thin is the only road to beauty.

Like YOU had happened all of a sudden.

But I knew you were beautiful already, Scarlet. And smart. So damn hilarious. "What did one snowman say to the other? I SMELL CARROTS!" No one could make me laugh like you did. No one else was that much fun to be with. We used hairbrushes as karaoke microphones. Cackled until milk squirted out our noses. I still can't eat Oreos without a glass of milk for dipping. But it's not the same without you, the best friend I ever had.

I can hear you now arguing with that statement. (You always did want to be a lawyer!) I picture you shaking your head and reminding me that I have Tuck. That I stole him from you and then we all stole something even worse. Something beyond words. And I don't disagree with you. I'm sorry we didn't tell you about us sooner. I suppose the secrets we keep can be as dangerous as the ones we share. Maybe more so.

Sometimes, I wonder how different our lives would be if the three of us had loved each other less. Or if we had picked a different time to share the truth. But since I promised to be honest here (and since you won't ever get this letter anyway) here it is:

After everything that's happened, I would still do what I did. And if you're honest, I think you would too.

Love,
Corie

P.S. More than anything, I want to hear your voice again.

Corie

Tuck and I live in a two-story Mediterranean at the edge of Conejo Springs two miles north of Chaparral Valley where Bets and I grew up. Ma's mid-century rancher has dark green shutters and beds of blue hydrangea. Out back is a shady sycamore with the tire swing my father hung. To this day the yard smells like love to me. And rubber. Falling leaves. Each November on my father's birthday, I sit on that swing and twirl.

This year the date lands on Thanksgiving, and as always Ma runs the show, recreating holidays from the past, trying to keep our father in the present. She dusts off trusty recipes and plays Christmas albums on her vintage turntable. But only after dinner.

Because carols before lunchtime on Thanksgiving is sacrilege.

While Cam and Wella play in the den, Bets stirs a pan of gravy on the stove, and I help my mother set the dining room table. My job is to lay two forks—one for the salad and one for the entrée—to the left of each gold placemat. Ma walks in front of me with a handful of spoons rubbing them on her pumpkin-colored cardigan.

"I like your polishing method," I say. She looks over her shoulder, and I smile at her.

"I can't believe Tuck is missing dinner." She shakes her head, sets down another spoon. "Even Joseph showed up today, and he's not family."

At this my smile goes stiff, although legally, Ma has a point. Joey and Bets never did get married, never settled down to raise their kids. They bounced from job to job, place to place, spending my sister's inheritance. After their final breakup, Ma labeled them both *aggressively transient*. She likes to say neither one can make a commitment. Not in relationships or in real estate.

"Joey is the father of your grandchildren," I remind her. "That makes him part of the family."

"So it does," she says. "And he made the effort to be here. I suppose that counts for something."

"It's not like Tuck is choosing to be away from us today."

From her, a lengthy *hmm*. "Isn't he?"

"He is *choosing* to remain employed." Besides an emphasis on the word 'choosing' my voice remains steady, my gaze even. If there is one thing I have learned in this life, it's the more you disagree with Ma, the more she thinks she is right. "But let's not argue," I say. "Please? That's not what Thanksgiving should be about."

She lifts her hands in mock surrender. "You're right. I won't say another word."

I count the place settings and realize Ma has left an empty space beside her at the head of the table. Wella's homemade *Uncle Tuck* name card glitters above the mat. When Ma notices me noticing, she shrugs.

"You never know," she says. "Tucker's case might cancel." She sets down the last spoon, then moves on to the dinner napkins, folding them into stiff white swans.

"Don't get your hopes up, Ma. Tuck texted me from the operating room an hour ago. The patient was being wheeled in already. If we're lucky, he'll be back here in time for your world-famous pecan pie." It's a clumsy compliment, but Ma nods.

"I still feel awful for his family," she says. "The patient's family, I mean. Not being together for Thanksgiving. It isn't right."

So much for not saying another word.

"The patient is a she," I tell her. "She was riding in the trunk of a car full of teenagers that crashed off an overpass just after midnight. Did you see it on the news this morning? Without surgery, the girl will be paralyzed. She might be even with it. Her family probably thinks her spine is more important than their mashed potatoes and stuffing. Or ours."

For a moment Ma studies the napkin swan in her hand. "Bethany!" she calls out. "I hope you're teaching Campbell never to ride in the trunk of a car!"

Bets emerges from the kitchen, her corn-silk hair gathered into a loose bun. She is wearing Chuck Taylors, striped leggings and a T-shirt with a sequined happy face.

"I put the kids in the trunk all the time." Bets points a gravy whisk at our mother. "It saves me room for my many, many shopping bags from Neiman Marcus."

"Very funny," says Ma. "And by that I mean you are not funny at all."

Before my sister can respond, Wella runs into the room, her doe-eyes wild with joy. "Hey there, princess," Bets says. She waves the whisk over her daughter's head. "What's got you so excited?"

"I beat Daddy at Go Fish again. I'm five for five!"

"Atta girl," Bets says.

"Daddy asked me to tell you Notre Dame is winning. And also that he needs another beer!"

"Tell him I'll bring one as soon as I'm done with the gravy. In the meantime, go easy on your father, OK?"

"Maybe I will." Wella grins. "Maybe I won't." She scampers down the hall, and my sister makes her way around the table, whispering to me behind her hand.

"Poor guy didn't get much sleep last night," she says. "If you know what I mean."

Across the dining room Ma twists the edge of another napkin. "I heard that, Bethany Jane, and I did not just fall off the apple cart. If you must know, I think being intimate with Joseph is a very bad idea."

"That's good, Ma," Bets says, "because he doesn't want to be intimate with you, either."

I toss a napkin at my sister, and it bounces off her head onto the floor. My mother frowns, and I am unsure what has gotten her more upset; the fact that I wrecked one of her perfect swans or that Bets is sleeping with her ex.

"Come on," my sister groans. "It's not like we did it in your den."

Ma folds her arms and stares at Bets.

"Hey." I take a step between them. "What can I help with next?"

After some thought Ma asks me to get the folding chairs, then she begins folding napkins again. Bets looks at me and mouths *Thank you* before returning to the kitchen.

I retrieve the chairs from the hall closet and stack them against the wall beside the piano. It's an old upright made of cherry wood that my parents bought when I was nine. I took lessons for seven years but haven't played a note since my father died. Opening the bench, I smell the dusty sheet music and let myself remember. Our favorite classical pieces. His applause at my recitals. *That's my girl*, he always said. From behind me, Ma appears and slides a chair into the spot with the *Uncle Tuck* name tag.

Under her breath, a *tsk tsk tsk*.

"Let it go, Ma," I say. "Tuck would be here if he could."

"It's not Tucker," she says. "I'm worried about your sister. The way she acts sometimes. The things she says. In front of the children."

"They are her kids," I say. "And Bets is just trying to get a reaction out of you. She's a toddler who won't grow up. A female Peter Pan. But she's only kidding. You must know that by now."

Ma licks her thumb, wipes at a spot on a wine goblet and dries the glass on her sweater. "I'm aware." She sets down the glass. "But certain topics aren't meant to be joked about."

"If we didn't laugh about her sex life," I tease, "we'd be crying all the time."

My mother picks up another glass and holds it up to the light for inspection. "Who says I don't?"

"What?"

"Cry all the time." She looks at me and sniffles. Her eyes are wet.

"Oh, Ma. I'm sorry."

My shoulders sink, and I try to imagine how difficult this

day must be for her. Another Thanksgiving without my father. On his birthday, no less. She wipes at her eyes, and I move to her side. "I miss him too. So much." I wrap my arms around her shoulders, and for a moment, she allows it. Then she slips away from me, adjusting her sweater with a tug.

"I'll be fine, Corie. It's been almost eight years, hasn't it?"

She asks the question as if she doesn't know. As if she hasn't kept track of every single day that has passed since my father died. I'm quiet while she arranges her mouth into a smile. I have no idea what to say to her.

"Oh! I almost forgot!" Ma snaps her fingers. "The special salt and pepper shakers!"

"Thank goodness you remembered," I tease. I reach out to touch her, but she's already gone.

When she returns with the pilgrim shakers, I appraise the table and pronounce it perfect. Sparkling crystal and polished silver. Miniature pumpkins. A cornucopia of gratitude. Even Wella's glittery place cards are just the right amount of messy.

"What else can I do?" I ask her.

"Nothing right now. Thanks." She glances at me sideways and adjusts a candlestick a half-inch to the left. "Why don't you get off your feet, Corie. You look a little tired."

"Yikes," I say.

"It happens." She smooths the edge of the tablecloth at one corner. "I was exhausted myself, you know."

"This morning?"

"No." Her smile is shy. "Back when I was expecting." She searches my face, and I stare at her.

"What?"

"You did turn down a mimosa earlier. A mother notices subtle hints like that. Just wait. You'll see."

Mother. A wave of nausea passes over me, and I take a step backward, knocking over a wine glass. I suspect she's trying to take the focus off her but to shift it to me?

To this?

"I'll be right back," I tell her, although I have no idea where to go.

Should I retreat to the bathroom and cry alone?

Hide in the den?

Bury myself in the backyard?

"I thought maybe…" my mother begins just as the doorbell rings. It is past noon so she has switched the setting over to seasonal mode. Above us a bell chimes the first seventeen notes of *Deck the Halls*. She lifts a finger for me to wait through the last *fa la la la la*. Then she says, "Would you see who's at the door? If I don't baste the turkey again, it will dry out."

"I'm not pregnant," I tell her.

"OK," she says before scurrying into the kitchen.

On autopilot, I trudge past the living room to the front door. When I open it my mouth hangs open. I can't help gaping at the person on the porch. Her hair is dull now and streaked with white. A web of wrinkles softens her once-sharp edges. But she still looks so much like her daughter, those fine features almost slipping off her face.

"Hello, Corinna," she says.

"Mrs. Hinden. Please. Come in."

Eleanor takes a step forward, hesitating in the foyer. We stare at each other until my mother emerges from the kitchen, wiping her hands down the front of her apron.

"Oh my, Ellie. It's been ages. Don't you look wonderful!" This is an exaggeration. Mrs. Hinden's denim shirt and pants hang loosely on her frame. Her eyes look haunted, the skin beneath them sallow. Before Ma can hug her, Eleanor Hinden turns to me.

"I was hoping you'd be around," she says.

"I am," I say. "Around." *Steady now, Corie. Just breathe.*

Ma's palm brushes my elbow. "This is silly, us standing here. Let's have a seat so we can catch up."

Before Eleanor can protest, my mother leads her into the living room, and I follow. They take seats on opposite sides of the couch while I settle onto the loveseat. Between us a glass coffee table gleams.

"Where are my manners?" Ma asks. "Can I get you a drink, Ellie?"

"No need," Mrs. Hinden says. "This won't take long."

My mother continues to smile, but her face is flushed, and I think back to the afternoon I questioned her about the meaning of the word *ostentatious*. When she asked why I wanted to know, I told her Scarlet's mom said our family was *ostentatious*. Ma left the room mumbling a sentence that ended in *lascivious*. I had to look up both words in the dictionary.

"You will stay for dinner, won't you?" my mother asks. "It's easy enough to add another place to our table. In fact, Tucker probably won't be here. You can have his seat."

Mrs. Hinden lifts a thumb to the hollow of her throat, and I will her to say no. "Thank you for the invitation. But I've got plans of my own. Pretty good ones."

"If you change your mind..." Ma says.

"I won't."

"Well. You know best."

An awkward silence settles over us, and my eyes cut back and forth between the two of them. "It's good to see you, Mrs. Hinden." I feel nothing close to good.

"You're a grown woman," she says. "Call me Ellie." Her lips peel away in a smile, and her teeth, although yellowed, are as even as I remember. The past decade may have ruined her, but the raw materials remain: Eleanor Hinden is a lovely woman. "I was wondering," she says, "if you'd maybe talked to my daughter lately."

"Scarlet?" The name leaps from my mouth, a foolish question. As if Eleanor Hinden has other daughters I might have been speaking to.

"I realize it's been a while." In her voice, a tremble. No sliver of sarcasm. "I thought maybe she would've tried to get in touch with you?"

"She hasn't." I glance at my mother. "I'd like to," I add. "Get in touch with Scarlet, I mean. But I don't think she feels the same."

Eleanor's face hardens. "My girl sure is a stubborn one. Never would listen to me. Or to anyone for that matter." As she speaks, I find myself nodding. *Stubborn* is one of the best words in the English language to describe Scarlet Hinden. But who could blame the girl for ignoring her mother's advice? Mrs. Hinden wasn't someone either of us wanted to emulate. Yes, she worked two jobs and managed to put food on the table. But she also came home wasted half the time and just as often with strange men. Scarlet said she was surprised Sam didn't take off sooner. But I always figured it would be hard for any man to give up on his kids no matter how much he wants to give up on his wife.

"Scarlet's a tough nut to crack," Ma says, trying to be agreeable. But Eleanor ignores the gesture and turns her attention back to me.

"I need you to deliver something for me, Corinna." Threads of color rise along her neck, and she reaches into her purse to pull out an envelope. The seal has been broken, and the Hinden's *less ostentatious* address is scrawled across the front in a looping cursive. I recognize the writing instantly.

Scarlet's ten-year letter.

"You didn't send it to her?"

"You know my daughter better than most people," says Eleanor. "Better than I ever did." She wipes her nose with the back of her hand. "Scarlet was here in August for a visit, told me she was thinking of moving in with her boyfriend. According to her, he's got a nice place. But the thing is, I never did catch where he lived. I'm sorry to say, I don't have an address where I can forward this." She blinks a few times, and I can't tell if she's dredging up information she wants to remember or try to forget.

"Scarlet's not home for Thanksgiving?" my mother asks.

"She was thinking about coming," Eleanor tells us, "but I screwed those plans up pretty good."

"Oh, I'm sure you didn't," Ma says.

"Think what you want, Laura. I didn't come here to see you." Eleanor regards me again silently, waiting for an answer to a question she has not asked.

"I'm sorry," I tell her. "I have no idea where Scarlet is."

"If it helps, she's still up in the Bay Area. She and that boyfriend of hers work at the same office. She's always going on about long days and billable hours. How many years it'll take them to make partner. Guess she's a pretty big deal now."

"Sounds wonderful," Ma says. Her enthusiasm makes me wince. As usual, it's too bright for the circumstances.

"Where do they work?" I ask.

"I couldn't tell you, exactly. Some law firm. It starts with an O. 'Oldman' I think. Or 'Olson' maybe. My brain isn't what it used to be."

She did it, I think. *Scarlet Hinden is an attorney. Just like she'd always planned.*

"Have you tried searching for her online?" suggests Ma. "I'm sure you could find information on the Internet."

Eleanor smirks. "That's funny, Laura. You thinking I've got a computer."

Ma remains undaunted. "Oh, but the library has—"

"I don't get out much these days," she interrupts. "And this is a delicate matter. One of those issues that needs to be resolved face to face."

"Then you should take the letter to her," I say. "Maybe you two could patch things up."

"Can't." The thumb returns to her throat. "Traveling is... difficult for me. So," she says, "Corie. You gonna help me out?"

"Me?" My heart is a hammer at my ribs. "I'm not sure what you think I can do for you. Or for her. For either of you."

"I need you to go to San Francisco and find Scarlet, of course."

At this Ma straightens. "Tucker's there all the time for work, isn't he, Corie?"

"Yes."

"Maybe the two of you could go up together," she says. "Get away to look up an old friend?"

My tongue is thick, and I'm afraid I might swallow it whole. *No no no no no no.*

"It's real important," Eleanor insists. Her words are rusty nails plucked from abandoned railroad tracks.

"It's just a letter," I say.

"No. It's more than that. You see, Scarlet won't listen to me, but I'm hoping she'll read this and listen to herself. Or maybe she'll listen to you. Remind her what she wanted to make of her life. Right now that girl is throwing her future away with both hands."

"But, Ellie." Ma places a palm on Mrs. Hinden's knee. "It sounds to me like Scarlet's doing quite well."

"She was," says Eleanor. "Better than quite. Until she went and got herself knocked up."

I suck in a breath. "Scarlet is pregnant?" My vision swims, and I'm afraid I might vomit.

"She had plans," Eleanor says. "Big ones. Better than anything I could've given her." Her chin inches upward, defiant. "Scarlet lost her way, is all. And we both know why."

"I wish I could help you, Mrs. Hinden." My offer is little more than a whisper.

"Then find my daughter. Tell her she can't have this damn baby."

"What?" The question is acid in my throat.

"Convince her to get rid of it. Adopt it out. Leave it at a fire station for all I care. As long as she doesn't try to raise this kid by herself."

Ma withdraws her hand from Eleanor's knee. "I thought you said she has a boyfriend. A nice lawyer?"

"Ha! Like he'll stick around. All men leave eventually, don't they, Laura? One way or another." Ice water courses through my veins, and I want to leap between Ma and Mrs. Hinden to shield my mother from Eleanor's words.

My father died. He didn't leave.

Scarlet's mother looks at me, and I freeze.

"It has to be you," she says.

"But why?" I ask.

"Because ten years ago you ruined our lives, Corie Slater. Don't you think it's time you made things right?"

Scarlet

She was in line at the service counter of West End Bakery when her skin sprouted fresh goose bumps and she caught herself in a familiar double-take. It had been a while since she'd seen the ghost. This time the vision appeared on the other side of the sun-streaked glass, white-blond ringlets moving past the crowded storefront. The apparition vanished from sight before Scarlet could repeat the mantra in her head:

She's not Corie. She's not Corie. She's not Corie.

Usually, by the third repetition, Scarlet had convinced herself. This morning, however, her fingers shook as she gripped the ticket stamped 94. If she hadn't promised Clara she'd take care of dessert, Scarlet would have fled the bakery and headed in the opposite direction. *She's not Corie*, she told herself a fourth time as she focused on the smell of buttery croissants. Warm ginger. Powdered sugar. When a minute of slowed breathing failed to calm her, she tried examining the pies in the display case.

Think about something else. Anything. Like what to bring today.

Two pies would be overindulgent, but one might shine a spotlight on the smallness of their group. Four people hardly constituted a party. Scarlet couldn't cancel now. She wouldn't. No matter how jumpy she felt. No matter how much she wanted to crawl into bed and forget about—

Stop!

It was Mama's fault, this ghostly vision. The frazzled

nerves. Her revving heart. More specifically Scarlet blamed the message Eleanor had left early that morning. While Gavin sat at their kitchen table Skyping with his family, Scarlet let her mother's call go to voicemail, retreating to her room to listen in private. On the edge of their bed, she'd sat. Both the door and her eyes were shut.

Don't be so bullheaded, girl. Having this kid will suck you dry. You'll end up alone, wishing you were dead. You should know that better than anyone.

Mama had grown increasingly agitated, taking long pauses, snorting her oxygen. By the time the message ended, salty tears streamed down Scarlet's face.

It should have been you, Eleanor told her. *Why wasn't it you?*

Digging into her purse now, Scarlet found her phone. Her fingers twitched, ready to hear the words again.

To punish herself.

Test her resolve.

"Ninety-four!"

A baker wearing a flour-streaked apron called out Scarlet's number. She stepped forward to place her order, her mother's words still ringing in her ears.

⋙⋘

Gavin swung their front door open while Scarlet was fumbling with her keys. She balanced two bakery boxes on the flat of her forearm: One pumpkin pie, one apple.

"Hello, beautiful." He kissed her cheek first, then rescued the boxes from her. "You were gone a long time. I was about to organize a search party."

"The line at the bakery was ridiculous," she said. "Turns out we weren't the only people who waited until the last minute."

"I should've gone."

"Don't be silly," she said. "I'm pregnant, not incapacitated."

You're bullheaded. It should have been you. Scarlet felt her cheeks drain of color.

"Everything all right?" Gavin asked.

"Yes," she told him. "I'm just a little hot."

She slipped off her coat while Gavin set the boxes on the counter beside two bottles of Pinot Noir. Lifting the box lids, he inhaled deeply. "These pies smell almost as delicious as you do."

"Someone's laying it on thick today."

"I speak only the truth." Gavin came to her side and sniffed around her like a cartoon bloodhound with his tongue hanging out.

"Stop!" Scarlet wagged a finger in his face.

"Come on. You know you love it."

"I love you," she told him. "Not being licked."

"Liar," he said.

"Never."

Gavin rummaged in the pantry for a paper bag with handles and lowered the pie boxes into it. Scarlet watched as he slid a corkscrew from a drawer and tossed it into the bag.

"So how's your family doing?" she asked. "Are all the Newstedts as marvelous as ever?"

"Everyone's fine, Scar. They're always fine."

"You Skyped with them longer than *fine*." She met his gaze, caught something in his eye. "Ah. So you told them?"

Gavin tilted his head. "I hope you don't mind. Too much."

"Not too much," she said. "Tell me. Were they happy?"

"Ecstatic. And so am I." She nodded, and he moved behind her, touched his mouth to the nape of her neck.

"This is really happening," she said. Gavin's hands moved over her stomach.

"Ready or not," he said.

Was she supposed to finish the phrase? *Here it comes.*

"You should have seen my mom's face," he said. "She's already calling herself Grandma. I hope your mother doesn't mind."

Scarlet swallowed. *Don't think about Mama.* She turned in his arms, and Gavin released her.

"Is your mom's arthritis any better?" she asked.

"Jury's still out," he said. "It could be a while before the new medication makes any difference. The doctor prepped her for so many possible side effects, Dad is worried she's not telling him the worst. Then again, Mom's not one to complain—much."

Scarlet slumped on a barstool. "I wonder what that would be like. Mama will still be complaining when she's dead. I don't think I'll ever escape it."

"Ouch." Gavin winced.

"Yeah," Scarlet said. *God. Change the subject. Now.* "Anyway, I saw something today. At the bakery." As she spoke, she adopted a false brightness, but still her face grew hot, and she didn't know whether she was reacting to the black thoughts about her mother or to her visions of Corie Harper.

Gavin peered at her, then shook his head. "OK, I'll bite. What did you see today while you were at the bakery?"

"Actually it was a *whom*. Another bout of mistaken identity. But it always feels more like a ghost. Someone from my past traipsing along the streets of San Francisco, oblivious to my existence. It wasn't, of course. It never is."

"So this has happened before?" he asked.

"Hmm."

"A Ghost of Thanksgiving Past," he said. "How Dickensian of you, Scar."

She groaned. "Now you think I'm crazy."

"Not any more than I did before." He smiled at her. "But this is the first I've heard about any potential paranormal insanity. Have you been holding out on me? Tell me everything."

"There's not much to tell," she said. "I used to believe I saw this person everywhere, but it's been years since… well, maybe not years. But at least since I met you. Or I would have said something to you about her."

Probably, she thought. *I probably would have said something.* But a Corie Harper sighting might have required more of an explanation than Scarlet would have wanted to offer. As a new couple she and Gavin had asked each other the usual questions: about successes and failures, hopes and heartbreak. She had been as honest as she could be while skipping the darkest parts of her past. Deflecting hard truths about herself was a learned skill.

"*Her?*" Gavin repeated. "I'll admit that's a relief."

Scarlet ignored the implication and dragged her index finger along the bullnose of their granite. "It was strange," she said, "her haunting my brain again after so much time."

Gavin studied her face, his green eyes soft. "Let me get this straight," he said. "Some *her* from your past is on your mind. Is it possible you're having second thoughts about not going home to see your mother for Thanksgiving?"

"Absolutely not." Scarlet laid her palms across her belly, thumbs hooked one over the other. She would keep this baby from Mama as long as she could. Forever, if she had to.

"I know seeing Eleanor is hard on you," Gavin said. "So the next time you visit, I'll come with you. In fact, we should probably try to get down there together soon."

"But… why?"

"I haven't even met your mother yet, and the delivery room would be a strange place to be introduced for the first time, don't you think?"

His question was rhetorical, but Mama's message echoed in her head. *Having this kid will suck you dry. You'll end up alone, wishing you were dead.*

"I don't want her there," Scarlet blurted out.

"Whoa," said Gavin. "Don't want her where?"

"At the hospital. When the baby's born." Scarlet lowered her eyes. *Calm down. You are safe. Everyone's OK. For now.* "My mother is too sick, and her immune system's shot. Being there wouldn't be good for her. For any of us."

Gavin touched her arm. "Sure, Scar. Whatever you say."

Scarlet lifted her head and held her breath.

"It can be just us," Gavin said. "If you think that's best."

She exhaled. "I really do."

"Then it's settled."

"You're my family now." Scarlet took his hand and placed it on her stomach. "You and this little one are all I need."

Gavin squeezed her fingers. "Then it's a good thing you're stuck with us."

"Good thing," she agreed. She pressed her mouth into a smile. And for a while, she let herself believe they could be happy.

৵৵

They were midway through their meal when Clara stopped to toast to friendship and the diners clinked their glasses across her tiny bistro table. On top of the sideboard were serving platters and a pitcher of cold water. Below that, a storage grid held bottles of San Pellegrino and wine. Every cabinet and shelf was full, each inch of space made useful. Scarlet cast her gaze around the place, a model of efficiency.

She missed the exposed brick walls. The duct work. The wood beams. But more than this, she missed the crowded days of her past. When she'd lived here, the smaller rooms had made her feel safe. There was almost too much room in her life now. Back then there had been nothing left she could not bear to lose.

"Can I make another toast?" Clara asked. "To the brilliant little fetus. She truly is as lucky as they come!"

"It may be a boy, you know," Gavin said. "My gut tells me I'm having a son."

Clara raised an eyebrow. "Boy or girl, this baby will be gorgeous with a capital G. And who knows? You may get a ginger out of the deal."

William Pendergast, Clara's new boyfriend, forked a mound of stuffing into his mouth. His hair was tousled as if he had just rolled out of bed, and his droopy lids made him look half asleep. "You lost me," he said while chewing. "What's a ginger?"

Clara sighed. "Poor Willie. Always behind the times." She spooned fresh cranberries onto her plate. "I was referring to the likelihood that the newest Newstedt will be a redhead. Take a look at that carrot top." She aimed her spoon at Gavin. "You'd better start stocking up on sunblock for your little girl."

"Or boy," Gavin said. He drained the last of his wine. "Please pass the Pinot, Scarlet." A ribbon of unease threaded through her as she handed him the bottle.

"You're not supposed to put sunblock on babies," she said. "Not until they're at least a year old."

"I don't know anything about sunblock and babies," said

William. "But I do know that once my brother had a kid, he never had sex again." He popped an olive into his mouth, and Clara socked him in the elbow. "Hey!" He spat the olive into his hand. "What did I say?"

"Are all men obligated to be disgusting?" asked Clara. "Or are you just especially good at it?"

"You're right." William nodded. "And I am definitely wrong. Because now that I think about it, the baby wasn't the problem. My brother stopped having sex the minute he got married."

"Bloody hell," Clara groaned.

Gavin smiled at Scarlet who was staring at her lap. "That's a charming anecdote, isn't it, Scar? We'll have to share it the next time someone asks when we're tying the knot."

William blinked at him. "You two aren't married? Clara didn't tell me."

"Because it's not your business," Clara said. "And also, it's no big deal. We do live in the twenty-first century, you know."

William turned to address her. "But Gavin strikes me as an old-fashioned guy. The type who would want to make an honest woman out of Scarlet."

"An honest woman?" Clara squawked. "Now you sound like a caveman. Or a nun!"

Gavin sipped his wine. "You're correct, Will. Scarlet and I aren't married. But the thought has crossed my mind. Yes it has." His tongue lingered too long on each *s,* and Scarlet's stomach twisted.

"Then you should do it, my man," said William. "Be spontaneous. Take control!"

"Do what, exactly?" asked Scarlet.

"Sorry to disappoint everyone," Gavin said, "but I'm not hiding a ring in my pocket."

"Scarlet can pick one out later," said William. "One she'll actually like."

"Oh, do shut up, Willie!" Clara said. "I'm sorry, Scarlet. Please forgive him."

"Hold on a minute." Gavin set down his glass, an exaggerated protest. "Is the idea of her being my wife so horrible you feel the need to apologize for it?"

"Of course not," said Clara. Her eyes cut to Scarlet.

"So, how 'bout it then, Scar?" Gavin wiped his mouth with a napkin. "Should I seize the moment? Would you like a caveman for a husband?" He grinned at her, but she shook her head.

Was he actually proposing? Here? Now? In front of Clara and some stranger?

"This is hardly the right time or the right company," she said. She hoped no one else heard the quiver in her voice. "How embarrassing. Especially for Clara and Will."

"I don't embarrass easily," said William. He produced an iPhone from his pocket. "And if you pop the question during dinner, I can post the video to YouTube before dessert. So. What should we title the clip?"

Scarlet removed her own napkin from her lap and placed it on the table beside her plate. "Excuse me for a moment." She rose from the table.

"Oh, Scar, we're only kidding around." Gavin reached out and grabbed her elbow. "I shouldn't have put you on the spot. Please don't be mad."

Scarlet inched away from him. "I'm not mad."

"Then where are you going?" he asked. "Clara cooked this enormous meal, and you haven't even had a bite."

"First of all, Clara ordered everything from the Mainland Market down the street."

"Well, I wasn't even born in America," Clara said. "Thanksgiving isn't my specialty. So who cares if—"

"And secondly," Scarlet interrupted, "I'm in a lovely mood. I promise. It's just that when Will mentioned dessert, I remembered we left the pies in the trunk. I need to get them before the filling congeals. Or cracks. Or whatever it is pie filling does when it's left inside a parked car for hours."

Gavin scooted his seat back, two thumps from the table. "Let me get the pies, then."

Scarlet demurred with a half-smile. "Thanks for the chivalry, but I could use the fresh air."

"Are you sure you're all right?" he asked.

"Yes." Her hand brushed her throat. "Just a bit queasy is all."

"Then I'm coming too," said Clara.

"Fine. But first admit you haven't lived in London since you were four."

Clara ignored her. "I won't take no for an answer."

"Oh, Clare. When do you ever?"

"Precisely," Clara said.

Scarlet turned then and walked out of the apartment.

ৎ৵৵

Descending the outdoor staircase, she drew her hand along the jasmine on the wall. Those tiny flowers clinging to the stucco. The sweet scent of the vines. She paused, took a breath, nostalgic for the days before Gavin. Life was less complicated when she believed she could be content.

Alone. Forever.

Not that Clara hadn't loved her then, didn't still love her now. But marriage was a different kind of commitment, another promise that could be broken.

As they approached Gavin's car, an ancient truck chugged up the street belching exhaust from its tailpipe in black, acrid puffs. A driver with a ruddy face and a bushy moustache leaned out the window and waved at them.

"Happy Thanksgiving, handsome!" Clara called out.

Scarlet turned and popped the trunk. "Maybe you should trade in good old William for Mr. Handsome in the pickup."

Behind her Clara scoffed. "Willie may be a bit rough around the edges," she said, "but at least he's fun."

"I see." Scarlet straightened. "And I'm not?"

"Not so much today. Although in your defense, it's hard to be fun when you're bloody miserable."

Scarlet rotated slowly then, a secondhand on a clock. "You're right," she said. "And it's not Will's fault. Or Gavin's. Or yours." Her voice caught, and she struggled to maintain composure. *You must be strong,* she thought. *Strong for the baby.*

"What is it?" asked Clara. "Tell me what's wrong, Scar."

She hesitated, considering how much to share. Clara knew Eleanor could be harsh, that she dreaded visits to her mother. But Scarlet had told Clara little about the worst part of their past. She didn't lie, she simply evaded. It was better than remembering, and she needed a friend who didn't know the truth. A friend who didn't pity her.

"It's just that I heard from Mama this morning," Scarlet began, but Clara turned and looked down the street.

Around the corner limped an old man with a long, stringy beard. He was barefoot, and his filthy trousers were belted with a rope. As he drew nearer, Scarlet searched his face. The sunken cheeks. His numb expression. It appeared as if he hadn't eaten in days.

"Wait," Scarlet told him. She reached into Gavin's trunk and pulled out the apple pie. "Have this," she said. The man took the pie, muttering something she couldn't understand. "You're welcome," she whispered as he shuffled away, hunched over the box as if it were a treasure.

When the man was out of earshot, Clara sighed. "That was awfully nice."

"We didn't need two pies."

"You've got me all misty-eyed now. Should I have done something too? Is it too late to invite the man to dinner?"

"Clare."

"No, seriously. If it's not too late, we can collect Mr. Handsome in the pickup as well."

"Are you making fun of me?"

"Absolutely not," said Clara. "I can't stand the thought of anyone being alone on Thanksgiving."

Scarlet swallowed. "My mother's alone today. In fact, I—"

"Oh, right!" interrupted Clara. "I'm a bloody idiot. You were starting to say you finally talked to her this morning."

"I didn't say we talked."

"But—"

"She left me a voicemail message."

"Ah." Clara nodded. "Wanting to mend fences, then?"

"The opposite," Scarlet said. "Mama insists I can't keep this baby."

"She what?" Clara's eyes went wide.

"My mother said if I'm too far gone to get rid of it, I should let someone else raise it." At Clara's gasp, Scarlet dropped her head. "Her own grandchild, Clare."

"Good Lord! No wonder you've been wretched." Clara lowered her voice. "What did Gavin say when you told him?"

"I haven't yet. I can't. He wants to meet her, for God's sake. He even mentioned flying his parents out this spring so we can all get to know each other. His family is thrilled about this baby. If they knew how Mama really felt about everything…"

"You're right," said Clara. "It would be terrible if anyone else found out. Especially Gavin. The man is clearly over the moon about being a daddy."

"But I can't keep them apart forever. And Mama will tell him how she feels the first chance she gets." At the thought of it, Scarlet's insides lurched, a dull and sickening shift.

"Are you absolutely sure that's what she wants? What did Eleanor say, exactly?"

"She told me becoming a mother was the worst thing that ever happened to her. That I pretty much ruined her life."

"God, Scar. How awful."

"I think a part of her believes if she hadn't gotten pregnant, she would be happy now. And healthy. Still married to Sam or to someone. '*Pop out a kid or two and men bolt*,' she says. '*You wait and see. That boy will be gone gone gone.*'"

"But that's ludicrous!" said Clara. "Anyone who knows Gavin can see he adores you. He was ready to propose just now over a plate of turkey and stuffing. You know what I think? I think your mother's a right bloody witch for suggesting Gav would ever abandon you. Especially after you have his baby."

"But I don't want him to want me because I'm pregnant."

"Oh, Scarlet. You can't believe that's why he's with you."

"I don't know what to believe any more." She shifted her gaze to the paper bag inside the trunk. It was torn at the edges and wrinkled. Not empty but almost. The lone pie box appeared small now by itself and insufficient.

"Life doesn't come with any guarantees," Clara said.

"No. But you can decrease your chance of being heartbroken by not wanting someone too much in the first place."

Clara shook her head. "That doesn't sound like much of a

goal."

"Maybe not," Scarlet said. "But I've been replaying Mama's message all day in my head, and I'm afraid." She paused now, choking on the words.

"Afraid of what?"

"Of letting myself need Gavin. What if I decide I can't live without him, and he leaves me? What if he leaves us?"

Clara gripped Scarlet's arm. "Listen to me, now. Not your mother. She's crazy. Scratch that. She's downright certifiable."

"That's just it, Clare." Something loosened in Scarlet's chest, her façade of strength unraveling. "My mother might be crazy, but that doesn't mean she's wrong."

Dear Scarlet,

It's been a few weeks since your mom revealed the Big News. Maybe you two have spoken by now. She might have told you what she asked me to do, and I hope you understand why I just couldn't. Why I'm still holding onto these letters and haven't come looking for you. Yet.

I simply cannot hunt you down for the sole purpose of convincing you to give up your baby.

But I also can't face you if you've decided to keep it.

You see, Tuck and I have been unable to do what you've apparently accomplished by accident. We've been trying for a while now. To the point where sex is practically a chore. We don't say that out loud, of course. But I've gotten pretty good at figuring out what's going on inside other people's heads. Even the stuff they try to keep to themselves.

Especially that stuff.

And even though it hurts me to say it, I hope you've decided to have this child. And I hope you're feeling the joy of it. Please, Scar. Let yourself embrace the possibilities instead of focusing only on the fear and uncertainty.

How do I know you're afraid and unsure?

Because I know you're terrified of becoming like your mother. You always have been. And I know she robbed you of some pieces of the human puzzle you can't get back: confidence, stability. The belief that when you love someone he or she won't betray you. I suppose I took a piece of that with me as well. But I've grown and changed, and I can only imagine you have too.

So forgive me now for suggesting that your mother is wrong. Again. This pregnancy won't ruin your life. Because you can raise your baby to be strong and independent just like you've always had to be. I believe you will shower your little boy or girl with the kind of adoration you've been seeking your whole life.

And whether or not the father sticks around, you'll be the center of this baby's universe. You will light up his or her world all by yourself. You have that spark within you. It's so bright. I read it in every word of the ten-year letter I've been keeping in my nightstand. Right next to the letter I wrote to myself.

At night I lie awake imagining the day I might be able to hand your letter over to you in person. Along with all these pages where I've been pouring out my heart. For you. For us.

For what we used to mean to each other.

I haven't forgotten.

And I'd be that for you again if you would let me.

Love,
Corie

Corie

When I arrive at the Conejo Elementary auditorium, a giant elf stands guard outside. Principal Anderson in a green velour suit, his pointy red hat decorated with sleigh bells. As I approach the double doors, he checks for stragglers over my shoulder. "Happy Holidays," I tell him. His shoes jingle as he ushers me inside.

The darkened auditorium is alive with voices, the smell of perfume mixed with peppermint. Inching my way along the back wall, I struggle to get my bearings. I can't see much, but most of the folding chairs appear to be occupied already. As I crane my neck, someone catches my elbow. A figure with straight hair and straighter shoulders. In the dim light, I can't make out her features, but I know them just the same. Long nose, sharp chin, full lips.

Kate Turlow. Head of the elementary school PTA.

It's a role she's been prepping for since she beat my sister out for senior class president. Like us, Kate still lives in our hometown. Unlike us, she married a man twice her age who just left her for an even younger woman. Kate's always been nice and quick with a smile. Perhaps overly friendly. But I sometimes think she's just pretending to be happy so she doesn't burst into tears.

"Well, well, well. If it isn't Corinna Slater sneaking in late." Kate gives my arm a squeeze. "Don't worry. Your secret is safe with me. But I am glad I caught you." In the dark her teeth glow blue-white, not unlike the artificial snow lining the stage. "A few of us are going to the Ice Cream Igloo after the show, and I was hoping you'd bring the kids." She leans in close, and her breath is sweet in my ear. "I hear Bets has to work tonight. Such a shame about her and Joey. But you know, some things just aren't meant to be."

"Yes," I say. "I do."

She pulls back and scans the crowded room, outlines of bodies short and tall. "Joey's around here somewhere," she says. "I guess it's not his night with the kids so he's keeping a low profile. He told me Bets gets mad when he—"

"Thanks for the invitation," I say. "But I'm meeting my mother tonight."

"She can come too, you know." Kate's laughter trickles out, sweet and airy like cotton candy. "Ice cream is an equal opportunity enemy."

"Maybe," I tell her. *No way no way no way.* "If the kids aren't too tired."

"Well, wake 'em up if they are, Corie. Life's too short to skip banana splits. Besides. I promised Brian Junior you'd bring Campbell. BJ's been missing their playdates ever since your sister started that weird work schedule. She never seems to—"

"I'll do my best," I say, cutting Kate off.

"Great. BJ will be thrilled." She breaks into another blue-white smile as the auditorium begins to quiet. My eyes dart toward the stage, and I cross my fingers that the spotlight won't come on while I'm still stuck here in the aisle.

"I'd better go find my mother," I say. "She absolutely hates saving seats."

"Take this as a peace offering." Kate hands me an extra holiday program. "And say 'hi' to your mama for me, won't you? That woman is such a sweetheart." I thank her for the extra program and promise to say hello. Then I shuffle up the aisle, deciding to be kinder to Kate Turlow. Sure, the woman tries too hard, and yes, she comes on way too strong. But at the end of the day, she is probably like the rest of us: a bit too lonely.

I tiptoe down the aisle, peering at the strangers in each

row. "Ma?" I whisper. "Ma?" One by one the audience members look up at me from their folding chairs. "Sorry," I say under my breath. "As you were. Carry on."

I am nearing the stage and desperate when I finally spot her. The left side of the stage is lit only by the bulbs on an artificial Christmas tree. The right side features a piano sporting an enormous plastic menorah. Between them, front row center, sits my mother, stiff and straight. In the almost-black room, Laura Harper's blond hair shines like angel's wings.

"Hey." I slip into the empty seat beside her.

"Where have you been?" she whispers.

"I told you. I had a curriculum council meeting. I got here as soon as I could."

"Sounds vaguely familiar." She shakes her head. "At least you're here now." My mother plucks a program from the chair on the other side of her. "Is Tucker coming, or is he working late again? And are you aware you're still wearing a name tag?"

"Shhh," I say as Principal Anderson steps onto the stage. He takes his place under the spotlight streaming above our heads. Dust particles float in the beam of it. In the back of the room, over a live microphone, members of the tech crew mumble instructions to each other.

"Welcome to our annual Winter Wonderland performance!" The principal bows, and the room erupts in ripples of applause. "Everyone here in Santa's Village is very excited too!" The mic screeches with feedback, and Mr. Anderson taps it before continuing. "We're kicking off tonight's show with our kindergartners singing *Up on a Housetop*. So keep your ears peeled for the sound of reindeer hooves!"

From behind the red velvet curtain comes the sound of tiny shoes shuffling and scraping their way onto hidden platforms. A woman in a polyester wrap dress and a pair of horn-rimmed glasses hustles from a side wing to the piano bench. While she plays a prolonged introduction to the song, the curtain rises to reveal the first performers of the evening.

"There's Wella!" squeals my mother, pointing to the second column on the left. "But why is she wearing a Star of

David on her head?"

"Shhh."

As she sings, my niece's mouth wags. Exaggerated *oh*s and *ah*s. When she gets to the part about the *click click click* of hooves, I slide out of my sweater and toss it onto the folding chair Ma saved for Tucker. Twenty children, wearing either antlers or star hats, lift their hands above their heads. *Snap snap snap*. Their fingers fumble. Small heads bob to keep time with the piano. Then, almost before it's begun, the song is over.

Wella nudges the boy standing beside her, but he is too busy picking his nose to bow. I clap for her wildly, fighting back tears stinging at the corners of my eyes. I love my niece. So much. She's like a daughter to me. But I want to be applauding a child of my own who is singing about Christmas in a Hanukkah hat.

After the show I pull into an empty space across from the Ice Cream Igloo. I cut the engine and hazard a glance at my mother, who is riding shotgun.

"Thanks for coming with me," I say.

"It's fine, Corie. You can drop me off at my car later after the school parking lot clears out. That place was a zoo."

"This place doesn't look much better." I lower my voice. "To tell you the truth, I'm not sure this is a good idea."

"What are you talking about?" Ma looks at me. "The PTA president invited us."

"It's not about that." I swivel my head to check on Cam and Wella. They are both too busy playing thumb wars to eavesdrop on us. "I'm allowed to get ice cream without an invitation from Kate Turlow."

"Then what's the problem?"

"I have nothing in common with the women in there. They're mothers. They volunteer for Hot Chocolate Fridays. Supervise field trips. Arrange crafts. Monitor circle time. And me?"

"And you, what?" She stares at me. Waiting. When I say nothing, she answers for me. "You open your home to your niece and nephew while your sister figures out her life. You read them bedtime stories before grading your own papers. You play games with them after a full day's work. You laugh.

Listen to their stories. Come to their shows. So don't you dare sell my daughter short, Corinna Marie."

"I'm not."

"You are," she says. "And you're underestimating the mothers in there too." My mother frowns at me. "When did you become a snob?"

"*I'm* a snob?"

"That's what I said. You are judging the people in there, assuming they're too shallow to appreciate how wonderful you are. That they think you're not good enough. Maybe you need to give them a little more credit."

My hands grip the steering wheel. "I'm not a snob."

"Prove it." Ma squares her shoulders.

"Hey!" Wella begins kicking the back of my seat.

Cam asks, "Are we getting ice cream, or what?"

I take a deep breath and release my hold on the wheel. "OK. We're going in."

"That's my girl." Ma pats me on the knee. "Kids, set the dial on your stomachs for triple scoops!"

We make our way inside the Igloo, already packed with families who came here after the performance. Each plastic chair contains a kid hunched over a bowl or a cone or a waffle cup. Ice cream drips onto red plastic tables. Our feet stick to the checkerboard floor. While parents crowd around their children, avoiding each other's elbows, Kate Turlow weaves between the tables taking pictures for the yearbook.

We line up in front of the counter, and Ma wrinkles her nose. "Smells like chocolate and disinfectant." Cam stands behind her studying the canisters of toppings. Wella, burrowing under my arm, asks if she really is allowed to order a triple scoop. When her construction paper hat falls off, I bend over to retrieve it. That's when I plow into BJ Turlow's giant cone of strawberry ice cream.

"Aunt Corie!" Cam gapes as his friend's triple-decker slides off my hair onto my shoe. With my bare hands, I try to pick up the fallen scoops. Two moms standing behind me take a big step back. "Sorry," I say to them. To Cam. To BJ. To everyone around.

"It was an accident," says my mother. "Don't be silly."

She asks an employee for a roll of paper towels and hands one of the mothers a five dollar bill. "Get the kid a new cone, would you?"

"Thank you, Ma," I say.

My cheeks are burning, and my hands are cold. Strawberry ice cream melts between my fingers.

Where is Kate Turlow? I think. *I hope she isn't seeing this.*

Someone orders BJ a fresh cone, and Cam orders the same. Wella and Ma wait for a table where they can eat their hot fudge sundaes. I retreat to the drinking fountain with a clutch of napkins to clean my hair. Afterward, chin held high, I look for a place to toss the sodden mess.

Both trash bins at the entrance are overflowing with Styrofoam bowls and plastic spoons. In search of a bigger garbage can, I back out the door and scan the lot. Around the side of the building, beyond the glow of the Igloo's neon sign, I find an open dumpster. I toss the napkins over the edge. On my way back inside I blink.

Then I blink again.

In the shadows it appears as if the side of the building has come alive. But then my eyes adjust, and I make out two people groping each other. Desperate. Unaware. I try not to look, but it's too late. My stomach heaves, and I slip back inside. And for the rest of the night, I can't stop picturing it.

Kate Turlow pressed against Joey Farinelli.

ప్రు

Hours later I awaken in the pitch black of my bedroom as Tuck gathers up Wella to return her to her bed. I keep my eyes closed so he'll assume I am asleep. I haven't yet decided how much I want to say to him. About what I witnessed in the Igloo parking lot. About my sadness over his long work hours and the increasing frequency of his overnight trips. About my fears that we, too, could slip away from each other without either of us noticing.

When Tuck returns, he kicks off his scrubs and slides into bed beside me, curling his body along the arch of my spine. His arm slinks around my waist, and he brings his lips to the base of my neck. I stir and stretch a bit, acting as if I've just awakened from the depths of a dream. Maybe a part of me has.

"Hi there," he says.

I roll toward him, pull the comforter up to our chins. "Hey."

"Sorry I missed the show."

I don't respond to his statement. The truth is, he has missed more than this performance. But it's a pattern with his job that is real and beyond his control. Cases run long. Flights home are delayed. It's not his fault, I know. But I don't always let him off the hook as completely as I should.

"How did everything go?" he asks.

"The kids were great. They didn't even notice Uncle Tucker wasn't there. Again." I hear him swallow and worry I was too harsh.

"They had fun?" he asks.

"They did. Ma took pictures of them running around in their costumes before the performance."

"Of course she did."

"Bets wasn't there. You weren't there. I wasn't there," I admit. "My meeting ran late."

Tuck presses a hand to my hip. "Work's a real bitch, Core. Sometimes, there's no avoiding it."

"Yeah." I settle into the crook of his shoulder. "It is. And you know who else is a real bitch that's hard to avoid?"

He sighs. "I can't wait to hear."

"Kate Turlow." My teeth bite off the Ts of her name, and I wish they could tear deeper.

"Interesting," he says.

He doesn't sound interested at all.

"Seriously, Tuck. That woman is a piece of work. Ten pieces. At least."

His chin bumps my head as he nods. "I see what you mean. She's clearly up to no good with all that volunteer work. And the party planning. Those PTA meetings. How dare she?"

"Don't tease me."

"I'm not," he says. But without looking at my husband, I know he is smiling. I can feel the amusement on his face.

"You have no idea what happened," I say. "I caught her making out with Joey in a parking lot after the show. She had her tongue so far down his throat I almost gagged."

Tuck snorts. "Thanks for the visual."

"This is not funny," I say. "I'm talking about my *sister's* Joey. Joey Farinelli!"

"I know who you mean, and I'm sorry." He swipes at his mouth, erasing the grin. "I'm not laughing. I swear."

"It sounded like you were."

Tuck drops his hand and cups my shoulder. "Not at all," he says. "But let me remind you that Bets is the one who left Joey. And you don't even like the guy. You never have."

"Bets does. And they're still sleeping together. Plus there's Cam and Wella. And oh my God. I can't stop seeing it."

"OK," says Tuck. "OK."

His voice is so calm I want to scream.

"What are we going to do about it?" I ask.

"We?" says Tuck. "We're going to do nothing. Because as mad as you are, it's really none of our business."

"My sister is our business."

"She's a big girl, Core," he says. "And she is well aware of who Joey Farinelli is. Kate too, for that matter. I wouldn't be surprised if Bets already knows what's going on. And if you ask me, they are two sides of the same coin. Three sides, if that's possible. Either way, they're entitled to their private lives. Whether we agree with how they live them or not."

"That's all you have to say?"

"There's nothing more to say. I don't live under their roof or walk in their shoes. I live here. And tonight my shoes couldn't wait to walk back home to you." Tuck runs a palm along my cheek. His touch is gentle. "I missed you," he tells me.

"I missed you too."

"So please, Core. Let's not do this again. It's not good for you. It's not good for anyone."

"Let's not do *what* again?"

He is quiet.

"What is it you think I'm doing, exactly?"

Tuck's hand freezes. "You mean well, Core." He lowers

his voice as if this will somehow soften the blow. "But sometimes you try to fix things or fix other people you think are damaged, and they end up even more broken than before."

Other people?

My throat stings when I realize what Tuck is hinting at. Or better yet, *whom*. The weight of his implication settles on my chest, and I have to force myself to breathe. "This situation with Kate and Joey," I say, "has nothing to do with her."

"Has nothing to do with *who*, Corie?" Tuck waits for my reply. After a silence, he answers his own question. "I'll take three guesses." With his fingers he counts the names. "Scarlet, Scarlet and Scarlet."

"Don't," I tell him. "Don't."

"I'm not doing anything," he says. "It's those damn ten-year letters. Ever since you got them, you've been trapped inside your own head. Obsessed. Reliving the past over and over. But it wasn't your fault, Core. Or ours. We were there, yes. But the rest of it... You need to let go."

"I already have," I say. "I swear. I'm not thinking about Scarlet. I didn't even—"

I cut my protest short. Should I remind him that I never looked for her? That Scarlet is, right now, somewhere in San Francisco, pregnant and successful, living her lifelong dream? I am not jealous. After all, Tucker chose me. But no part of me wants him worrying about our long-lost best friend who is not only beautiful but fertile.

"You can't save everyone," says Tuck. "You couldn't then. You can't now."

I shut my eyes. "I didn't want anyone to get hurt."

"Of course you didn't. And that's my point. Sometimes, you try to protect other people, and you only make things worse."

"So you're saying I am to blame. At least a little bit."

"That's not what I meant. I'm simply asking you to stay out of this situation with Bets and Joey and Kate. You already harbor enough guilt. For both of us. It's exhausting."

I suck in a breath. Loudly.

"I didn't mean it that way," he says.

"No. I guess I have been pretty hard to be around lately."

"Don't put words in my mouth," he says. "You're fine. We're fine."

"Are we? Really? Admit it. These days it must be easier to be at work than to be with me."

Tuck's arms stiffen around me. "Is this because I was late tonight?"

I don't answer him because it is not about tonight. It's about always. And in the wake of my quiet, Tuck moans. A deep rumble in his throat. "Dr. Merchant took forever in the OR," he says. "And then I couldn't get a flight out of SFO until ten o'clock."

"I didn't ask why you were late," I tell him. "I know why you were late, and I understand. I asked if we are *really* fine."

Tuck shifts, gathers my hand in his. "As far as I'm concerned we're great."

"And what do other people think about us?"

"I don't care what other people think."

I withdraw my hand. "Maybe that's part of the problem."

"Maybe if you focused less on what's wrong with other people and more on what's right with us, you would be a whole lot happier. Maybe we both would." Tuck rises from the bed and grabs his shoes and scrubs from the floor.

"Where are you going?"

"My legs have been twitchy since I got off the plane. I need a walk. To clear my head."

"At this hour?"

"Fresh air still works after midnight," he tells me. "And I didn't mean to wake you in the first place."

"Yes you did," I say. In the moonlight, I see his shoulders sink.

"I love you, Core," he says. Then he whispers, "Try to get some sleep." I listen as the stairs creak under his weight, fourteen times in all. Then in the silence that follows, I am alone with my dark thoughts and our cold sheets.

And no one else to share them with until morning.

Scarlet

The city streets were decked out for the season. White lights. Red bows. Giant trees in storefront windows. The effect was warm and magical, but Scarlet rushed past the holiday tableaus without a second glance. The fatigue and nausea of the first trimester had mostly passed, but they had been replaced by a gnawing pit in her stomach, the heaviness of what lay ahead.

Motherhood. Child rearing. How would she survive?

She told Gavin she was heading downtown on her lunch break in search of maternity bras. What would he think if he discovered the truth? If he knew that for more than a month she had been grappling with her mother's dire warnings? Would he be angry or think her weak? Would he even want to have a baby with someone who had so many doubts in him?

At her first appointment she'd been surprised. Scarlet had assumed a space like this would be cluttered with official papers and serious books. The air, she thought, would be thick with shame. The guilt and anger visible. But the office was bright and sparsely furnished. Scarlet felt clean when she was here. She'd now been to two appointments and already felt as if she'd been baring her soul for the better part of forever.

Today her gray jacket and trousers were especially tight, the waistband held together by a rubber band rather than fastened. Dr. Kagawa, as usual, was dressed in dark slacks and ballerina flats. Her white blouse had tiny buttons at the collar.

She made Scarlet feel enormous.

The room smelled so strongly of cinnamon, Scarlet could almost taste it. Since she'd become pregnant, her senses were overly sharp. Not always in a good way. The only perfume she could tolerate was given to her by Gavin. She wore it now, a subtle lavender, and the cinnamon overpowered it. Scarlet almost asked Dr. Kagawa if she'd bought a candle or put a sachet in her desk. But what if noticing a new scent revealed that she was crazy?

The doctor flipped backward through the pages of a yellow legal pad, and Scarlet found herself shivering. Dr. Kagawa looked up from her notes.

"Are you cold?"

"No," Scarlet said.

She was imagining what Mama would say if she were here. *Some shrink. She's not wearing glasses. And shouldn't you be lying down on that couch? Guess the upholstery is too fancy for that. What is it? Suede? Leave it to you to find the only head-trip doctor in San Francisco who doesn't know what the hell she's doing. This place is for crap, Scarlet. Mark my words.*

"So." Dr. Kagawa turned to a fresh page in her notepad. "Still no thoughts of harming yourself or your baby?"

Scarlet nodded.

"Is that a yes, you have those thoughts? Or a yes, you do not?"

"No," she said quickly. "I mean no, I don't want to harm myself. Or my baby." Scarlet's mouth twitched. "I'll plead the fifth when it comes to harming anyone else." Her tight laughter echoed off the walls, and she lifted a hand as if to wave the sound away.

"You like to joke about serious topics," said Dr. Kagawa. "Especially when they're about you." There was no inflection at the end of her sentence. The doctor wasn't asking. She was telling.

"I hadn't noticed. But it's probably true."

"Why do you think you do that?"

"I don't know. Maybe to beat everyone else to it. I'd rather laugh at myself than have others laugh at me."

The doctor regarded her for a long moment. "Do you

worry about being the object of ridicule?"

"Not so much now," Scarlet said. "Let's call it a leftover habit from when I was a kid."

"Were you often teased as a child?"

"Weren't we all? Being a kid is awful. I made an easy target."

"Why is that?"

"I went to school with a lot of rich kids. And I wasn't. Rich, I mean. Also, I was kind of overweight. For girls, that's pretty much a cardinal sin." *Kind of. Pretty much.* Scarlet cocked her head as if she were listening to those chants in the cafeteria.

Hindenberg. Hindenberg.

The doctor nodded, an invitation for her to continue.

"I tried being funny first. And smart. But boys didn't line up for girls who were hilarious and brainy. They still don't. So I lost weight and borrowed clothes from a friend. I wore make-up, plucked my eyebrows. Grew breasts. Almost overnight, I looked like an entirely new person."

"How did that make you feel?"

"Good," admitted Scarlet. "Great, even. For a while." She looked away, noted a small square window across from her. Could she squeeze through it now if she tried?

"For a while?" the doctor prompted.

"Yes."

"And then what?"

"In the end," Scarlet concluded, "none of it mattered."

"What did matter?"

Scarlet bent her head, focused on her lap. Dr. Kagawa was patient with her and kind, but how much should she share? Some things she had never told anyone. Not Mama. Or Clara. Or Gavin. This was the doctor's job, of course. She was paid to listen and not judge. But she was also a virtual stranger. She hadn't earned Scarlet's trust.

"What did matter?" Dr. Kagawa asked again.

"I don't know."

"What do you know?"

Scarlet had expected this question. It was the way things went in these sessions. She lifted her head again to find Dr.

Kagawa resting the tip of her pen against her lip.

"I know I worked hard," she said. "Graduated top of my class. Got a full ride to Berkeley. They couldn't take that away from me."

"They?"

Scarlet paused, considered her answer. "Everyone."

The doctor leaned forward, black hair neat at her shoulders. "Do you feel like people take things from you?"

"They try," said Scarlet. "But they can't."

"Why is that?"

"I make sure I don't have anything worth taking," she said. "Not any more."

Dr. Kagawa set down her pen. "That must be difficult."

"It's easier than you think." Scarlet crossed her legs, and the wool of her pants scratched her knees.

"What is easy?" asked the doctor.

"Winning. Winning is easy."

"But you can't win all the time."

"Yes," she said, "you can."

"How?"

"You keep changing the rules."

Uncomfortable now, Scarlet trained her eyes on the wall above the doctor's head. *She should have a clock there.* Instead there was a plant—a Creeping Charlie, maybe—hanging from a macramé pot holder. Did the tendrils ever grow long enough to tickle the doctor on her head, or did she always trim the branches just in time?

"What would you do if you discovered you were still losing?" asked the doctor. "Even after changing the rules?"

Scarlet shook her head. "I'd stop playing."

Dr. Kagawa tented her fingers above the pages of her pad. "Quit before someone else can beat you?"

"Now you're getting it."

"What would happen if you didn't quit? What if you stayed in the game?"

Scarlet's hands balled into fists. "I've had my heart broken before," she said. "I won't let it happen again."

"Who broke your heart?" asked Dr. Kagawa.

Eyes closed, Scarlet fought the despair. She smelled

rubber from Sam's tires. Tasted Tucker's lips on hers. Heard Corie's stricken keening. Pictured Mama's good black dress. Felt strangers lifting her chin.

I'm sorry for your loss.

She opened her eyes, and Dr. Kagawa was watching her. Had she spoken the words out loud?

"I asked who hurt you," said the doctor.

Scarlet swallowed hard. "Who hasn't?" Dr. Kagawa was quiet, and Scarlet shrugged. "Whatever doesn't kill you makes you stronger, right?"

"Do you believe you're strong?" asked the doctor.

Scarlet placed a cool palm against her cheek. "I have to be," she said. "Otherwise I would be dead."

೪ↄ৶

Stepping out of Dr. Kagawa's office building, Scarlet hunted in her purse for a pair of sunglasses. The crying had stopped, but her eyes felt hot and swollen. Sunlight glared off the sidewalks, sharp and white. Even after she adjusted her lenses, Scarlet still found herself squinting. Not at the brightness of the afternoon but at a man in hospital scrubs. He was leaning against the building, arms folded across his chest.

Tuck Slater. Standing fewer than ten feet away from her.

He looked exactly as he had when she ran into him last August. His black hair, a bit too long across his forehead. A tentative smile. That tiny gap between his two bottom teeth. They hadn't planned to meet. Not after so many years. But deep down Scarlet had been unsurprised to find him at the cemetery.

As teenagers she and Tuck had often visited, two wounded birds in a place where they weren't the most broken. They always invited Corie, but she stopped going early on. The statues made her shudder, and she hated concrete evidence of her own mortality. As for Tuck? He felt deeply connected to the space after his mother's death. And when his dad remarried, Tuck spent hours at her graveside talking things out with her. Mr. Slater had found a new wife, but Tuck still missed his mom.

The boy was heartbroken. Vulnerable. Irresistible.

Scarlet pretended not to hear.

She had come for the silence, anyway. The contemplation of inevitable peace. In the cemetery, she wasn't alone. Pain was something to be shared. Tuck's being there with her had started out as an unexpected bonus, but over time, something shifted. She began to imagine they might fix each other's hurt. Too late she learned what Tuck wanted more than Scarlet's pieces was the wholeness of Corie Harper and her family.

Scarlet approached him now, and without thinking, she walked into his arms. For a moment they held each other. She breathed him in, then pulled away. Tuck took a step back, lowered his eyes. She surveyed his scuffed tennis shoes, moved upward to the dimple in his cheek. Having spent countless moments staring at his profile, she knew its shape by heart. How many times had she dreamed of tracing that face with her finger? Of kissing the rough edge of his jaw with her own soft lips?

"You're looking well," Tuck said, finally. She lifted a hand to brush him off. "No," he insisted. "You are." She nodded then, relenting.

"Been standing here long?" she asked.

"Long enough."

"Want to sit?"

When he nodded, she led him across the street to a grassy park. The concrete benches were cold despite the sunshine. Behind them children scrambled around the sandbox and playground.

"Nice outfit," she said as they sat. Tuck looked down at his scrubs, loose cotton pants and a matching top. In his shirt pocket he had an envelope. A pen. A pair of glasses.

"No big deal," he said. "Just work."

"And *just work* happened to bring you to downtown San Francisco?"

"I'm up here a lot now," he said. "At UCSF Medical Center. Sometimes Saint Francis. They're part of my new territory. I sell spine implants."

"You told me," she said.

He met her eyes. "I remember. At the cemetery."

"And out of nowhere you decided to find me."

"It wasn't hard. Were you hiding?"

"No," she told him.

"Good."

"Does Corie know?" Scarlet kept her voice steady and the question open-ended. What part of it would Tucker end up answering?

"She knows I'm in San Francisco."

"But you didn't tell her you were planning to look for me." Her words were bait. Scarlet was fishing for answers. *Had he been planning this?*

Tuck shook his head. "I guess I wanted to wait until there was a reason to tell her."

Scarlet smiled. "That is how you operate, isn't it?"

He brushed a hand through his hair. "If you say so." Before she could gather the courage to ask him what it was he really wanted from her, a buzz sounded from inside her purse.

"Excuse me." She checked her phone. A text from Gavin.

Hey, beautiful. How's the lingerie search going? Can I get a fashion show later? After the ultrasound?

The ultrasound. She had almost forgotten. Without texting back, Scarlet shoved the phone into her purse. She had been gone from the office for more than an hour. It was time for her to leave.

"I have to go," she said.

"Something wrong?"

Instead of answering, Scarlet said, "I'm sorry."

Tuck stood, reached out to help her up from the bench. She took his hand, and he slipped her a business card. She looked down at the card, back at him.

"I'd offer you a ride—" he began.

"I've got it," Scarlet said.

"If you need anything…" He nodded at the card.

"Thanks," she said. "I won't."

Still, she slid the card into the pocket of her jacket before turning in the direction of the bus stop. A part of her hoped Tuck would call after her. Ask to speak with her a bit longer. Tell her why he'd come. All she heard though was the clicking of her heels along the sidewalk.

ॐ

In the exam room, while she lay on the table, Gavin held Scarlet's hand. An ultrasound technician (*had she said her name was Andrea?*) squeezed a line of cold gel across Scarlet's belly. Her voice was bubbly and lyrical as she apologized for the gel's temperature. Then her tone evened out when she set about her work.

From a tray beside the monitor, Andrea (*yes, it was Andrea*) picked up a wand and drew the tip along the tight drum of Scarlet's abdomen. The wand's pressure was light, belying the weightiness of what gathered on the screen. First there was static, like a television without a signal. Next a blob in varying shades, something out of Picasso's blue period. Then, miraculously, a blurry skull materialized atop a throb that had to be a tiny heart.

Scarlet felt a jolt of recognition.

So you're the one who's been invading my body. Sapping every ounce of energy, killing my appetite. Stealing our sleep. Hello, little one. Hello, my baby. It's your mama.

Mama.

Scarlet's pulse raced with the strangeness and the wonder of it all. She felt both thrilled and terrified. *Oh, God. What have I done?*

"Looking good," said Andrea. "Looking really good."

The technician began to identify a litany of parts, growing organs, pieces of an incomplete human in the second trimester of development. Scarlet nodded, trusted that she was, in fact, looking at two legs, two arms. Ears. She accepted Andrea's professional assessment that everything seemed to be progressing normally. The baby appeared healthy. On the large side for its due date.

"When did you say your last cycle started?" asked Andrea.

Scarlet closed her eyes and kept them shut as she answered.

"Beginning of August, I think, but I'm not positive. I've never been regular. It's why I was on the pill in the first place," she explained. "I went back to my hometown that month, and

I skipped a few days by accident." Scarlet opened her eyes, met Andrea's gaze.

"It happens," said the technician. "Lucky for this little one, right?"

Scarlet smiled.

While Andrea continued her measurements, Scarlet thought about her encounter with Tuck, about how life truly could change in an instant. Human beings begin each day with assumptions about how the hours will proceed, forever unaware of which rug might be ripped out from under them. Out of nowhere, a thunderstorm might strike. Or the minutes might tick by without a drop of drama.

We never know which outcome we will get.

"Are you sure you don't want to find out the gender?" asked Andrea. She wore a smock covered in candy canes and a headband with pointy elf ears. Earlier, when she'd left the room in search of a missing form, Gavin had whispered that he didn't think he could look directly at her without laughing.

Like staring at the sun without risking blindness.

"We want to be surprised," Gavin told Andrea. "At least that's what the boss here has decided." Scarlet turned toward him and eked out a smile.

"Mr. Newstedt," Andrea said, "that is the correct answer." She returned her attention to the screen. "Good thing, too, because this baby is *not* cooperating. You've got a shy one here. Or a rebel. Pick your poison." Her laughter echoed in the sterile exam room, bouncing off the ceiling tiles.

"You OK?" Gavin asked Scarlet.

I am the opposite of OK, she thought. She closed her eyes and ignored the smell of her skin, clean sweat mixed with lavender. Instead she focused on the beat of the baby's heart. Her own blood coursing through its miniature veins.

Whoosh. Whoosh. Whoosh.

Lost in the rhythm, she wondered why Tucker hadn't asked if she was pregnant. Had he not noticed the swell of her stomach, the fullness in her breasts? True, she had gained only a few pounds after months of morning sickness. And in the stress of recent weeks, the hollows of her cheeks had grown more pronounced. Scarlet realized she might have appeared thinner today than she had when Tuck saw her last.

So why didn't I tell him about the baby myself? A waste of breath. That's why. Tuck Slater was happily married to her ex-best friend.

Wasn't he?

"Scarlet? Scar?"

The voice sounded foreign to her, as if it were coming from some faraway place. Or filtering through the layers of gel Andrea was wiping off her stomach. Scarlet turned her head, faced Gavin.

"Where did you go?" he asked. The sound was once again familiar in her ear, and Scarlet smiled.

"I'm right here," she said. As she reached out to him, the sheet of butcher paper underneath her crinkled. "Where else would I be?"

Andrea stood then and rolled her stool across the room. "I'll leave you to finish cleaning up," she said.

"Thanks, Andrea," Gavin said.

"My pleasure. And strong work, Mama!" She flashed Scarlet a thumbs-up, then she was gone.

Sitting up slowly, Scarlet adjusted her clothes while Gavin pored over the pictures Andrea had printed out.

Her baby.

"That was by far the coolest thing I've ever seen." He shook his head as if he still couldn't believe it.

"Hmm," said Scarlet in reply.

"You want to grab dinner? Celebrate?" Gavin studied her face. "Or we could go home if you're too tired."

"I need to tell you something," she said.

Gavin's gaze strayed to the stool abandoned in the far corner, then back to Scarlet. "Don't keep me in suspense," he said. His mouth twitched. "They'll need to get this room cleared out soon."

Scarlet dropped her chin to her chest, the straight view to the floor partially obscured by the small rise beneath her blouse. She would be, at the end of this week, eighteen weeks pregnant.

"I lied to you," she said. "The truth is, I've been seeing a psychiatrist." At her confession, Gavin exhaled as if he'd been storing all the oxygen in the room.

"I knew that," he told her.

A tilt of her head. "You did?"

"You're very loud when you're on the phone with Clara. Plus, you hate shopping. For bras or anything else."

Scarlet cracked a smile. "You think you've got me figured out."

"I do." Gavin crossed the room now and put the ultrasound pictures in her purse. "If that's it then, let's get out of here," he said. "I'm absolutely starving."

And so they left together, holding hands.

Dear Scarlet,

My niece and nephew are curled up with me on the couch watching The Wizard of Oz so I probably don't have to tell you what I'm thinking about, do I, Dorothy? That costume you made for Halloween our sophomore year will forever be the greatest I've ever seen. Better than Tucker's aluminum foil Tin Man. And let's not mention my Scarecrow outfit. Those overalls, hat and hay were already pretty lame. Then you had to go and rescue a dog to use as a real-life Toto.

I'll never forget how hard you cried when your mom made you bring Toto Two back to the shelter. It's been what—thirteen years? (You know how I hate math.) But I still like to tell myself that some nice family adopted that old dog; that someone who really loved him held on tightly in the end.

Sorry if that's depressing, but my thoughts these days are dark, and you're the only one who I can share them with. The only one who would understand.

Take tonight's dinnertime conversation. Ma was there (Isn't she always? Not that you'd know, but she is.) and Tuck and Bets were at work (Aren't they always?) so it was just the four of us: Ma, me, Campbell, Wella. And then Wella said it was too quiet with only four of us, and I said something sappy back to her like, "It doesn't matter how many people are around your dinner table as long as you've got love for the family that is there."

And that's when Wella started asking about my dad again. So I had to tell the kids (again) about their grandfather's heart attack. About how nobody expected it, except for maybe him. I had to watch (again) as their eyes grew wide and shiny at the details. This happens every time they hear the story, their morbid curiosity. After all, Cam was just a baby when my dad died, and Wella wasn't even born. I guess there's something safe about a tragedy that hasn't touched you with its stone-cold fingers.

While I was talking about Dad, Ma wiped her nose with the sleeve of her sweater, in short, choppy swipes, like it was itching. She almost never lets herself cry. At least not in front of me. And I'm not sure if that's a good thing or really bad, but I am sure I'm grateful for her control. For better or worse, I hate to see tears in her eyes. Or anyone's. Even yours. Especially yours.

Anyway, before I sat down to write this letter, I got to thinking. My father loved you like you were his own daughter, and this probably made everything both better for you and worse. I mean, sure, your life was brighter for a while because he was in it, but he was also one more person you stood to lose. And you did lose him even before he died when you walked away from us. By the time I lost him, you were nowhere to be found. I understand why, but it hurt. It always will.

But I'm ready to stop crying now. About what happened to us and to the people we loved. I'm ready to stop comparing pain. And I'm more than ready to stop hating myself. Are you?

Oh, Scarlet. I don't want to be mad at us any more.

Love,
Corie

Winter

Corie

Midterm staff development meetings are almost always a bore, and this year's program, sadly, is no exception. While our students enjoy a day off between semesters, the entire district's faculty gathers for stilted keynote speeches, agonizing break-out sessions and new PowerPoint presentations on old lessons we are retaught each year:

- How to treat bloodborne pathogens in the classroom
- Preparing kids for success on standardized tests
- Food allergies: myths and realities

Per tradition, Bart Kominski saved three seats in the back row, and Stella Womack brought a dozen Krispy Kremes, half powdered and half glazed. Unfortunately, the lattes I contributed were not enough to counteract the boredom, and by the time Superintendent Marta Iglesias took to the podium to discuss sexual harassment, I felt myself drifting off. Midway through her lecture on behavior that could result in a lawsuit, there comes a tap on my shoulder, and Stella whispers, "Who is that?"

I open my eyes to her dark ringlets dangling in my face and follow the point of her nose to the latecomers standing along the back wall of the gym.

"Which one?" Bart pokes his sandy head over Stella's shoulder.

"Him," she says to us.

With the tip of her finger, she gestures to a tall man with

broad shoulders. He has a shaved head and smooth skin the color of black coffee. He peers at his watch and leans against the wall, his posture both confident and loose.

"The one with the khaki pants and no tie?" I ask. She nods, and I swallow a mouthful of tepid latte. Bart scoots closer, his metal chair squeaking across the floor.

"That's Rick Roosevelt," he tells Stella. "In the old days, Corie was one of his students."

"Wait! He worked at CHS?"

"Shhh," I say.

"How come I've never seen him?" Stella asks.

"Dickie left the year before you were hired," Bart says. "Maybe two."

"Dickie?" Stella raises a brow. "Really? Dickie?"

"He goes by Richard," I correct. "Or Rick."

"*Dickie*'s got more zing," Bart says. "The guy gave up teaching to go to law school, wanted to spread his wings and whatnot. But he must've missed the classroom because I heard he's over at Conejo City College now. Teaching English to pre-law students. Or pre-law to English students. One of those."

"At CCC?" Stella asks. "Seriously?"

"Yeah."

"So he's smart too." Stella straightens in her seat.

"Shhh," I say again.

Bart bumps me with an elbow. "Looks like Stella found a subject to be interested in today."

Before I can shush Bart, Superintendent Iglesias finishes her speech and thanks us all for our careful attention. The crowd begins a half-hearted clap, and as she exits the stage, a wisp of a man in an ill-fitting suit steps up to the platform. He tugs his tie and introduces himself as Paul Fenton. He's an educational consultant. His voice cracks twice.

"For the next hour," Mr. Fenton informs us, "we will be articulating with our academic departments here on campus. The list of locations for each meeting is posted on the back doors." His words echo in the gym, but most of the teachers are no longer paying attention. "Please make your way to the correct classroom. Then after lunch we will gather back here for our series of breakout sessions."

Bart, who is in the social studies department along with Stella, looks at me and shrugs. "Guess this is where we part ways."

"Or... we could take an early lunch," Stella says. She checks our surroundings for potential spies. "Come on, kids. What do you think?"

"We can't," I say.

"Why not? No one will know we're missing, and I'm craving a margarita from Don Consuelos. Extra salt."

"Thanks a lot, Stell," I groan. "Now, instead of *articulating* about language arts assessments, I'll be fantasizing about chips and guacamole."

"At least you won't be fantasizing about Dickie Roosevelt," quips Bart.

"Stuff it," Stella says. "Unless you can set me up with him, in which case, please keep talking."

I proclaim them both ridiculous, then corral them to the back of the gym where the room assignments have been posted. As I scan the list of locations, I find myself wishing I were anywhere but on this campus. Discussing language arts. With other English teachers.

Especially Richard Roosevelt.

"Wait!" I say before I can reconsider. "Let's go."

"Let's go what?" Bart says.

"Oh my God!" Stella's mouth hangs open. "I think Corie Harper just agreed to ditch with us."

᠅

The main dining room of Don Consuelos is packed when we arrive so a waitress in an off-the-shoulder blouse leads us to a table on the patio. Mariachi music trumpets from palm tree speakers, and a green and red striped awning billows in the breeze. Our waitress deposits a ramekin of salsa and a basket of tortilla chips on our table.

"Who knew this place would be so crowded?" Bart asks.

Stella grins. "I told you their margaritas are to die for."

When we order our drinks, Bart sticks with plain iced tea.

"Someone's got to get this group back to work in one piece," he says.

"You're a prince," Stella tells him.

Bart salutes her. "Don't forget it."

When our margaritas and tea arrive, she licks the salted rim. "See, Corie? Isn't this better than sitting in a room full of English teachers?"

"Stella, you have no idea."

We decide on Supreme Enchilada and Consuelos Nachos platters to share. "With extra plates and forks, please," Stella requests. "Please." Hazy sunshine warms my skin, and my mouth waters at the scent of grilled onions and peppers.

"Cheers to cutting class," I say, and the three of us toast to freedom.

For the next half hour we talk about work, Bart railing against standardized tests while I suggest we get Don Conseulos' enchiladas in the CHS cafeteria. On her second margarita, Stella asks what we think about our assistant principal. More specifically, how we think he handled his first semester.

"I can tell you one thing," Bart says. "I *think* Henry Callaghan *thinks* plenty about Corie." Stella steals a cheesy nacho from my plate. "So true. That boy is nursing a mad crush on you."

I spit an ice cube into my glass. "Are you two insane?"

"Sure," she says. "But that's not the point."

"Henry knows I'm married."

"But he isn't," Stella says. "Married, I mean. And believe me, he has his eye on you. It's kind of cute the way he's always creating excuses to talk to you in the faculty lounge at lunch."

"That's because I sit in a corner by myself."

"Hey! That's your choice," says Bart. "We only leave you alone so you can write."

"Henry doesn't know that," I say. "He's just being nice."

"Aha. There's your answer," says Stella. "Corie thinks our new AP is *nice.*"

"I do not!" My nose stings, and I tell myself it's from the salt on my margarita and not because I sometimes watch Henry Callaghan cross the quad from my classroom window.

"I don't think about anyone but Tucker," I say.

"Then your life is more depressing than I suspected," says Stella. When I frown at her she adds, "There's nothing wrong with a little fantasy now and then. In fact, it can spice things up."

Bart takes a forkful of enchilada, talks with his mouth full. "I agree if we're talking about Dickie Roosevelt. But please. No fantasies about Henry Callaghan."

"I take it H.C. isn't your type?" Stella asks.

Bart shakes his head. "He's a math/science guy. He doesn't get the way a history class should be run."

Stella squawks into her drink. "So you got a bad mid-year review from our AP?"

"Hell, no! He gave me a five-star rating. Then he told me I should put more maps up on my walls. Maps!" Bart drops his fork. "As if we don't have bigger issues than—" He breaks off mid-sentence, his focus shifting over my shoulder. I swing around and see Rick Roosevelt walking toward us across the patio.

"Speak of the devil," Bart says.

My mouth is an O. I gape at him like a fish.

He reaches our table and looks down at our graveyard of plates and glasses, eyes poring over each item like an inventory. Then Rick Roosevelt smiles.

"I didn't mean to interrupt."

"You're not," Bart says.

I take a long breath, an attempt to calm my racing heart. This was exactly the encounter I'd been hoping to avoid when we left school.

"I don't believe we've met." Stella bends over me and sticks out her hand. "I'm Stella. Stella Womack? I teach at Conejo High."

"Rick," he says. "It's a pleasure."

"All mine." Stella flashes her teeth, then she asks Rick Roosevelt to join us.

No no no.

"Wish I could." He glances around the patio. "I'm meeting the other afternoon presenters here in about five minutes."

Bart groans. "Don't tell me you got roped into running one of those things."

"I did." Rick ducks his head. "But only as research for my dissertation. The district's letting me administer a survey during my session."

"On what?" asks Stella.

"It's another study on the role gender plays in academic success. But I'm hoping my angle is original." He smiles at Stella. "I won't bore you with the details."

"On the contrary," she says. "It sounds fascinating. Maybe I'll attend your session instead of the one I signed up for. Who needs more practice of online grading programs? Am I right?"

"You'll get no argument from me," Rick says. "But I didn't stop by to talk shop." He shifts his attention to me as I sit in silence, dreading what's to come. "I wanted to ask if you got your ten-year letter, Corie. I mailed them out months ago, but I always worry some of my old students won't receive theirs. People move. Addresses change." He pauses. "The perils of time."

I nod, force myself to speak. "I did get it. I absolutely got it." My tongue tangles on itself, a jump rope that's been stepped on.

"I'm so glad," he says. Then he clears his throat. "Do you know if Scarlet's letter made it to her?" My mouth goes dry. Full of wool. I fumble for a way to answer him honestly.

No, Scarlet's letter is collecting dust in the top drawer of my nightstand alongside several others I've been writing to her.

"Sorry," I say. "I haven't talked to her in years."

"Huh." Rick Roosevelt studies my face. "She didn't tell me you two weren't in touch." My blood is ice, and my brain thaws his words.

She didn't tell me.

"You saw Scarlet?" I ask.

"In August. I ran into her on campus at CCC. Actually, she ran into me. And I expected to see all of you at the ten-year reunion." He hesitates. "But I understand why that might have been difficult."

"It was my anniversary," I tell him, although this wasn't the reason Tuck and I skipped it. Neither of us wanted to revisit those memories over banquet chicken and small talk.

"Fair enough. You are forgiven."

Rick nods, and I nod back. I almost tell him *forgiven is the last thing I feel*. Instead, I steer us back to the fact that he and Scarlet saw each other last summer.

"Why was Scarlet at CCC?"

"Setting up a scholarship. Her firm agreed to sponsor a deserving student each year. Someone who wants to pursue law school but can't afford tuition."

"That's... wow... that's really great."

"Yeah." He nods again. "She wants to make sure other kids like her get a shot. It's pretty wonderful."

She always was, I think.

"I offered to work with her," he says. "To do what I could to get the program going. We outlined a plan together. I wanted to help her." His eyes remain fixed on mine. "And the kids who need the money, of course."

"Of course," I say. "That's very generous."

"Not generous enough. I never heard from her afterward. I have no idea if she followed through."

"At least you tried," I tell him. "I mean it. Sometimes people don't want to be helped."

Rick puts a hand on my shoulder. His expression is gentle, but I don't want it to be. "I'm sure you tried to help her too. You and Tucker. You three were tight."

Yes. We were, I think. "That was a long time ago," I say.

"My second year teaching, as I recall." He runs a hand over his head as if even he can't believe it. "I was twenty-five when I started that ten-year letter assignment."

I do the math in my head. Rick Roosevelt is still young.

"Not that it's any of my business," Stella interjects, "but what's this about some old letters? Am I being nosy? I hate being out of the loop."

"It's a long story," I say.

Against my will, I picture Scarlet the week after we wrote to ourselves. Her pale face. Eleanor's fake pearls. The stench of flowers in baskets, vases, wreaths. Organ music wailed all day, but my best friend never did.

"Jeez, Corie." Stella pokes my shoulder. "Serious much?"

I lift my head, and find Rick Roosevelt staring at me. "I'm sorry about you and Scarlet," he says.

"I am too."

"If you hear anything from her..." he says.

"I won't," I tell him.

"Well." His head bobs at Bart and me. "It was great running into you two again. And nice meeting you, Stella. Maybe I'll see you again at my breakout session?"

Her face is flushed, and she grins at him. "One o'clock. In the theater. I'll be there."

Bart aims a thumb at Stella. "Good luck getting a decent survey out of this one," he says. "She might skew your results."

Rick smiles and runs a hand over his dark scalp. "I'm sure she'll do just fine."

"Either way, I hope your survey goes well," I tell him. "And I hope you hear from Scarlet."

Rick looks at me, and his smile tilts. "So do I, Corie. So do I."

Scarlet

"I thought you were meant to be over the morning sickness by January," said Clara. "Haven't you reached the second semester yet? You know. The good part. Before you get too big and uncomfortable?" She handed Scarlet a cup of tea with lemon, then slid a chair up to her desk.

"It's second *trimester*," said Scarlet. "And I'm well into it, thank goodness. But these circles under my eyes are not from pregnancy. For better or worse."

"What's got you so looking so wretched then?"

"Wretched? Ouch."

Clara shrugged. "If the circles fit..."

"Right." Scarlet took a sip of her tea, stalling. She didn't want to explain the reason for last night's lack of sleep.

"It's nothing." Scarlet blotted her lips with a napkin even though her mouth was already dry. "Why can't it be nothing, Clare?"

"Because it never is," she said. "Not with you."

"I promise I will figure it out myself."

Clara furrowed her brow. "I'm worried about you. Please. Let me help."

"Fine." Scarlet cleared her throat, kept the details vague. "It's just that I found something," she said. "Last night before bed. And after I found this something, I couldn't sleep."

"So?"

"So. That's it then," she said. "I'm tired. Not baby sick."

Scarlet looked away from Clara and fidgeted in her chair.

"I meant *so what did you find.*"

"It doesn't matter. I shouldn't have been searching in the first place."

"Searching," Clara pressed.

Scarlet looked back at her and gave another inch. "In Gavin's gym bag."

"For what?"

"Tylenol," she said. "Pregnant women are allowed to take Tylenol. I checked."

"But your medicine cabinet is practically a pharmacy, Scarlet. Why on earth would you search in Gavin's bag?"

"He was already in the bathroom taking a shower," she explained. "It was steamy in there, and I didn't want to disturb him." Scarlet scooped a lemon slice from her empty cup and shoved her napkin inside.

"Reasonable excuse," said Clara. "I suppose."

"In any case, I didn't find any Tylenol."

"What did you find, then?"

Scarlet skinned the rind off the lemon and slipped the wedge into her mouth. Why had she thought she could keep last night a secret? Her lips puckered around the word even as she answered. "A ring." Her voice dropped to a whisper. "The diamond kind. Gavin has a diamond ring in his gym bag."

"Bloody hell!" Clara slapped Scarlet's desk.

Scarlet sighed then. Relieved. Worried. Pleased. "And after that," she said, "I couldn't sleep."

"Of course you couldn't," said Clara. "Why didn't you tell me?"

"I just did."

"Jesus, Scarlet!" Clara covered her mouth. "This is huge news!"

Scarlet laid a hand on her belly. "Almost the hugest."

"If you spill every detail now," said Clara, "I might forgive you for not calling me immediately. So. What happened next? Don't leave anything out. Not a word."

"First, Gavin came out of the shower." Scarlet crumpled the Styrofoam in her hand. "Then, I pretended to be asleep. The end."

"That's it?"

"Yep."

"So he didn't ask you?"

Scarlet shook her head.

"But he is taking you out tonight."

Scarlet nodded. "For the anniversary of our first date."

"Sounds like the perfect opportunity for a proposal. Oh Lord, what I wouldn't give to be a fly on the wall. Or in your soup. Or something!"

"Well you can't be." Scarlet tossed her cup at the trashcan, and it ricocheted off the edge before landing on the rug. Clara retrieved the cup, napkin and lemon rind, and threw the whole mess in the garbage.

"Can I at least be your maid of honor then?" she asked. "I'm very helpful. See?"

Scarlet frowned. "What you are is very relentless. But we can talk about that later. Right now, we have to get to court."

In the elevator on their way to the lobby, Clara hummed the wedding march while Scarlet drummed her fingers against the strap of her leather bag. "Remember, I haven't said *yes* yet. And Gavin hasn't asked. We don't know for certain that he will."

Clara stopped humming. "Why else would he be carrying around a ring, silly? He's obviously going to propose. Probably tonight. Which means we have the rest of the day to figure out what you're going to say to him."

"We?"

"Fine. You." Clara held the elevator door, and Scarlet stepped into the lobby. The odor of disinfectant slapped her in the face, the marble floors still slippery from a mopping. "But seriously, Scar," said Clara. "What *are* you going to say when Gavin asks?"

"Honestly, I'm not sure," she said. "But I can promise you one thing: You'll be the third person to know."

৩৯৫

She'd been composing a mental list of pros and cons since discovering the ring. Reasons to say *yes* to Gavin. Reasons why saying *yes* was a terrible mistake. Neither side was winning. The scales were too easy to balance. When Judge Noonan called for a break, Scarlet tried Dr. Kagawa's office, hoping for some last-minute advice. But the doctor couldn't schedule a session on such short notice. Scarlet was on her own with this one.

God. What should I do?

She needed time. To shower. And think. To decide what was best for both her future and the baby's.

After court she took a taxi straight to the apartment. But when the driver pulled up to their building, Gavin's car was already parked across the street. Scarlet dug in her bag for her phone.

He's home, she texted Clara. *Wish me luck.*

Without waiting for a reply, Scarlet climbed the stairs to their apartment one foot at a time. Like a bride walking up the aisle toward her groom. Or an inmate to the electric chair. Why was she so terrified to face the man she loved?

Their door was locked. Gavin was forever sliding the deadbolt in place, an old habit he seemed unable to break.

Gavin threw open the door before she could knock. "Hello, beautiful."

"What a surprise," she said. "You're never home early." Scarlet hoped she sounded happy.

"I was excited for our evening."

"Sorry to keep you waiting." She swiped at her forehead and kicked off her shoes in the entryway. "The cab was hot. I'm a little sweaty."

"You're glowing."

Scarlet smiled. "You're equivocating."

"OK, let's compromise: I'm glad you're all right. When you didn't come back to the office, I thought maybe you weren't feeling up to dinner."

Scarlet scanned the room. No flowers. No candles. She hadn't said as much to Clara, but she suspected Gavin might propose at home, not at the restaurant. He seemed the type of man who would want to celebrate all night, not wait until its end.

Gavin pulled a chair out from their table. "Have a seat."

"I need a shower."

"In a minute." He patted the cushion of the chair. "Please. Sit."

She took a step forward, then stopped. "Since when did you become so bossy?" Her lip turned up at one edge.

"So you've finally noticed." He cupped a hand around his mouth as if revealing a long-held secret. "For your information, Scarlet Hinden, I have been in complete control of this relationship from the beginning."

"Is that right?"

Gavin nodded. "Do you remember our first unofficial date?"

"Ugh." She scrunched her nose and lowered herself into the chair. "Not this tired story again."

"I know, I know. You hate to be reminded of the single clumsy moment in the history of your life."

Scarlet grimaced. "It's not that."

"Of course it is. But allow me to disabuse you of your shame."

"What are you talking about?"

"When you plowed into me that morning? Coming out of the copy room?" Scarlet rolled her eyes, and Gavin grinned. "I orchestrated the entire fiasco."

"You're crazy."

"Nope. I knocked into you. On purpose. I wanted those papers to spill so you'd finally notice me." She studied his face, noted the rise and fall of his Adam's apple. As far as she could determine, Gavin was not lying.

"It took forever to sort through those piles," she said.

"Yes. Just the two of us. Sitting *this close* to each other."

"You were practically in my lap," she said. "I was furious."

"You were dying for me to kiss you." Gavin smiled. "And that's exactly why I didn't. I was patient. Waiting you out. Until you couldn't resist me any longer." He took her hand.

This is it, she thought. *He's going to ask me. Right now.*

"When you were hired," Gavin said, "you pretended to be so tough. Storming around like you were angry at the whole world."

"What makes you think I wasn't?"

"I could tell. Deep down inside you were soft."

"Soft?" Scarlet withdrew her hand and sat up straight. "You really are crazy."

He leaned toward her, insistent. "I'm not," he said. Then he paused, as if making sure she was truly listening. "That first month, I heard you crying. Over that little girl from Oakland. The one the police found chained to those box springs in her basement. Do you remember? Her name was Madison, I think."

Scarlet stiffened, recalling the news reports, the gruesome network coverage. Everyone at the firm gathered around televisions watching her rescue. The child was filthy and emaciated. Terrified of people. Scarlet's coworkers were outraged. They took bets on the parents' defense strategy. She listened to their protests and prayers. It was a miracle the girl had survived.

How had she survived?

"Madelyn," she said. "Her name is Madelyn."

"She was five."

"I didn't cry," said Scarlet.

"Not in the lounge," he said. "But afterward. In the conference room. I was outside the door."

"You were spying on me?"

Gavin shook his head. "There was something in your eyes that day," he said. "Something about that girl's story crushed you."

"That makes me human, Gav. Not soft."

"Exactly. Human. I liked that about you. I still do. But I'm not stupid, Scar. I could tell even then you didn't want comforting. Not from me or from anyone for that matter. You'd built a wall up so damn high I couldn't even wave to you over it. So a few days later I bumped into you. Literally. Papers everywhere."

"You risked months of my research."

"I gave you a reason to need me," he said. "It's OK to need someone, Scarlet."

She shifted in her seat. Gavin looked so hopeful sitting next to her adding this new thread to their story. Was he trying to melt her? Loosen her up for the big question?

"Why are you telling me this now?"

"Because I want you to know," he said. "I see you, Scarlet Hinden. The real you."

"I'm not who you think I am, Gav."

"You're wrong. I've watched you all this time. I've looked under that thick skin of yours. In front of everyone else, you spit nails. But you cry alone. Over other people's hurt. You can't stand it when someone else is in pain."

Scarlet dropped her head. She did not deserve this praise. Gavin was giving her too much credit. He wouldn't if he could see inside her heart. "You don't know me," she told him.

"I'm trying damn hard to."

"Well, you can stop," she said. "Just be satisfied on the surface. It'll be easier for us both." She stood quickly, and Gavin caught her chair to prevent its toppling over.

"Easy is overrated," he said. "I don't want to be on the surface."

"Maybe not. But I don't want to be fixed."

She spun around, then realized she had nowhere else to go. She imagined Gavin's eyes boring into the nape of her neck. He loved the spot below her ponytail where a few stray hairs would fall free to brush against her white skin. Gavin favored the parts of her that were most vulnerable whether she wanted him to or not. She feared if he reached out to touch her at this moment, she might break.

"Please, sit, Scarlet."

His request was quiet, and she turned slowly to face him. Then she squared her shoulders, teeth sliding against each other. A voice came from her that did not sound remotely familiar.

"Gavin Newstedt." Her words were low and steady. "Will you marry me?"

His head bent, but he did not break eye contact. He rose to his feet and collected both of her hands in his. "I don't want to fix you," he said.

"That's not an answer."

"Is this your way of proving you're the one who's in control?"

She raised her brow. "Are you going to keep asking

questions?"

"Do you really want to marry me?" Gavin asked.

Still clutching his hands, Scarlet dropped to one knee and closed her eyes. Then, although she didn't realize it, she held her breath. Gavin freed a hand and placed it below her chin. He lifted her face and bent for a kiss.

"Yes," he said into her mouth. She opened her eyes.

"Yes?"

Gavin nodded and helped Scarlet to her feet. She pressed a palm against her forehead. "Did we just get engaged?"

"I believe we did." Gavin grinned. "I also believe you're the tiniest bit insane."

"Oh, I'm a lot insane," she said. "And yet you claim to know me."

Gavin drew Scarlet to him, and she let herself be held. She wanted to rest her head on his shoulder. To pull him into the bedroom and sleep for hours. Instead she peeled herself away from him and smiled. "I'll be right back. If you're going to make an honest woman out of me, I'd like to take a shower. Maybe put on clean clothes. A dress."

"You probably should," said Gavin.

"I won't be long," she told him.

"Take your time," he said. "I'll open up some champagne. And a bottle of sparkling cider for you."

In the bathroom, she removed her trousers and blouse with trembling fingers. She placed the clothes on a towel hook where they hung like empty husks. Turning on the shower, she slid the knob toward its highest setting. Her skin rippled with goose bumps. She should have waited to undress.

Scarlet leaned over the sink and peered at her reflection. "Hello, beautiful," she said, an imitation of Gavin. She tried on different smiles. None of them felt real.

I will do this one thing right, she thought. *I have to. But how?*

While she waited for the water to warm, hot tears gathered in her eyes. Then Scarlet watched her face disappear inch by inch in the steam-covered mirror.

Dear Scarlet,

We interrupt this regularly scheduled broadcast to bring you an important message:

I am angry! At the universe. My uterus. At my mother and Bets and Tuck. I'm angry at myself.

And my job. I hate my freaking job right now. Because I really want to be writing—I have a novel in me or maybe even two, dammit!! But how can I possibly write anything worth publishing when I'm busy teaching my students how to analyze Huck Finn?

I know. Shame on me for complaining. I have a great career, a great family, a great husband, great friends. (Except you of course. I don't have you any longer.) OK, so I also don't have a father any more. Or a book deal. Or a baby. But we can't always get what we want, right? Shit. Now I'm angry at the Rolling Stones. You know what else makes me angry? Spilling my guts to you and then sticking every letter in a drawer. But I need to blow off steam, and Tuck is out of town (on my birthday) so I have no one else to vent to except you. Congratulations, Scarlet! You win! Proceed directly to Go and collect TWO HUNDRED DOLLARS! Am I making any sense? Probably not.

Right now, you are probably thinking I'm being 'overly dramatic' and I guess I always tended to be emotional. You used to accuse me of being too sentimental, like when I cried during those Sarah McLachlan commercials. But what I would like to know now is how come you never did?

Those dogs were so pathetic, their eyes all goopy and wet and their fur so matted. Their skin completely flea-bitten, for God's sake. But you would shrug and say there were plenty of people in this world who have it worse. Why should we cry over a dog?

You were full of shit though, because then you went and rescued Toto Two. Even though you knew your mom would make you take him back. It's almost like you wanted to torture yourself or something. You tried pretending nothing bothered you, that nothing, no one, no dog really mattered. But the truth is, you were scared. Scared to want something. So you lied to yourself, my friend. Maybe you're still lying.

I didn't know you loved Tuck because you never admitted it to me. Or to him. You joked that kissing him would be like kissing your brother, or worse, your loser cousin. And you started to keep me at arm's length too. Like you still couldn't trust me. And when I'd try to get closer, you would pull away. I understand now that you were kidding about Tuck. And protecting yourself from needing me—or anyone else—too much. But your attitude made it easier for Tuck and me to pick each other. I loved you first, but he loved me back. I couldn't risk losing him so I left you.

We were young, Scarlet. And stupid. So very, very stupid. But I'm all grown up now. And I sometimes wonder if I'm being punished now for the past wrongs I've done. For being a part of your life's worst pain. For being the wrong person at the wrong time. Always the wrong time.

Am I rambling? I think I'm rambling. Can you tell I drank most of a bottle of wine by myself? I was saving it for my birthday, and I would have shared it with Tuck, but he's not here and I have no idea where you are.

So, cheers to us. All three of us. Better drunk than lonely.

I miss him. I miss you. I miss me. Is that possible?

Can a person miss herself?

Why do I feel like I'm about to find that out?

Love,
Corie

Corie

My sister removes her empty coffee cup from its saucer and squirts a puddle of ketchup onto the tiny white plate. "I still can't believe Miss Goody Two-Shoes played hooky from school," she says. "And that we're wasting your day off at Barbecue Bobby's."

"I'll be back for afternoon classes." I spin a fork in my pasta primavera. "And if I didn't take the ten o'clock appointment, I would've had to wait until March." I shove the ball of fettuccini into my mouth and slurp the noodles from my chin.

"I wish you would've let me come with you." Her fingers hover over a basket of French fries. She selects two stuck together. "I'm not good for much these days, but I can drag myself out of bed for moral support."

"You're sweet," I tell her. "But I was fine. And you're here now."

"Still. I could've been there in the waiting room. Brought along some trashy magazines. Made it fun."

"With your kids around, I get plenty of fun these days." I sprinkle more parmesan cheese on my pasta, then set the dispenser back beside a plastic cup of crayons. "What I need is a cooperative embryo."

"It's like the doc said. You've gotta take the calendar and ovulation kits out of your bedroom." Bets snatches another fry and aims it at my face. "It's Valentine's Day, Core. Make love. Not schedules."

"I would be naked without my ovulation chart."

"Naked is sort of the point, isn't it?" Bets cocks her head. "Speaking of which, what's Tuck got planned for you two tonight?"

"Who knows? He was in surgery all morning. Right now he's probably at a lunch meeting trying to win over some new doctor."

"Sounds dazzling. Almost like foreplay."

We stop talking as a waitress in a short skirt and apron stops by to refill our water glasses. Before I can take a drink, my sister's cell phone vibrates on the table. Bets drops her burger and snatches her phone in one swift move.

"It's rude to text at lunch," I say in my best imitation of our mother. "Where are your manners? Next you'll be putting your elbows on the table."

"In case you hadn't noticed, this isn't Buckingham Palace." Bets nods at the cup of crayons. "Our table is covered with butcher paper. To color on."

"I was being Ma," I tell her. "Don't you get it? A joke?"

Bets ignores me and taps out a reply.

"So?" I say when she turns her attention to me again.

"So what? You want me to ask the waitress for more crayons?"

"So... who's the message from?"

"Right," says Bets. "Because *that's* your business." She studies me with a raised eyebrow.

"Oh my God." I lower my voice as if someone in the noisy lunchtime crowd might overhear our conversation. "You're not still hooking up with Joey, are you? Today of all days? Come on, Bets. He's seeing at least one other woman that we know of. What happened to your pride?"

My sister's tongue rolls across her teeth like she's checking for lettuce. Then she says, "I seem to remember one of my sisters promising not to judge me. Wait a minute. I only have one sister. YOU."

"Lucky me," I say.

"Anyway, what's wrong with a casual dip in the Farinelli pool every once in a while? I get to splash around for a bit, then Kate Turlow shows up to deal with his crap. Like the goddamn cavalry. With fake boobs."

"Wait. You think they're fake?"

Bets frowns at me. "That's not the point."

"Then what is?"

"Just because Joey can't keep it in his pants doesn't mean he's not great in bed." She leans over the table. "There's a reason ladies toss their panties at him."

"And you want to be one among many?"

"I'm no lady," she snorts. "And why do you care? Is this all hitting a little close to home for you?"

"No." I sip my water again. It drips onto my lap. "I never have to worry about Tuck. Ever."

"I think the lady's protesting a little too much," says Bets. "Did I get that right?"

"Close enough. But I'm not protesting. And Tuck and I are great."

"You should be thanking me then," says Bets. "Because I'm taking the kids and staying at Joey's place tonight, which means you guys have the house all to yourselves."

Her phone buzzes again, and my stomach churns while she responds to her ex. *Tuck and I might be going through a rough patch,* I think, *but we're nothing like the two of them. How could she even try to make a comparison?*

"I hope you at least asked him to get tested for STDs," I say when Bets finishes her text. My sister is quiet for a moment. Then she drops her phone into her purse.

"That wasn't Joey," she says. "It was Tuck. He tried to text you, but you didn't respond so he got worried."

"Oh." I wrestle a red crayon from the plastic cup and draw a long oval on the paper next to my glass. I avoid the stray drips of water around it. "What did you tell him?"

"That it's rude to text during lunch."

"Ha." My eyes burn, but I refuse to cry in this restaurant with butcher paper tablecloths. "No, seriously. What did you say?"

Bets grins. "I told him to pick up some chocolate and wine because he's having chart-free sex tonight."

"Thank you," I say. "For real." Dragging the red crayon

across the paper, I extend my single red oval into a two-sided one. It is twisted in the middle like a figure eight.

Or the symbol for eternity.

※

Greer Larson creeps into my classroom a full five minutes before the after-lunch bell. Behind her the door shuts with a *hush,* and she slips into her seat, hunching down as if to hide. From me. From everyone.

"You're early," I say. She withdraws into the hood of her sweatshirt. Other kids begin to shuffle into the room alone or in small packs. They laugh. Shove. Posture. Greer lays her head down on her desk. I walk to her aisle and bend down to whisper. "Are you all right?"

From under her hood comes a sound. Maybe a sniffle.

"If you stay after class," I tell her, "we can talk during the break. I'll write you a pass if you need one." Her shoulders jerk by way of response. The bell rings, and I return to the front of the class to begin our lesson.

As usual, I have put a journal prompt on the board, this time a quotation from T.S. Eliot's *Love Song of J. Alfred Prufrock.*

What does the statement "I have measured out my life with coffee spoons" mean? What activities signal the passing of your day? In other words, what is the routine of your life, and why is this routine significant? There is no right or wrong answer. Think deeply. Answer honestly.

While the kids write, I roam the classroom pausing to read what they've come up with or to redirect a student who is distracted by something else. Most of them follow directions. A few of them work hard. Others spend more time staring into space, pretending to "think deeply."

When I reach Greer, I stop to check how she's doing.

The girl's journal, a navy blue spiral with college-ruled paper, is open on her desk. Only a few lines are scrawled across the page, and her arm curves around them shielding her words. I gather my skirt and crouch down close. Greer pulls her arm back so I can read what she has written:

My days are measured out by a lot of puking. This is significant because morning sickness sucks and whoever said it stops in the first trimester sucks too. Now it's too late for an abortion which sucks the most.

I go numb and move away from her like a zombie. One of the undead. I want to crawl under my desk right now and wait for the world to end. Instead I peel a post-it off the pad next to the computer. My breath whistles through the pen's cap as I write out a pass for the health office. I sign and date the note then drop it on top of Greer Larson's almost-empty journal. On unsteady legs, I continue to make my way up and down the other aisles.

I'm about to stop the journal-writing session when my cell phone vibrates on my desk. Troy Solomon says, "Busted, Ms. Harper!" but I ignore him and check the incoming text from Tucker.

Can't wait to see my favorite Valentine tonight.

I turn off the phone and place it in my purse. Then I clear my throat and face the students who, by now, look at me expectantly.

"All right then," I begin, willing my voice not to crumble. "What can you all tell me about Michelangelo?"

୨୦୶

That night Tuck drops his box of chocolates when he opens our bedroom door. I'm sprawled on the bed in a black negligee, my stomach sucked in, both calves flexed. My husband surveys the champagne, the rose petals. My coy smile.

"Am I in the right house?" he asks.

"Welcome home," I say. "I've been expecting you."

Tuck glances over his shoulder then back at me. "I must be dreaming because it seems like we're alone here."

"Well, it is Valentine's Day."

"So I've been told."

He moves into the room, and I imagine myself pressed against him, shirt off, lost in the moment, skin to skin. In the earliest days of *us*, we could drive each other crazy fully clothed, lying side by side on the bench seat of his truck. We hadn't told anyone we were together yet—had barely admitted it to ourselves. We took slow steps toward intimacy. Inch by

inch. Touch by touch. It was thrilling. Breathless. Urgent.
Neither one of us could get enough. That was before the
sadness. Before loss and pain and failure.

Tuck tilts his head. "What's that look for?"

"Nothing." I meet his eyes. "I was just wondering if
you're thirsty."

"I'm parched." He smiles at me and rescues the dripping
champagne bottle from the ice bucket. After pouring a small
amount in one of the two flutes, he offers it to me. "You
first."

"No, thanks." I slip off the bed and approach him while
he freezes, a half-filled glass of champagne in one hand. "I feel
like celebrating in a different way." I take the glass and set it
on the dresser.

His mouth is a question mark, and I hoist myself onto the
dresser, coaxing him into the space between my legs. He
moves his hands up my thighs. Our breath quickens when his
fingers reach my hipbones, and I free myself from a tiny strip
of underwear. Tuck unbuttons his jeans, and we lock eyes as
his keys hit the floor. I almost don't notice when the glass of
champagne tips over. I think only of our lips and tongues and
skin. Salt mixed with sweetness. My teeth braced on the hard
bones of his shoulder.

Afterward we are quiet. Tuck's damp forehead rests
against mine. He inhales. I exhale. There is no space between
us. All too soon he backs away from me to peel off his shirt.
Then he tosses it in a heap next to his jeans. His eyes search
mine as if he's figuring out a secret. The answer to some riddle
he cannot solve.

Without a word he grabs a handful of tissues from the
box on the dresser and offers one to me. Then he uses the rest
to mop up the champagne dribbling onto our rug. I clean
myself and readjust my negligee while he heads into the
bathroom. I'm on the bed when he returns, a towel wrapped
around his waist.

"So tell me, Core. What exactly was that?" His arms are
limp at his sides, and I lean back against the pillows.

"That," I say with a smile, "was Valentine's Day." I survey
the planes of his face, expecting the blank slate of satisfaction

he usually wears after sex. But tonight he just looks confused. His mouth is a downward arc, and I feel suddenly naked even though I never got undressed. "You're not mad, are you?" I ask.

He lowers himself onto the mattress beside me. "No, Core. Of course not. But let's be real. We haven't exactly been rocking the world of romance lately. It's been... clinical... I guess you could say. With all the planning and coordinating and manipulating. It's been a long time since you went at me like that."

"*Went at you?*" I laugh, hoping to keep the mood light, but in truth, I am bewildered. "I'd say you met me half way."

"You flashed your panties at me," he says. "What did you expect?"

"My panties render you helpless, do they?"

"A little bit." Tucker rakes a hand through his dark hair.

I shrug. "I thought you'd appreciate the spontaneity."

"I did," he says. "I do." He scoots closer, and his eyes move over my face, like he is memorizing my features for an exam. "What about you?"

"Me? I'm fine."

"Did you even enjoy yourself?"

"Hey!" I protest. "Did you forget I was the initiator?"

"Yes," says Tuck. "You were." His tone is gentle, although a part of me wishes he would yell if that's how he's feeling. At least then I would have a reason to yell back. "Be honest, though," he says. "You don't really want me like that any more."

"Not true."

"Should I review the definition of 'honest' with you?" His eyes open wide. He is pausing for me. Expectant. And for a split second, I consider telling him everything.

That I adore him and think he is the most handsome man alive. That I want to be with him even more now than I did when he first kissed me. That I have let sex get tied up with having a baby. That "romance" is important, but I can't stop thinking about "zygotes." That Henry Callaghan thinks my writing is work, that Greer Larson is pregnant, and that these things make me want to burst into tears and cry for the rest of my goddamn life.

But I don't say any of this. Instead I place my hands on top of Tuck's and say, "I love you. So much."

"I know," says Tucker. "I love you too."

"We've been too stressed out lately."

"We."

"Yes," I say. "We." I drop my hands and square my shoulders. "All right, I. I have been too stressed lately. And I wanted tonight to be special." I smile at Tuck and wait for him to respond, but he stares at me, speechless. "So I put on this outfit, and I chilled some champagne. I waited here on this bed to tell you I officially threw away our chart. I mean my chart. Dr. Hassagian told me to. I was all set for the big reveal, but then you walked in here looking like a kid on his birthday. So cute and irresistible. I couldn't help myself. I skipped straight to dessert."

Tucker's eyes wrinkle at the edges. "Really?"

"And truly."

"So basically, you're telling me you couldn't keep your hands off me?"

"Basically," I say. Tuck lowers his head and kisses me. Our first real one of the evening. Then he hops up from the bed and lets his towel drop to the floor.

"Don't move," he says. "I'm going to make us roast beef sandwiches."

"Naked?"

"The house is empty," he reminds me. "Gotta take advantage when we can."

While Tucker heads downstairs to dig around in our fridge, I collect his clothes and put them in the hamper. Then I pour us both fresh champagne.

As long as you're not pregnant, I think, *you might as well enjoy this.*

Before the bubbles have subsided, I hear Tuck outside the bedroom door. He lingers in the hallway on the phone, and his voice is low. I can't make out what he's saying. The hairs at the base of my neck prickle. I'm on alert. Preparing myself. *What will it be this time?* I do not want to know. Sharing my husband is part of his job description, but the timing couldn't be worse.

I sit on the bed and wait. Who is Tuck prioritizing now?

A minute later he strides into the room with no sandwiches but plenty of apologies. "Dr. Aminpour needs an implant at Memorial," he says. "Right now." Without making eye contact, he grabs a fresh pair of scrubs from the closet, then hurries to dress while I sip my champagne. "I've been trying to convince him to use us for months and of course he picks tonight."

"Then you can't say no," I tell him.

"Thanks for understanding." He slips his feet into his shoes without untying the laces. "I'm so sorry," he repeats as I follow him downstairs and onto the front porch where he pauses for one more kiss.

"I'll be back as soon as I can," he says. Then he jogs out to his car.

"Be careful!" I call out. He doesn't look back at me.

What do I do now?

Bart is out with his boyfriend, and Stella's on a date. Bets took the kids to Joey's. And Ma? I can't call her. Instead of sympathy I'd receive another earful about Tuck's choices. Grading papers is always an option, but working on Valentine's Day is too depressing. I wonder what Henry Callaghan is doing. Is he with someone? Does she iron his pants? I hope she bought him a new pair of glasses.

Draining the rest of the champagne, I head back into the house not just alone but also very lonely. In the silence of the foyer, I consider writing another letter to Scarlet. She's probably spending tonight with the father of her child. Savoring her last taste of freedom. Soon they'll have an infant on their hands and...

Stop.

I pad into the living room and curl up on the couch. Behind me a patch of moonlight peeks through parted curtains.

The house is peaceful now, not empty.
February 14th is a Hallmark holiday.
My husband is gainfully employed.
He would be here if he could.
This is not the time for complaints or fantasies or regrets.

These are the things I tell myself—but still. Watching Tuck back out of the driveway and disappear down the street made me feel like half of a twosome being kicked off Noah's Ark. And so I dream of drowning when I finally fall asleep waiting for Tuck to come back home to me.

Scarlet

You're the one who proposed. She reminded herself of this each time Gavin brought up the wedding. This was what engaged couples discussed. *When they might have the ceremony and where. How many people they should invite. Who would actually attend.* Each question was a ripple from the stone she threw into the pond. So she took deep breaths. She hemmed and hawed. Blamed her indecision on hormones and exhaustion. And for a while she successfully avoided making plans. Then one Sunday morning, Gavin suggested they elope.

"How about Hawaii?" He flipped through the travel section of the newspaper. "Managing a wedding will be too much with a newborn. Let's do it now. Tie the knot and enjoy some sun, sand and cocktails before it's too late. What do you think?"

Scarlet grabbed a saltine from the box sitting between them on the table. "I think it's a little selfish."

He set down the newspaper. "I was trying to be romantic."

"Keep trying."

Gavin regarded her for a long moment. He appeared confused.

"I can't drink, remember?"

"Ah," he said. "I see. I mention Hawaii, and you get tripped up on the issue of umbrella drinks." He shook his head. "I didn't specify alcohol, Scarlet. Not specifically."

She popped the cracker into her mouth and crunched it while she spoke. "So. Cocktails mean something else to you, then. Unspecifically? Like, maybe *cocktails* is some new code for a visit to the Pearl Harbor Memorial?"

Gavin chuckled. "Sometimes I forget how funny you are."

"Oh, I'm hilarious."

"And I'm interested in whisking my fiancée away to take our vows before she has our baby." He smiled at her. "Besides. You would look damn sexy in a bikini with that cute, round belly of yours."

She glanced down at the swell of her stomach. She was wearing what Gavin referred to as her *sleep uniform*. A pair of sweatpants, fuzzy socks and one of his old T-shirts. "I guess I'm just sick of flying," she said. "And the older I get, the more I hate airplanes." Scarlet took another bite of cracker.

"Is that why you haven't visited your mother in so long?"

She coughed a cracker crumb into her hand.

"I know it's a touchy subject for you," he continued, "but since you won't tell me what happened between you two…" He paused. "I'm sorry. I shouldn't have brought it up."

She swallowed, her throat newly dry. "But you did." Rising from the table, she trudged to the couch and settled herself between two oversized cushions. Gavin came to her side holding out the box of saltines like a peace offering.

"Forget I mentioned your mother. Or eloping. Or cocktails. From now on, we'll take each month, week, day as it comes. How does that sound?" He placed a hand on her knee, and at his touch, Scarlet sucked in her breath. "Want another cracker?"

Her mouth quivered at the edges. "I want to be alone."

"Fine."

He set the box of crackers on her lap, then grabbed his keys from the console. Scarlet waited for him to say something more. She could practically hear his voice. Smooth as river rock and nearly as strong. Gavin. Ever rational. He would apologize, and she would tell him she was sorry too. *I didn't sleep well,* she'd explain. Then he'd offer to take her to the movies or maybe downtown for lunch. Some activity that would spoil her, she was sure.

But Gavin didn't do any of the things Scarlet had come to expect. Instead he walked out the door without another word.

༄✌

The next day she stood in the corner of a Hallmark store studying what remained of the Valentines and sorting through the pink and red envelopes. She was hoping to find a card to break the iceberg between Gavin and her. Was it foolish to imagine she could win him over with some printed, store-bought sentiment?

She glanced at Clara browsing next to her. "Any luck?"

Clara grimaced. "Sydney and I are in that awkward stage between 'thanks for the lovely shag' and 'can I leave a toothbrush at your place?'"

"I did warn you not to break up with Will so close to Valentine's Day."

"But Willie wouldn't stop complaining about my long hours at Olson Brickman. I mean, bloody hell! I'm an attorney at law not some check-out clerk at Hallmark." She glanced around the store and lowered her voice. "No offense to Hallmark clerks, of course."

"Of course," agreed Scarlet. "In fact, I kind of wish you worked here. Then you could help me find a card that says, *Sorry you might have knocked up a total bitch!*"

"Maybe you're a bitch? Or maybe Gavin knocked you up?"

"Right," said Scarlet. "Ha, ha."

She continued sifting through the picked-over rows of cards. Some featured roses or Cupid's arrows. One or two were covered in Dalmatians. The smell of old strawberries and dust lingered in the air. Was it coming from those potpourri balls in the baskets at their feet?

Scarlet rubbed her aching forehead. "Do you think Gav will forgive me?"

"Hmm. You did steal his thunder by proposing to him first. And then you shot down his attempt to take the lead by eloping."

"God, Clare," she said. "That's exactly what I did."

"It may take a little time for him to get over it. But mark my words: He will." Clara selected a card with a baby in a diaper clutching a cotton-ball heart to his chest. "I mean, it's Gavin. He's a saint, or he wouldn't be with you in the first place. You're not exactly an easy one to love."

"Stop it. You adore me. Admit it, or I'll go insane."

"Yes," said Clara, "I do. But I can also walk out of your life at any moment and never look back."

"You wouldn't."

"Of course not," she said. "But Gavin can't."

"Sure he can."

"And leave his baby? You know him better than that." Clara pointed at Scarlet's two carat diamond ring, the one Gavin had produced from his gym bag the night Scarlet asked him to marry her. "He is a part of your life forever now. For better or for worse."

Scarlet worked the inside of her cheek. "I do give him plenty of worse, don't I?"

Clara sighed. "Gav loves you. We both do. But sometimes you can be a bit prickly. And then it hurts to get too close. You understand?"

She nodded, and her eyes grew wet. She could certainly stand to soften her edges, let Gavin past the gates of her defenses. But could she risk truly needing someone else? Surrendering again? The thought of it, of being broken, made her shudder.

"All right then," Clara said. "The next time the poor boy tries to sweep you off your feet, try to remember you are not living in some soap opera. You can't treat him horribly and expect he'll wait around on the sidelines until you need a kidney transplant, or else."

"Or else what?"

"That is not the bloody point, Scarlet. But death, of course. In soap operas, everything's always life or death."

"Or kidney transplant?"

"Right," said Clara. "And you're a smartass who is horrible at changing the subject."

"I think they have a card for that."

"Are you actually smiling?"

Scarlet said, "I'm trying to." Then she chose the card nearest to her without reading it. "Let's pay for these and go."

"But you didn't even look inside! Is that a *sorry I'm a melodramatic witch* card or a *thanks for being a miserable sap* card?"

"I believe it says *quit while you're ahead, Clara Broxton.*"

༄༅

They hurried back to Olson Brickman talking over the noise of passing traffic. "I hope Gavin brings you a big fat box of chocolates for Valentine's Day," said Clara. "There's been talk around the office, and some of the ladies were hoping you'd be waddling by now. Patricia, in particular, seems annoyed you're not bigger."

"I've got three months to go," said Scarlet. "I'm not supposed to be a complete hippo. At least not yet."

"Good." Clara looped an arm through Scarlet's. "Then we've got something to look forward to."

Scarlet was quiet for half a block. "Did you mean it, Clare?"

"That I want you to look like a hippo?"

"No." She stopped and turned to face Clara. "About Gavin staying with me. No matter what."

"Absolutely."

"But the people I love always leave me, Clare. I'm not sure I can take losing another one."

"I haven't left," said Clara. "And you're never getting rid of me."

"Promise?"

Clara wrapped her arms around Scarlet, the Hallmark bags crinkling between them. A yellow taxi honked, and Clara flipped the driver the bird.

"Thank you," Scarlet said.

"For what?"

"Always talking me off the cliff."

"You're welcome." Clara smiled. "And everything will work out." She pulled back to look Scarlet in the eye. "You need to believe it now too."

"I'm trying," she said. "I'm just so afraid."

"Of what, exactly?"

Scarlet laughed now. "Of everything. It's why I see a psychiatrist, remember?"

"I'm no doctor," said Clara, "but I do recall something my mum used to tell me when I was upset. It was pretty helpful. *Clara*, she would say, *when you're eighty years old, all of this will have sorted itself out.* So just imagine it, Scar. Being old and happy. And none of this nonsense will matter."

"But don't you get it?" Scarlet sniffed. "That's when it will matter most. When I am wrinkled and gray and utterly abandoned because I screwed up every relationship I ever had. I don't want to end up alone in fifty years."

Clara squeezed her arm. "Then I suggest you stop walking away from the ones who love you now."

❦

In the courtyard outside Olson Brickman, Scarlet dug a pen out of her purse. She filled out Gavin's card with all the words she hadn't shared. About her past. And their present. About the future she imagined. When the blank space was used up, she reread what she had written. On her way back into the building, she threw the card in the trash.

❦

By the time she spied him strolling across the almost-empty office, Scarlet had begun to think he would not come. But there he was, headed her way in the cashmere sweater she gave him for Christmas. He was carrying a vase of red roses, and when Scarlet stood to embrace him, he smiled.

"I got you something," she said. "I swear."

Gavin set the flowers on her desk. "I'll take a singing telegram, please."

Scarlet shook her head. "I mean, I don't have anything for you."

"Which is it then? Something or nothing?" Gavin scanned the room in an exaggerated search. "Are we on candid camera?"

She fumbled for the right words to explain. "I bought you a card."

"OK."

"But I don't have it any more."

Gavin tilted his head. "Well. That clears the situation up completely."

"I'm sorry."

"Don't be."

He stuck out his hand, and Scarlet took it. Where he was going, she would follow.

∽∾

"So what's the plan?" she asked. Gavin eased his car through the parking garage and onto the one-way street.

"It's a surprise."

"As long as we're not eloping to Hawaii." Out of the corner of her eye she saw his mouth twitch. "I can't believe I said that. I don't know how you stand me."

"Not your fault." Gavin changed lanes to pass a Jeep crawling down the one-way street. "I was out of line springing an idea like that on you," he said. "And then I brought up your mom. You hadn't even eaten breakfast yet." He smiled. A weak one, but still.

Scarlet grabbed his hand again and laced her fingers in his. "I shouldn't be so damn sensitive," she said.

"I knew what I was getting myself into when I fell for you, Scar." He cut her a glance, then looked back at the road, braking smoothly at the red light.

"So you've told me," said Scarlet. "But did you really know? I mean, I am a Guinness-Book-of-World-Records-Worthy Pain in the—"

Before she could complete the sentence, a delivery truck slammed into them from behind, and her words were eclipsed by the roar of shattered glass, of metal shrieking as their car was pushed across the intersection. Scarlet thought she heard a scream.

Then her world went black.

∾∾

The next images were of ceiling tiles and blinding walls. Bright circles danced across the inside of her lids. How long had she been sleeping? It hurt to think. Everything hurt. She opened her mouth to say *Turn off the white* but nothing came out when she tried to speak. She listened to Gavin weeping softly, his head lowered to the edge of her bed.

Am I dying? she thought. *Already dead? Is this what death feels like?*

Gavin gripped her hand, and she tried to return the pressure. Just a flutter. Would he feel it? After a moment he lifted his stricken face.

"Hey. That's my girl," he said. "Wake up, now. Come on."

Let me sleep.

"Shhh." He wiped at her cheeks, his fingers wet and trembling. Had she been crying too? "Don't worry," he said. "The baby is fine."

The baby. Yes. I need...

Her body felt unbearably heavy, strapped down by wires and tubes. Something beeped, a steady rhythm. She wished it would stop.

"I know you didn't want to find out," said Gavin, "but they did an ultrasound. To be sure he was all right."

A boy, thought Scarlet. *I'm having a boy.*

Her throat wheezed on the word. "He..."

"The doctor slipped," Gavin admitted. "But I can't un-know it now."

Neither can I.

She turned her head, but the throbbing was a knife at her skull. She smelled soap in the air and something else. It was coppery and thick.

"We're all going to be fine," Gavin told her. "The police said we were lucky the airbags were disabled. The baby could've been—" He cut himself off.

A vein pulsed at the edge of his forehead where skin gave way to hair. She had never noticed it before. He took her hand again and rubbed at her clammy palm. Then he bent his head and blew on her fingers. A monitor hiccupped near her bed.

Blood pressure. Pulse. She didn't know what it was for. She did know her tongue was a desert and her teeth chattered between parched lips.

"She's shivering," Gavin told a nurse checking the notes on Scarlet's chart.

"Normal," she replied, nodding toward the IV. "It's the pain meds and the shock. Happens to a lot of people." From a cabinet she retrieved a salmon-colored blanket and handed it to Gavin. Then she shuffled from the room, her rubber soles squeaking on the linoleum.

The IV continued its steady drip, drip, drip, and Scarlet's body shook as if she had been plunged into an ice bath. Gavin covered her with the blanket and rested his hand on her knee. "You're going to be fine," he said. "You and the baby."

She angled her face toward the slope of her belly. "He…" she gasped again before her lungs emptied.

"I told you, Scar." He squeezed her leg. "Our boy is going to be fine. He's perfect." She stiffened and opened her eyes wide. Two words croaked from her throat as if from a muddy swamp.

"Not. Yours."

Gavin froze, but the pulse at his temple kept beating. The thinnest of lines appeared between his brows, and he dragged his hand up her leg, pausing at the mound of her stomach.

"I didn't think you'd say it out loud," he said. When he stood and shoved his chair back, it hit the wall with a hollow thud.

In that moment Scarlet could not have moved, even if she wanted to. There was nowhere in the world for her to go. And as Gavin walked out of the room, she watched his shoulders sink. Then the door shut with a whisper in his wake.

Dear Scarlet,

Tuck is keeping secrets from me. There. I wrote the words.

I don't know what he's up to, but something feels off. For one thing, he's been in my nightstand. The things in my drawer have been disturbed. But why? What is he looking for? Has he been reading these letters?

And a couple of months ago he came home from a work trip smelling of perfume that wasn't mine. Lavender. I caught the scent when I was doing the laundry. He stuck his scrubs in the hamper with the rest of our clothes as if he had nothing to hide. And maybe he doesn't. But the women in his hospitals don't wear fragrance as a rule.

I haven't told another person about my concerns. Especially not Tuck. But lately I've been tempted to look at his phone records and his credit card statements. At the bills that he is always so careful to sort from the rest of our mail. He claims he wants to keep an eye on our balances and doesn't mind being in charge. After all, his salary is higher than mine, and it varies because of commission checks. Plus, everyone knows I've always hated math. Having Tucker balance our checkbook makes good sense.

You would probably say that if my spine is tingling there must be a reason. That instinct is the best detective, and I should snoop around a bit. But I'm not sure I'm prepared to rifle through his files. First, I would have to explain my sudden interest in our financial affairs (no pun intended). And secondly, I am flat-out terrified to discover something is wrong. Because if Tuck has his eye on someone else, I don't know what I'll do.

It's not like we've got children to bind us together going forward. Just a marriage license and some wedding vows. Pre-written ones at that. Everyone knows these things are easily ignored. And as pathetic as I feel admitting it, Tuck could walk out of my life with no strings attached. At least if we had kids he would have to keep seeing me. Not that I would want to be like Bets, slipping back into bed with someone who didn't want me enough to fight for us in the first place.

Still. Bets has solid proof that Joey Farinelli finds her desirable. The man can't keep his hands off her every time they exchange their kids. And even though Bets hasn't said as much, I know their continued attraction makes her feel powerful. Sexy. Sneaky. Like she's getting away with something without breaking any rules.

And if you're thinking my doubts about Tuck stem from my own guilt— like when your mother accused Sam of the stuff she was doing herself— you would be wrong. When Tuck chose me, I promised we would stay together forever, and I meant it. I know you believe I went after him just so you couldn't have him first. That on some level, I wanted to prove to people that Tuck would pick Corie Harper over Scarlet Hinden.

But I swear that wasn't the case. In fact, if I was jealous of anyone back then it was Tuck, not you. I hated your bond with him. All those afternoons in the cemetery. I couldn't relate to that at all. Even worse were the inside jokes that started up between you. When you two would laugh together, I couldn't stop crying. Not because he was close to you but because you became closer to him. I wasn't your first choice any longer, and I never felt more alone.

So you see, I know what it's like to lose you both at once. And by the time I turned to Tuck, you had already been pulling away from me. The void began the minute you two began sharing something that I didn't. In fact, I think he might have hurt me more than you did by stealing my best friend. So I guess what I am saying is this:

If you wanted revenge, you got it before Tuck and I got together. And you'll be happy to hear that karma is probably still kicking my ass. But don't you think the statute of limitations should have ended by now? Either way, Tuck's on his way home from work so my investigation will have to wait. He leaves for his national sales meeting in the morning. I'll start with the bills he keeps locked in the desk drawer. Don't worry. I know where the key is hidden.

Yes, Scarlet. My husband hides the key. So wish me luck.

Love,
Corie

Corie

Tuck could walk back in the door at any moment to collect something he forgot. His toothbrush. The flash drive for some presentation. A better kiss goodbye. What would I tell him I was up to? I have no good explanation. My fingers shake as I fish the key from the mug on top of our refrigerator.

Tuck claims he started locking his desk drawers to keep Cam and Wella out. *They'll go looking for glue or tape or scissors,* he said, *and mess everything up.* I pointed out that my sister was far worse. That she could do more damage than the kids. The funny thing is, Bets would tell me this was a terrible idea. That I should not spy on my husband who is away and trusting me.

Nevertheless.

I tackle the Amex folder first. A quick check of his most recent statements reveals nothing out of the ordinary, but I remind myself not to be naïve. He could have a secret card he uses on the sly, the bills sent to a P.O. Box. *God.* I chew on my lip. *Who have I become?* I place his credit card statements back into the drawer before moving on to his AT&T bills.

Last month's envelope is fat and crammed with folded pages. My gut churns. Heat blotches my cheeks. Even my nervous system is afraid. Tuck is constantly on his cell, and when he's not, he keeps the phone pass-coded. That way the kids can't play with his apps. At least that's the reason he gives me.

Most of the numbers are recognizable or calls placed once or twice. These I can easily rationalize. I would expect Tuck to have a large number of calls he makes only a few times. His day is one long string of information-gathering and messages to return. Appointments to schedule. Doctors' questions to answer. What I am hunting for is unexpected repetition. If he has been contacting someone special, the number would reappear multiple times.

By page eight, a prefix I can't identify or explain keeps popping up. So I Google it and find my answer: Tuck's been making a lot of calls to San Francisco. Sometimes in the middle of the night.

My insides roil. *This is what it's come to?*

The bill still clutched in my hand, I dig in my purse for my phone. Then, although I am alone, I hole up in the bedroom. *Our bedroom.* In the house Tuck and I bought with the money I inherited when my father died.

As I dial, my throat constricts. *Will I even be able to speak if she picks up?* I brace myself against the corner of our dresser, next to the stain from the champagne on Valentine's Day. The phone rings and rings, sharp jolts to my heart. The line engages with a muffled thud. Then a female voice.

"UCSF Medical Center?"

The reception desk at one of Tucker's hospitals.

Of course.

I drop the phone and dash for the bathroom where I throw up in the sink. Saliva threads from my lips to the drain. *How could you have doubted your husband? What is wrong with you?* But even as I scold myself, new questions flood my mind. What is it about our marriage that has me searching through Tuck's things? *Is there something else to worry about? Something wrong that I am missing?*

I wipe my face with a damp washcloth, rinse the basin of the sink. When I try to drink some water, the rim of the cup tastes like Tuck's toothpaste. His quick kiss from this morning. Gagging once more, I decide I cannot stay inside this house. So I dress in the shadows without turning on the closet lights, then I grab a sweatshirt and rush out the door.

❧

With no better plan in place, I drive to the grocery store because Tuck loves it and I want to feel connected. In the middle of the frozen foods aisle, I get his text.

Boarding now. Miss you already.

I shiver in my sweatshirt and do not reply.

How did I stoop to this? To snooping for receipts in my husband's pockets and perfume on his scrubs? The man has been knocking himself out to provide for me (and my sister and her kids and sometimes—more often than we'd like—my mother) and I reward his efforts with suspicion and deceit?

God help me.

This morning before he left, I let him embrace me, the smell of sleep still thick in the air. He pecked my lips, told me he loved me. And I said it back to him, knowing that as soon as he was gone I planned to dig through his bills, sift through his laundry, seek signs that he had been lying. That he was keeping secrets and wasn't worthy of my faith in him. As it turns out, I am the one who isn't worthy.

I wipe my nose on the sleeve of my sweatshirt and toss three boxes of Eggo waffles into the cart. I've moved down the aisle to the Tombstone pizzas when Kate Turlow comes around the corner. She's wearing designer jeans and a gray blouse that matches the circles under her eyes. When she sees me, she freezes. A statue holding a small basket of groceries.

"Hey, Kate."

Her gaze travels upward from my Converse shoes to the baseball cap. "Hey, yourself." She blinks as if fighting back tears, and I notice her top is misbuttoned.

"Are you OK?" I ask.

"I'm not, actually. But thanks for asking. Especially since you don't like me."

"What are you talking about?"

Kate sighs. "Come on, Corie. It's too early in the morning to pretend. Anyway, being liked is overrated."

Her mouth trembles now, and I almost feel sorry for her. Kate Turlow looks miserable. Fragile. But then I remember what she has been up to and with whom. *Does she know I saw her with Joey outside the Igloo? I hope she does. And I hope she knows he still loves his own family and my sister more than he will ever care about her.*

Kate glances into my cart. "You must really like waffles."

"They're Wella's favorite," I tell her. "You remember Wella, don't you? Bets and Joey's youngest?"

"She's a beautiful girl." Kate nods, and I feel my edge slipping. "Bets is lucky," she says. "I always wanted a daughter."

"You've got Brian Junior," I remind her, as if she might have forgotten her own son.

"Of course," she says. "And he's great. But."

"But what?"

"It's just hard," she says. "You become a mother, and your life isn't your own any more, you know?"

"No," I tell her. "I don't."

"Well, trust me. It's hard."

I clutch the cart handle now, my knuckles white. "Love isn't supposed to be easy," I tell her. "But like Bets always says, family is the only thing that matters."

"Don't kid yourself." Kate sighs. "There's nothing harder than a family. Nothing."

ço~ç

I pull into the garage and sit in the parked car for several minutes before unloading the groceries. By the time I head inside the house, a sweating milk carton has soaked through its paper bag, and the seam splits as I step into the kitchen.

"Shit!" I leap over the bubbling puddle and place the rest of my armload on the counter near the sink. "Shit, shit, shit!"

"Hey there, sis." I spin around to find Bets standing beside the kitchen table, her mouth dipped into a smile. "Hasn't anyone ever told you not to cry over spilled milk?" I notice she is still in her cloak from the 24-hour pharmacy. A red plastic nametag is affixed above the pocket.

Bethany H., it reads. *How can I help?*

"I thought you'd be in bed already," I say.

"I waited up for you."

"The kids are at Ma's."

"I know," says Bets. "I called over there on my way home. I mean on my way here. To your house."

"You live here too," I remind her. "It's fine to call it home. Take advantage of the peace and quiet while you can. Wella and Cam will want to play all afternoon once Ma drops them off. This may be your best chance to rest before Sunday."

Bets doesn't agree with me or disagree. Instead she crosses to the dishwasher where two towels hang on the handle. She grabs the one with tiny lemons embroidered above its hem and stoops to wipe the milk up off the floor.

"Please go to bed," I tell her. "I'll mop as soon as I get the rest of the bags inside. You and I both know this won't be the last thing I spill today."

"I'm not tired," she says from her knees. "I will be soon. But right now I'm on a second wind." She tilts her head as if counting. "Or maybe a third."

"How long ago did your shift end?"

"A while," she says. "But I got sidetracked in the middle of it."

My arms drop, and I wrestle with a sigh. My sister's track record at various jobs has never been stellar. It's why she's stuck working the graveyard shift in the first place. I open my mouth to question her, and she says, "Relax, worrywart. Mel covered for me."

"Melvin Barclay?" I groan. "You didn't leave him in charge, did you?" Melvin graduated from Conejo High two years after I did. Back then he was heavily into drugs, and he still dabbles in pain killers.

"The only people who come in after midnight have diarrhea," she says. "Or they're drunk. Or both. It's easy enough to suggest Pepto Bismol or a cup of hot coffee. Mel can handle that level of responsibility if I can."

Bets stands to rinse the towel in the sink, and I marvel at her confidence. She glides through life certain of herself. Everywhere. At all times. Meanwhile, I'm haunted by insecurities, doubts from a ten-year-old ghost.

"I know it's not my business," I say. "But you're a single

mom. You have to protect your job for the sake of the kids."

Bets rings out the towel and drapes it over the faucet. Keeping her back to me, she says, "That's what I wanted to talk to you about."

"Oh no," I say. "You lost your job again."

She turns toward me, wipes damp hands down the front of her smock. "Thanks for throwing the 'again' in there." The corners of her mouth curve up. "You really know how to make a girl feel good."

"Sorry, Bets," I say. "I didn't mean—"

"You did. And I deserve it. But no, I didn't lose my job. And yes, Mel handled the large number of people who entered Clark's after I left. Which was exactly zero." When my eyebrow lifts, Bets says, "Of course I called to check in on him. I'm not an idiot. I just had to leave for a while. It was important."

"What was?" I am bewildered. "What's this all about?"

"It's about me. And the kids." She glances at the floor. "And also Joey." Bets hesitates, then lifts her head. "He showed up at the store tonight crying, and he begged me to come home so we could talk in private. I mean home to our house. Not yours. And we talked for hours, Corie. More than we have in a long time. Maybe ever. And we didn't just talk. We also yelled a little. And said things that should've been said way back when. Before everything broke. And then suddenly, it was like everything was clear for both of us again. Or maybe everything was finally clear for the first time. Either way, what I wanted to tell you is that Joey wants to get back."

I bob my head as if this might help me understand her. "Get back what?"

My sister smiles.

"Together, Corie. Joey wants us to be a family again." Her chin juts like the edge of a knife. "Don't look at me like that. You have no idea what it's been like."

I shake my head in two swift jerks. "I've got an inkling."

"No," says Bets, "you don't. And you are not going to make me feel guilty about giving him one more shot. About giving *us* another chance. I love him. He's the father of my kids."

"Ha!" A laugh cradled in a sob.

"I know this is unexpected," she says, "but we're going home. Cam and Wella and me. Joey's bringing his truck by tomorrow. We'll pack our stuff up today."

I suck in a breath, then discover I can't let the air back out. Bets sniffs and reaches for a paper towel. I stand across from her in the kitchen silently. A glacier. That's how I feel. Like stone. Cold and hard and heavy. Like I would fall down and shatter if someone pushed me.

Wella and Cam are moving out.

My throat aches with what I'm about to lose. Their bright laughter rang in our corners, their bones lengthened, their muscles stretched. Under this roof I watched their small hopes and dreams grow. *They are thriving here*, I think. *How can you take this life away from them?*

How can you take it from me?

I wish I hadn't let myself imagine a future where Cam and Wella were mine, vague fantasies of Tuck and me adopting them someday. A family of four, just like that. What could be easier? I conveniently skipped the part of the story where Bets and Joey would be gone.

More realistically I told myself Bets and the kids were better off here, and I trusted that my sister felt the same. While she worked nights and slept all day, I attended the kids' school events. Arranged play dates. Read them books. I cooked healthy meals and washed stains from their clothing. I let myself play house. Not just structurally or practically. But emotionally. And now, after settling into these new patterns, after making room at our table and in my heart, I have to face the end of my sister's *temporary arrangement*.

On the very day that I'd been questioning the foundation of my marriage, Bets is going to make her own relationship work. As hurt and angry as she was when she walked out on Joey, she plans to box up her pain and leave it behind. With me. Here. Again.

Please, I think. *Let Cam and Wella stay. Experiment with your own life. Not with theirs.*

Not with ours.

But when I manage to speak, the words that come are:

"Does Ma know?"

"No," Bets says. "I didn't want to tell her over the phone. And I thought you should hear it first." She blows her nose. "I'm sure this is hard on you, Corie. And I'm more grateful to you and Tucker than I can ever say. I need to know you're OK with this."

My sister implores me, but I do not reply. Inside me a chasm spreads, and I am not ready to face it. Not in front of Bets. Not while Tuck is on a plane.

Not until I figure out how to survive being alone.

Scarlet

Scarlet lay on the bed in the room that used to be hers, before it became Clara's office, before it became her bedroom again. The digital clock on the nightstand flickered at her in the dusky light.

6:43. 6:44. 6:45.

She caught her breath but failed to hold it until the clock glowed 6:46. She was out of practice, or perhaps the baby had stolen too much space from her lungs. More likely still was that she had been weakened by the bed rest ordered by Dr. Nguyen. After the accident Scarlet was supposed to stay off her feet as much as possible.

Each morning Clara left water bottles and a sandwich by her bedside so Scarlet got up only to brush her teeth and use the bathroom. Afraid of preterm labor, she languished in her bed. It was a sacrifice she made willingly, but time slowed to a virtual standstill.

Tick tock.

6:50.

She heard Clara banging around the kitchen prepping a dinner she had no doubt purchased on her way home from Olson Brickman. The girl never would be a cook, but this limitation didn't keep her from trying. In truth Scarlet sometimes felt stifled by Clara's constant service. She would appear in the doorway soon, a dark outline lit from behind, her face half-hidden by the shadows. *Get up now. Food's ready.*

Scarlet would drag herself from bed to face another evening in the cusp between winter and spring.

6:53.

She rolled over now (the left side, she had been told, was better for the baby) and caught a whiff of freesia from the vase on the dresser, another attempt by Clara to lift her prodigal roommate's spirits. Scarlet tried to act more cheerful or at least less consumed with worry. But she had no idea what this next stretch held for her or her baby.

Dr. Kagawa had sounded unsurprised when Scarlet called to cancel their standing appointment. She could have told the doctor about the accident, a reasonable explanation for her quitting. Instead she claimed her insurance wasn't covering their visits.

The cost has become prohibitive.

"This is not uncommon," the doctor reassured her. "If you'd like, we can explore—" But Scarlet thanked her and hung up without listening to her options. She did not want to visit Dr. Kagawa any more. She was home now, whatever that word meant. She had Clara. She was still pregnant. And tomorrow the rising sun would bring with it a brand new day.

7:00.

In the kitchen a buzzer shrieked, and Clara slammed the oven door. Scarlet wondered what her friend was doing. Sticking a fork in another frozen lasagna? Opening the bag for a Caesar salad kit? She expected Clara to suggest they go out for a more celebratory meal tomorrow. They'd had enough delivered pizza. Too many roasted chickens from the market. *Perhaps,* Clara would say, *we can find a restaurant close to home. One birthday dinner won't jeopardize your rest.*

Either way the calendar would mark yet another day of growing older, followed by another one and then another until Scarlet became a mother.

"Lasagna's ready!" Clara called from the kitchen. "Come on out now, or I'll be forced to eat the whole pan by myself."

"In a minute," said Scarlet.

She reached under her pillow and slid a thin box from beneath the case of slippery satin. Sitting up, she pulled off the top and removed the envelope Gavin had left with Clara back when Scarlet was recovering in the hospital. The seal had been torn open then re-affixed with a small strip of tape. Scarlet never asked if Clara read the note.

It was 7:05, and the light had all but faded from her room. Good thing she'd already memorized every word he had written.

Scarlet,

I'd like to say "no hard feelings," but that just wouldn't be true. I feel worse than hard right now, and I can't stay here. I've decided to give up the apartment and move back home. Leaving Olson Brickman is a risk, but my father knows a partner at a small firm outside of Lincoln. Guess I'll finally be a big fish in a little pond. You always thought that would suit me better, didn't you?

In any case, Clara said you could stay with her as long as you need. You and the baby. This is a relief to me because, despite everything, I wish you well. All of you. And I hope you find what you're looking for because clearly, I was not it. Some things just aren't meant to be, no matter how much you want to make them work. And I did try, you know. For a long time. But loving someone should be easier than this.

Anyway, you can keep the ring. I don't want it any more.

I'll settle now for taking back my pride.

-Gav

Scarlet tucked the note back into the box with her small collection of photographs. There were only a few. She'd always had difficulty deciding which moments warranted a shot at permanence. If nothing lasted forever, why step out of the present to preserve memories for the future? It was easier to remember happiness without the evidence of loss. So everyone else was busy snapping images with cameras and phones while Scarlet was left with rare glimpses of her life, recorded by others, saved in secret.

The first picture was from her sixth birthday, a strip of

three frames taken in a photo booth at Chuck E. Cheese. In the top shot she smiled naturally, then she stuck her tongue out for the middle one. In the last picture Mama had popped her head into the booth to kiss her on the ear. It was a nice day and simple. One of the rare ones she could recall, the nice days having grown rarer still in the years after Sam left.

The next picture was her favorite from an afternoon with Gavin. A sunny day at Ghirardelli Square. He asked a passerby to take it while they posed, and as Scarlet studied their smiles, she could practically smell the salt in the air, taste hot chocolate on her tongue. *You're a beautiful couple,* the stranger had said. Gavin turned to Scarlet and grinned. "She's the beautiful one. I'm just the lucky guy who gets to tag along."

She placed the photograph back into the box and picked up the last one. Creased down the middle, smudged with fingerprints, it was a candid of her at prom. She was with Corie, of course, and Tucker. They'd been a threesome on that night and every other night until the last one. *Their last one.* Who had given her this photograph? Someone from the yearbook committee? Scarlet couldn't remember. She did remember she was happy that day.

"Are you coming?" Clara called. Scarlet nodded to herself.

Surely she'd be happy once again.

৯৵

She sat on the couch and kicked off her slippers. Using a bare heel, she pushed aside a stack of magazines to rest her feet on the wooden coffee table. "This place is a mess," she said under her breath.

"I heard that." Clara poked her head around the corner. "When you blow out your candles tomorrow, wish for something useful. Like a housekeeper. Or perhaps somewhere else to live."

"Great idea," Scarlet said. "At least then I won't wake up to a naked man in my bathroom."

"*Your* bathroom?"

"Mine. Yours. Ours." She waved a hand in front of her face. "Let's not argue over pronouns." She grabbed the current issue of *Us Weekly* and began flipping through the pages. Clara approached, a set of salad tongs in her hands, and took a seat opposite Scarlet.

"I would expect you'd be thrilled to see a naked man these days," she said. "You may be stuck eating for two, but I'm stuck having a love life for two."

"Oh." Scarlet's smile was wry. "So we're calling your behavior *love* now, are we? Honestly, Clare. Mr. Tall Dark and Hairy? I don't even know his name."

"First of all, it's Timothy. And secondly, you haven't liked any of my previous boyfriends so why protest this one? You never know. He might be the one."

"I see." Scarlet laid the magazine down upon the swell of her belly. "Timothy's the one."

"I said *he might be*. And anyway, this is all a bit of the pot calling the kettle black, isn't it?"

"Pot? I'm no pot." Scarlet shifted on the sofa. "Gav left me, remember?"

Clara stared at her if she couldn't quite make the connection, exaggerating her confusion for effect. "Which is relevant because…"

"Because you, my friend, do not get dumped. You do the dumping. Regularly and without warning."

Clara swallowed, then said, "I was only kidding, *my friend*. But if you listen to yourself, you might discover the two of us have more in common than you think."

Heat spread across Scarlet's collarbone, flushing her throat. What was wrong with her? Of course Clara had been joking. The girl was born spewing sarcasm. And yet Scarlet had baited her, angling for a fight. Why did the topic of love shove her so quickly off the rails?

"I'm sorry, Clare. I didn't mean—"

"No, no. You're right," she said. "Everyone knows it's a bad idea to call a pregnant lady a pot. I'm sure that's Chapter One in the *Caring for a Pregnant Lady Handbook*." Clara grabbed the remote control and clicked on the television.

"I'm sorry," Scarlet said again, her apology little more than a whisper.

"So you mentioned."

"It's not you."

"That's obvious." Clara shook her head. "Next time, try to have a sense of humor, and I'll try to get Timothy to put on some pants."

Scarlet choked out a laugh. "I'm a terrible person."

"No," said Clara, turning to face her. "You're not terrible. You're just terribly sad." She reached out to wipe a fat tear rolling toward Scarlet's chin. "Let's skip this soggy act, shall we? You'll get the lasagna wet."

Scarlet sniffed. "You're too good to me."

"I am, aren't I?" Clara tilted her head. "So. Are we staying here or having a proper meal at the table?" By way of answer, Scarlet plucked a tissue from the box on the side table and blew her nose. "Right." Clara handed her the remote. "I'll get the napkins and silverware. But if we're going to eat on our laps again, I'm using paper plates instead of dishes."

Scarlet smiled. "Good. Less clean up after."

"Ha! As if you ever clean." She patted Scarlet on the head, then disappeared into the kitchen.

While Clara clanked around collecting utensils for dinner, Scarlet scrolled through her favorite channels willing her tears to stay put. Why succumb to despair now after weeks of careful stoicism? She'd barely flinched when Clara told her a moving truck had delivered boxes from Gavin's apartment to her doorstep. "You'll be OK," Clara kept repeating. "You. The baby. Even Gavin."

"Maybe," Scarlet told Clara from her hospital bed. "Either way, it's over now."

In the weeks that followed, Clara took care of everything, filling Scarlet's prescriptions and their refrigerator, unpacking boxes of clothes and toiletries. It was Clara who arranged a storage unit for Scarlet's small furnishings, then she remade her home office into Scarlet's bedroom. She'd moved in a sleigh bed and a dresser, painted the walls Scarlet's favorite color: robin's egg blue. But despite her best efforts, Clara hadn't known how to make her friend *happy*. Unfortunately Scarlet didn't know how to do that either.

So she perused magazines in which she had no interest, channel-surfed until her mind went numb. Occasionally she opened her laptop hoping to distract herself on the Internet. But inevitably these searches unearthed information Scarlet was disinclined to learn. About her pregnancy. About the traits her baby might inherit. Reminders of its lineage she didn't wish to see. *His lineage*, she corrected. *It's a boy.* One she would have to support by herself in every way. Emotionally. Physically. Financially.

In a gentle voice full of concern, Larry Reisman from Human Resources had told Scarlet the partners at Olson Brickman were so sorry about her accident. In light of her bedrest, she'd be paid a full salary until she exhausted her maternity leave. After that, if she were unable to return to work, Scarlet would receive disability compensation. According to Larry, this should afford her ample time to figure out a long-term plan.

Long-term plan.

Scarlet was grateful she was on the phone and not in Larry's office. He had no idea she was covering her mouth to keep from laughing out loud.

Clara returned from the kitchen with lasagna and a green salad. "Here we go," she said. She arranged their meal on the coffee table while Scarlet pulled an afghan from the arm of the couch and stuffed it behind her back for support.

"This looks delicious," Scarlet said.

"No, it doesn't," Clara told her. "But thanks for saying so anyway."

For several minutes, they ate together in silence, the evening news droning on the television. As the weather segment began, Clara cleared her throat.

"Are you choking or making an announcement?" Scarlet asked.

"It's just that a few people have asked me if they can stop by for a visit tomorrow. Maybe have some cake. Open a few presents."

"You mean you've asked a few people to stop by. No one wants to see me on their own."

"That's rubbish," said Clara. "Everybody from Olson Brickman misses you. Poor Alice and Patricia ask after you constantly. And at the yoga studio Izzy is relentless. It's all, *how's Scarlet,* all the time."

"Your nose is growing, Pinocchio."

Clara opened her mouth to argue, but the phone rang in the kitchen, the old land line Scarlet had installed when she lived here years ago.

"Seriously?" Clara muttered. "I thought I put a block on telemarketers. Who even has this number any more?" Scarlet shook her head, but then the answer presented itself. Her skin prickled. Speaking of blocked numbers.

Mama.

It had been months since Scarlet blocked Eleanor's calls, months since she'd felt her stomach twist each time her cell phone rang. Still. Mama was a stubborn woman, and tomorrow was her daughter's birthday. Of course she would try one more time. Here. The last place she knew Scarlet had lived.

She wrapped the afghan around her shoulders while Clara headed into the kitchen. "Broxton," Clara chirped into the phone, the same clipped tone she employed at Olson Brickman. "Yes," she said. "I'm still in touch with her."

Scarlet shivered, and there came a long pause. *If Mama insists,* she decided, *I will take her call.* Clara had been her go-between in too many awkward conflicts already, and Mama could no longer intimidate or coerce her. No one could. She was free now. For better or worse, she had taken control of her life in the most sweeping way possible.

"I'm not sure what you need," Clara told Scarlet's mother. After another few beats Clara said, "No, I don't think I can do that."

Sweat beaded on Scarlet's forehead. *What did Mama want?*

"I wish I could be more helpful," Clara said. "But I will give her the message." Scarlet sighed and shrugged off the afghan. Birthday or not, Mama hadn't fought very hard to speak with her only daughter. What a fool she'd been. Why was she disappointed or even slightly surprised? When it came to motherhood, Eleanor went through the motions. On autopilot. Nothing more.

Clara emerged from the kitchen then, and Scarlet immediately apologized. "I didn't expect her to track me down here so thanks for running interference."

"I almost told her you were home," Clara said. "But..."

"If she tries again," Scarlet said, "I'd be willing to speak with her." She took a breath and steadied her voice. "I guess a part of me wants to talk to Mama, tell her I'm doing just fine. That we both are." The baby moved then, a heel rippling under her skin. Scarlet laid a palm on her belly and pressed back at the foot poking her there.

"Scar—"

"I know my mother's crazy," she said. "But I hope she wasn't too awful to you. Did she sound at all upset? Should I go ahead and call her back or wait for her to make the next move?"

"That wasn't Eleanor," said Clara. She placed her hand on Scarlet's shoulder. "It was someone named Laura Harper."

"Corie's mother?"

"Who is Corie?"

Scarlet suddenly felt sick.

Laura had probably learned about the car accident in the hair salon or the grocery store. Or perhaps from a coworker at Conejo Realty who was eager to spread bad news. Scarlet pictured them whispering together about the poor Hinden family. What terrible, terrible luck! Laura would rest a hand on her heart. The Harper family and their goddamned sympathy.

"Scar?"

She looked at Clara. "Did Laura ask you about the accident?"

"No," she said. "Who is Laura Harper?"

If not the accident, what was she calling about?

Scarlet thought back to the August afternoon she'd spent at the cemetery with Tuck, pictured him waiting for her outside Dr. Kagawa's office in December. If Corie had discovered they'd seen each other, she would have told Laura for sure. Maybe Mrs. Harper was calling to defend her daughter like a normal mother would.

But I never asked him to come, Scarlet thought. *I swear, Tuck Slater found me.*

Clara tilted her head. "Are you all right?"

Scarlet squared her shoulders.

"I'm asking because this Laura Harper person, whoever she is, she didn't have good news."

Scarlet took a breath, and the baby rolled again inside her. This child was her life now. The past no longer mattered. *Let it go.* She spread both hands across her stomach and exhaled.

"Clare," she said. "Out with it."

"It's your mother," Clara said. "I am so sorry."

Dear Scarlet,

I like your friend Clara. She reminds me of you, smart as hell and sharp-tongued to the point of wickedness. She works the same kind of sarcasm you turned into an art form so I figure the two of you must be really something when you're together. I wanted to ask her if you're still funny like you used to be, but every time I opened my mouth, I couldn't find the right words. And I don't suppose you'll be joking around with me again anytime soon. So in the end, it doesn't matter if you've changed.

I was terrified to meet your new best friend, you know. And also a little jealous. The truth is, I haven't replaced you. I never could. Sure, I have Ma and Bets. And Tuck, of course. But a really close girlfriend? I haven't had one of those since you. I don't think I will take that risk again. It hurt too much to lose what we had. It hurt even more to consider that you and I were never as strong as everyone thought we were.

I gathered from the way Clara hugged us that you haven't filled her in on our story. At least not all of it. She thanked Ma and me for holding down the fort, then she cursed a bit and got right down to business. She was matter of fact about everything. Which I suppose is par for the course if you're a lawyer. She filled out paperwork and signed on dotted lines. There were a lot of them, you know. So much red tape. But she didn't mind being your stand-in. I could tell.

She didn't question me at all, even though I was almost hoping she would. I wanted to tell her everything so she could pass it on to you. That I am still with Tuck, but we haven't yet had kids of our own. That Bets just moved out and took with her the next best thing. That I still have your ten-year letter sitting in my nightstand. That I saw Rick Roosevelt, and he looked great. He also seemed quite interested in you.

Ma tried to pry information from her, but all we learned is that you couldn't travel for medical reasons. The baby, right? Your girl is a discreet one. She seemed surprised when Ma asked her if you couldn't fly because you're pregnant. I guess your mother never got around to telling you she let that cat out of the bag. And you must still be carrying that baby, or you would have come down here yourself.

Because I know you, Scarlet. No matter how angry you ever were with your mother, there was a part of you that wanted her approval. Forget that. Her love. Or are you still too proud to admit you need someone else? I sometimes wonder what direction our lives would have taken if you had been more open to it. With me. With Tuck. Yourself. We might still be best friends. Or maybe you and Tuck would be together. We'll never know. What's done is done. And we have to live with the consequences. All of them. We both made our beds, and we are lying in them for better or worse. Because in real life? There are no do-overs.

Are there?

Love,
Corie

Corie

When the garage door grumbles open, I'm on the floor of the room Wella and Cam used to share, leaning against the bunk beds Tuck found for them on eBay. He spent a weekend painting them red. I bought quilts with white boats sailing on blue stripes. The room is nautical with a side dish of patriotism, and the kids love sleeping here.

Loved.

It's been a month since my sister left, but the kids' pillows still wear dents from their heads. I haven't had the heart to change the sheets. I look up from my game of solitaire and catch my husband in the doorway watching me.

"Whatcha doing down there?" he asks.

I offer him a small smile. "Plotting world domination."

"Lofty goal." He crosses to the lower bunk and ducks to sit at one end. I wait for him to continue the joke, but he simply looks at me, head tipped to one side, weighed down by unasked questions.

"I saw Bets and the kids today," I tell him. "They brought pizza from Mario's. Wella and Cam said they wish they could've seen you."

"Box in the oven?"

"We finished the whole thing." I collect the cards into one pile and begin to shuffle them. "There's ham from Monday night. I could make you a sandwich or something."

"I'll fend for myself, thanks."

The cards slide between my fingers with a *thwack,* and I set the deck on the rug in front of me. "Did you know that when the sun shines through this window it makes a big patch of light here where I'm sitting? When I was little, I used to find Ma reading in some strip of sunshine. All the time. She was never on a couch or bed. Always on the carpet. Said it was easier to soak up the warmth like that." I look at Tucker and shrug. "I try it sometimes too."

"Makes sense." He slides off the edge of Wella's bed onto the floor beside me. "Not much sun at this time of night, though."

"The kids and I were playing Go Fish in here," I tell him. "I wasn't ready to stop when they left." Tuck stretches out a foot and pokes my leg with his tennis shoe. I tell him all the time that he should double-knot the laces, but he forgets, and one is usually untied.

"How's everyone doing?" he asks.

"Great." I shake my head like I can't quite believe it myself. "They all seem great. And happy. You know. For now."

Tuck's face falls. Just an inch, but still. A frown. "You want your sister to be happy, right, Core? This is a good thing."

"Of course it is," I say. "It's just... I worry."

"About?"

"When the other shoe will fall." I nod at his sneaker. I think back to the Saturday afternoon my sister showed up on our doorstep, kids in the backseat of her car, their SpongeBob suitcases stuffed with clothes and toys. I couldn't even pretend to be surprised that she had left Joey. Or disappointed that she wanted to stay with me and not Ma. Bets claimed the situation would be temporary. Cam and Wella weren't mine to keep. But still. I expected her to find a place of her own someday— not reconcile with her ex and move back in with him.

Away from me.

"Maybe Joey's got them tied up tighter these days," Tuck says to me.

"Huh?"

"You know. His shoes."

I glance at Tuck, confused.

"Forget it," he says. "I was being stupid."

I nod at him without trying to figure out what he's talking about. "I miss them," I say. "Is that crazy? We finally have our home back, and I miss them?"

Tuck blinks at me, runs a hand through his black hair. "I'm not the best barometer." He was barely eighteen and just off to college when his father moved with his second wife to New York. Tuck has no siblings and no cousins. There's one uncle in the Midwest. My husband has lived most of his life with a hole where a family should be. To him, mine feels unusually full.

Tuck stands now and offers me his hand. "You wanna come watch me work some magic with leftover ham?"

I stare at the ropey veins of his forearm, the muscles tight under his skin. I love this man. I have for almost half my life. But we've spent half of that half picking ourselves back up again. I'm beginning to think staying down might be easier.

"Core?"

"Hmm."

His tongue clicks against the back of his teeth, and I think for at least the hundredth time that I do not know my husband. That in the end, none of us ever actually knows each other. No matter how many nights we spend lying next to someone else, each morning we wake up to our own selves again. Alone. Separate. Secretive. Two souls sharing only what they want the other one to know. I reach up, and he pulls me into his arms. I let myself believe, for just this moment, he can keep me safe.

"It's going to happen for us," he says. "We'll have our own kids someday. I promise."

I press my chin against his chest and listen to his heartbeat, a steady pulse in my ear. I don't want to hear anything else. I can't stomach my own doubts. Or worse, his hope.

My mouth opens against the jut of his shoulder, and I fight the urge to bite down hard. It's not that I want to hurt him; I simply need to brace myself on something solid, to stifle the sob rising in my throat. Yes, I've wanted children since I was a child myself, but other things have brought me gladness. I can be glad again. I should be grateful we are alive. That we have our health and each other. We can be happy. In fact, we should be. We will be. I know we will.

We will.

We.

ॐॐ

Before my period comes the next morning, I already know I am not pregnant. I'd told Tuck I wouldn't take a test, at least for another day or two. He has seen my face collapse too many times after peeing on a stick. He's become a fan of waiting to let nature be the first indicator. Nature and time.

"Give it a few days," he asks me each month. "Please." And I say I will.

But patience is more his strong suit than mine, and after he fell asleep last night, I crept into the bathroom seeking results. I didn't have to visit the drugstore. Anyone who's been trying to get pregnant for more than a few months has at least one test in the back of her cabinet. Next to a box of tampons. I've got more than one brand by now. Why would I trust EPT when Clear Blue Easy might tell me something better? Also the two-pack is cheaper, and if the line doesn't show up on Tuesday, it might darken into itself by Thursday. Maybe this time.

Except not this time.

So I rinse my underwear, shower and dress before heading into work. During my brain-dead drive I try to lose myself in the day's lesson plan. *Macbeth*. That old queen had trouble with bloodstains of her own. And she didn't have children either, despite that weird quote about nursing a baby.

I have given suck and know / How tender 'tis to love the babe that milks me.

Each year my students and I theorize: Did she mean she nursed a plot to kill Duncan like she would a baby? Or that she had a child who died before the play even began? Either way, Lady Macbeth was no mother, and Shakespeare was onto something. Ambition can be deadly when taken to extremes.

Maybe I shouldn't aim for things out of my reach, either.

When I arrive on campus, the faculty workroom is empty, and I'm the first one at the copy machine. That's what I get for showing up at the crack of dawn, time and space to prepare myself. I arrange a picture of a wood carving of King Duncan on the copier and print out eighty-five. I have two senior classes, each with thirty-eight students, but some will lose theirs or turn them into airplanes.

Kids.

When the copies are complete, I stuff the stack into my bag. I'm eager to get to my classroom, to dissolve into my day. Checking my watch, I round the corner of the office and plow full speed into Henry Callaghan.

"Sorry!" I blurt out as his faculty newsletters flutter to the floor.

"Corinna," he says. "Good morning."

We bend down at the same time to collect the fallen papers, and our heads bang against each other hard. I rub my temple, and Henry looks up at me from a crouch, glasses crooked now, mouth grinning.

"Sorry," I say again.

"I'll survive," he tells me.

He returns his attention to the newsletters, and my fingers twitch with the urge to reach out and straighten his glasses. I never would, of course. The idea is ridiculous. A leap of imagination. My brain's lame attempt to shock me out of my own sadness. And yet I stand here. Not helping him. Looking at his spiked up hair.

Ridiculous.

Papers gathered, Henry rises to his full height. "I'm surprised to run into you, Corinna. Literally. Don't you usually blow into the parking lot a few minutes before the bell? Not that I keep track."

"Sorry," I repeat for the third time.

He laughs. "Don't worry. I won't report you."

I try to smile back, but my mouth feels stiff. When the words finally come, they are rushed. "You see, my niece and nephew used to make me late. Before. But I've been getting here early now. Better parking spots. And I have more time for lesson planning, of course. I love extra planning time."

"Sure you do."

"No, really."

"Uh huh."

Before I can figure out what else to say to convince him, Stella emerges from the ladies' room, an oversized briefcase rolling behind her.

"Good morning," Henry says.

Stella regards the two of us standing side by side, and her lips go crooked. "Just another day in paradise," she says.

I offer up a half-wave, one I hope says *nothing unusual going on here*. But Stella sidles out of the faculty workroom without another word.

"She's a shy one, isn't she?" asks Henry.

I laugh. "She's the furthest thing from it." I'm still laughing when the attendance secretary and a counseling assistant walk into the office together. I hitch my book bag higher on my shoulder. "Anyway, I should go."

"To prepare your lessons," he says. Not a question.

"Yeah," I tell him. "Yes."

"If you don't mind my asking, why don't they make you late any more?"

"What?"

"Your niece and nephew," he says. "You told me they made you late. Before."

"Oh, right," I reply. "They were living with us for a while."

"With you and Tucker?" He keeps his focus steady, but the tips of his ears redden.

"Yes."

Henry cocks his head. "But not now?"

"No," I tell him. "Not now."

I break eye contact and grab the mail from my box. And as I turn to leave, he says, "Don't forget your copy of the newsletter."

But I ignore him and keep walking out of the building and across the quad to my own classroom where I can shut the door and finally be alone.

༜

Ma is waiting for me after work on the top step of our porch. As I come up the walkway, she remains seated, the afternoon breeze blowing blond strands across her face. She wears a green golf shirt with Conejo Realty embroidered on the pocket, and she hasn't bothered to belt her khaki pants. When I see her chewing on her lower lip, I know for sure she has something *not-so-great* to tell me. Poor Ma does not wear her heart on her sleeve.

My mother wears her teeth upon her lips.

"Nice to see you," I say. "I wasn't expecting a visit." She looks up, shades her eyes with one cupped hand.

"I've been missing my little girl these days," she says, and I believe her. She hasn't spent a morning at the house since Bets moved out.

"Keeping busy?" I ask.

"Busy enough," she says. "I'm meeting new clients to show a property on Heron Lake at five-thirty, and I've got bridge with Maggie and the rest of the girls tonight."

I set down my bag and sit beside her. "Sounds like fun."

"You really should learn to play one of these days, Corie. You have no idea what a good time it is."

"I can't manage anything beyond solitaire."

At this, Ma smiles. My dad was never any good at cards either. My parents would return home after an evening spent playing with other couples, and he'd lament his poor performance while she patted him on the back. "George," she used to say, "you've got lots of strengths. But everyone has weaknesses." He'd shrug, appeased by her assurances while I was tempted to ask what she thought her weakness might be.

I reach into my bag now and withdraw an apple left over from my lunch, biting a chunk out of one side. A line of juice dribbles down my chin. "So what's up?" I ask her, chewing. She's returned to sucking on her lip.

"I went to New Horizons earlier," she tells me. "I hadn't stopped by in a week so I figured Ellie might be lonely today."

"She's probably always lonely."

My mother nods. She knows I'm right.

The day Eleanor Hinden almost died it was a neighbor, Jed Perkins, who discovered her, alone and half-dead in her silent kitchen. He'd been checking in on Eleanor every day to see if she needed anything. That morning she was slumped in a chair, tank empty, skin all but blue. Ma's number was circled in an address book lying open on the counter.

After calling 911, Jed contacted my mother. Since her number was right there, he assumed she'd be the one to call. Ma went straight to the ICU where Eleanor lay unconscious for days. Later, we both agreed this was a merciful thing. Until Clara Broxton showed up, Eleanor had no other visitors. And who wants to awaken to the cold hard fact that hardly anyone gives a damn?

"According to the receptionist," Ma says, "Clara calls once a week to see if there's anything that needs doing."

"That's nice of her," I say. In my gut, a stab of jealousy.

"It is."

I take another bite of apple, feeling awkward now and guilty. But since my father died, I get ill at the thought of a place like that. *A long-term care facility.* Ma thinks the name New Horizons sounds lovely, even hopeful. But to me it's an ironic thing to call a series of buildings where people wait for their lives to end.

Ma's eyes drop to my chin. With a thumb she wipes the juice, then she dries her hand on the leg of her pants. "The phone rang while I was there today," she says. "And Ellie was visiting the ladies' room so I answered."

"Let me guess. Clara?"

My mother smiles. "Her accent is adorable."

"Do you think it's real?" I ask. "She told me she lived in England for only a few years." On my tongue, the taste of apple core. A seed sticks in my tooth. "Maybe the whole *bloody hell* thing is a play for attention."

"I like her," says Ma. "She's a good sport. Coming down here, handling Ellie's transfer from the hospital."

"A better friend than I ever was, right?"

My mother frowns. "That's not what I'm saying, and it's not a competition."

"Good. Because I'd lose."

"Oh, honey." She sighs. "We've all lost a lot. Too much. Each one of us."

I study my mother's face, note the tremble at her jawline. This sharing of emotion is a rarity for her. Then and now the Harper instinct is to pretend pain isn't there, to ignore the bad and focus on what good life still affords. It's not a terrible way to look at the world. It's just difficult to heal a buried wound. Such darkness requires sunlight or at the very least acknowledgment.

"Sometimes I forget how hard it's been for you," I say.

"It's been hard for you too," she says. "And I know I didn't ask you often enough—or ever, really—about your feelings. A person gets busy mourning in her own way. Forgets to support her loved ones when she's hurting herself. But it's about time for some mending, don't you think?"

"Sure, Ma. Sure."

"I'm glad you feel that way."

"Why?"

Her gaze is fixed across the street.

"Ma." I lean toward her, yet she refuses to look at me. "Ma. What did you do?"

"It's really no big deal," she says. "But Clara asked for your address and phone number."

"And?"

"I gave it to her."

I exhale, relieved. "You scared me for a minute."

My mother turns. "I also told her. About Scarlet's ten-year letter. I said you have it and that you'd send it to Scarlet."

"Oh, Ma. No."

"Yes." She puckers her mouth. "Don't worry. I explained to Clara that you were simply holding onto it for a while."

"For months," I correct, mortified. "God, Ma. Why?"

"Because, Corinna Marie. That letter isn't yours to keep. Ellie trusted you to deliver it."

"I didn't know where to find Scarlet!"

"You didn't try."

I shake my head. "She won't want to read it."

"You don't know that."

"I know Scarlet hates me."

"Maybe so. And maybe this is your chance to fix things."

"We tried Ma. Ten years ago. Tuck and I both did." I swallow hard. "In the end, she's the one who turned her back on us."

"Do you think she sees it that way?"

"There's no other way to look at the situation."

"Really, Corie? Because from what I recall, you and Tuck weren't being honest with her. And when you finally told the truth." A pause. "Well."

We are both quiet now. After a minute, I speak again. "Tuck chose me. He loves me. We had to be together."

"I'm not disagreeing with you."

"If Tuck had wanted her instead of me, Scarlet would've done the same thing."

"Now with that I might have to disagree."

The breeze returns, and I recall an afternoon years ago when the sway of my backyard hammock was a rhythm I knew by heart. I pumped both legs to keep us rocking while Scarlet held my new video camera. It was an early graduation gift from my parents. She loved it more than I did.

We should interview each other, she said. She made up questions on the spot. I laughed when she asked me if I had a crush on Tucker. She must have known, had been begging for the truth. And I could have told her that day. But I didn't.

God, Scar. That would be like me having a crush on you.

She snorted. *Come on. You know you want me.*

I replayed that tape at least a thousand times wondering how different our lives would be now if I'd been honest with her then. If I hadn't been so selfish. So damn scared.

"I didn't want to lose either of them, Ma. I wanted to have Tuck and keep Scarlet too. Both of them. Somehow."

She looks at me. "I think a part of you was afraid."

"Afraid. Of what?"

"That if Scarlet found out about you and Tuck, she might make a play for him."

"*Make a play*? Ma. No." I shake my head. "Definitely not. And even if she had tried, it wouldn't have worked."

My mother is quiet. She takes my hand. "What about now? Are you worried about Tuck now?"

"No," I say.

"Are you sure?"

For a moment I can't breathe. "No," I say for the third time.

"All right, then." Her fingers press against mine, and I withdraw my hand.

"But what if it's not all right?"

My mother sighs. "Love's a messy business. Everyone gets a little dirty." For a minute silence stretches between us. Then Ma pats my knee. "I should go," she says.

"You should."

"I hope you aren't too mad." When I don't answer, she pulls herself up by the porch rail and walks to her car without looking back. A bank of cloud blocks out the sun, then continues across the sky.

"I'm not mad," I say to no one. Above me tree branches rustle, and my skin prickles at the brush of cool air. But I remain on the porch, knees tucked to my chest. Waiting.

For what, I do not know.

Scarlet

Scarlet watched, skeptical, as Clara positioned a pair of powder blue baby booties above each place setting at the head table. She'd already draped it with a crisp white cloth and sprinkled glitter around the centerpiece: an enormous stuffed stork with a diaper in its beak.

"Shouldn't I be buying all this stuff myself?" Scarlet leaned over and poked at the diaper, watched it swing. "This seems like begging to me. Be honest, Clare. Will it seem like I'm begging?"

"Don't be silly." From a paper bag, Clara produced a large plastic knife. "And don't worry. I'll make sure Izzy gets pictures of you cutting your cake."

"I wasn't worried."

"As for drinks, remember to stick to the punch bowl on the right. The one with the floating sherbet balls. The other one has champagne." Clara glanced at her again. "I hope we won't run out."

Scarlet still had trouble believing two dozen women liked her enough to put on dresses and heels and come to The Bayside Tea House this afternoon. Did they realize they had RSVP'd *yes* to finger sandwiches and conversations about spit up and breast pumps? Scarlet feared a few were merely curious. That she, once again, had become a source of pity. Some poor victim left to raise her child alone.

But Clara had insisted on throwing her the shower, told

her this is what women do for each other. Last month Patricia Keeling helped Scarlet register online at a store called Baby Bliss, and this morning Alice Barnes took her to Le Chic Salon for a pedicure and blowout. Now as Clara led her to an overstuffed armchair and instructed her to sit, Scarlet felt like a doll in a dress and wedge sandals. Fussed over and fragile, her limbs arranged by someone else.

"I realize this might be difficult," Clara told her, "but you simply must let other people wait on you. Patricia will be in charge of your food and punch. Alice agreed to handle the presents. She'll stack them near this loveseat here and record the gifts as you open them. All you have to do is smile and stay off your feet."

"Or I could skip the whole thing entirely."

"You, my love, are not funny in the least." Clara produced a tube of pink gloss from a pocket in her skirt and slicked it onto Scarlet's lips. "Anyway, your hair is far too pretty not to share with everyone, isn't it?"

While Clara appraised her handiwork, Scarlet twisted a dark strand around her finger. "You will tell me if I start making weird faces at any point today, won't you?"

"Stop it," Clara said. "You'll be brilliant."

"It's just that sometimes I can't control the shape my mouth takes on. Not when I'm nervous."

"Then don't be. Remind yourself that everyone is positively thrilled to see you today."

"So you've told me."

"And I never lie," said Clara. "But I do have a few things left to do so don't distract me. Where is that list?" As she hurried off in search of her checklist, Scarlet gazed across the room to the entrance to the Tea House.

She still had plenty of time to run away.

ৎৄৢৎ

In the end, however, she didn't run. *Couldn't,* was more like it. Clara hovered close to her all afternoon making escape impossible. Not that she actually would have skipped out on the party Clara worked so hard to plan. Still, being the object of attention was the last thing Scarlet wanted. Each time a guest greeted her with a gentle hug or a knowing look, she tried not to worry about what they might have been thinking. *Or whom they were speculating about.*

She endured Izzy Garcia's third retelling of her emergency C-section and listened patiently to Patricia's warnings about the dangers of epidurals. Eventually, after surviving two long hours of finger sandwiches, cake and presents, Scarlet found herself on a loveseat with a paper plate secured to her head.

Well-intentioned Alice, a young coworker from Olson Brickman, had collected ribbons from each gift, threading them through a hole in the center of the plate. She finished the hat off with a bow in the center then tied her creation onto Scarlet's head.

"You have to wear it for at least one hour," Alice announced. "For good luck!"

"But I feel so lucky already," Scarlet said.

"Psst," said Clara. "You're making a face."

Scarlet lifted her upper lip above her teeth. "Is this better?"

"Keep trying," Clara whispered. Then she stood and clapped her hands. "All right, everyone! Who's going to help me finish off the cake?"

As Clara led a trail of women over to the dessert table, Scarlet leaned her head against the loveseat. *Almost done,* she thought. *Then we can go home.* She was just closing her eyes when Izzy Garcia sat beside her. A jangle of bracelets hung from yoga-toned arms, and her braid smelled like incense and coconut oil.

"Long day?" Izzy asked.

"The longest," Scarlet said. "Do I sound ungrateful?"

"You sound pregnant." Izzy pulled a ribbon off Scarlet's face and tucked it onto the top of the plate. "After Charlie was born, I was a zombie for nine months. But if I can survive being a single mom, anyone can. You'll be back to your old self soon enough."

"Really?"

"No," admitted Izzy. "But would you rather hear that your life will never be the same?"

"Probably not." Scarlet rubbed her belly, wishing she could feel the baby kick. "In any case, the reality can't be worse than what I'm picturing."

"Keep believing that," Izzy said. "And you'll be fine." She put a hand on Scarlet's knee. "And I hope you don't mind me saying I think it's a good thing Gavin left you when he did. Especially if he wasn't up for the long haul. Not everyone's cut out to be a daddy."

And there it was.

Scarlet had assumed everyone at the shower would be wondering about Gavin, but she'd hoped to make it through the afternoon without anyone bringing him up. She looked at Izzy now, her dark eyes full of concern, and nodded absently in the way of someone who'd become an expert at not telling the whole story. Izzy was a lot of fun to be around, and she taught a fabulous hot yoga class. But trusting her with the truth, trusting anyone for that matter, was an entirely different issue.

"Will we see you back in the studio after all this?" Izzy waved a hand over Scarlet's stomach like a psychic with a crystal ball. "I've got a Mommy and Me class on Tuesdays. You can bring the baby. Charlie loves it."

"I might give that a try."

"Just don't tell Clara," she said. "She would kill me for suggesting you abandon Bikram." At that moment Clara approached with a cake plate in one hand and a cup of punch in the other. "Were your ears burning?" asked Izzy.

"No. They're frozen," Clara said. "I brought sherbet balls!"

Izzy stood and offered Clara the spot next to Scarlet. "Sit. You've been going hard all day without a break."

Clara collapsed onto the loveseat. "Don't mind if I do." She handed the punch to Scarlet and swallowed a forkful of cake. "So, Mommy-to-be," she said. "Are you ready for your speech?"

"My what?"

Clara licked frosting off her lip. "Your speech."

"Oh. My. God!" said Izzy, grinning. "Where is my phone? I need to get a picture of Scarlet's face!"

Scarlet's heart banged against her ribs. There was no way she could speak in front of these people. Right here. Right now. She would rather go into labor in the middle of The Bayside Tea House. She grabbed Clara by an elbow and squeezed. "Thanks for the lovely shower, Clare, but if you make me give a speech, I will hate you forever."

"Sorry, love. But you're doing it." Clara scarfed another bite of cake, then leaned in close. "Seriously, Scar. There's been a lot of speculation today. Not just about you but about Gavin and the baby. Your plans. The minions want to hear what's going on from the horse's mouth. Not that you're a horse."

"Or that it's anybody's business."

"Of course it isn't. But if you don't say *something*, they will fill in the blanks themselves. They already have been, frankly. With theories that are worse than what's truly happening."

"I don't owe anyone any explanations, Clare. They're just being nosy."

"Or maybe they care about you. Genuinely. So stop being suspicious and start treating these women like they're your friends."

Scarlet's shoulders slumped. "Didn't I do that today? I tried, Clare."

"Yes, you did," Clara said. "But you also avoided having any real conversations." Scarlet opened her mouth to protest, but Clara cut her off. "Talking about strollers and car seats does not count."

"What else—"

"And for someone who is supposed to be taking it easy, you visited the bathroom at least half a dozen times."

"That's what pregnant women do," Scarlet said. "And Dr. Nguyen upgraded me to modified bed rest, remember?"

"I know that, but no one else does. And I'm tired of Patricia asking when and if you're coming back to work." Clara shrugged. "For the record, I wouldn't mind hearing what's next for you, either."

Scarlet's eyes fell to her lap.

She knew she was being unfair to the people in her life. To Clara. Even to herself. Perhaps she could offer up something without spilling every detail about her past, present and future. Maybe this was another opportunity to establish control. To set the record straight or in whatever direction she chose.

"Fine." Scarlet set down her cup of melting sherbet balls. "Give me a minute."

"How about five? I'll gather the group by the cake, and you can thank everyone one more time. Tell them whatever parts of the story *you're* ready to share." Before Scarlet could consent, Izzy returned waving a cell phone in her hand.

"Don't you dare move," Izzy said. "First, I want a picture of you panicking. Then I want another one after you've done some relaxation techniques. I can use them as *Before and After* shots advertising the benefits of yoga. But should we lose the crazy bow hat? What do you think? Do the ribbons help or make it worse?"

"Both," Scarlet said. A smile tugged at her mouth.

Izzy held up her phone. "Try to look terrified!" It was then that Scarlet caught a glimpse of something—*someone*—out of the corner of her eye. She turned to get a better look at who was standing in the doorway, and her smile disappeared. The paper plate slid off her head onto her belly.

"Oh, no you don't!" said Clara. "You heard Alice. You have to wear the hat for one whole hour."

"Clare," said Scarlet. "What did you do?"

She cocked her head. "Um… I threw you a shower."

"I'm talking about her."

Scarlet nodded toward the woman coming through the French doors of the Tea House. Her halo of blond curls had been corralled into a twist and a few loose tendrils floated down her face. She wore linen pants with a blouse in the same turquoise as her eyes, and the light behind her almost made her glow. The effect was otherworldly, but Scarlet knew this was no ghost.

It was Corie Harper Slater, all grown up.

Clara squealed. "She made it!"

"You knew?" Scarlet felt the breath squeezed from her body as Clara flew across the room to greet their guest.

"Who is that?" asked Izzy.

Scarlet blinked twice. "Somebody from a lifetime ago." Her vision swam, and she feared she might faint as Clara led Corie over to present her as the best gift of the day.

"Look who's here!" gushed Clara. Scarlet could barely breathe.

"Can you believe it?" Clara nudged Corie. "Scarlet Hinden is speechless!"

Corie, pale as ever, held up a shower invitation. "Hello. Hi."

"I wanted this to be a surprise," said Clara. "But then Corie's flight was delayed, and I wasn't sure she would make it before the fun was over." She paused, her gaze shifting between Corie and Scarlet. "Don't worry, you two. We've got this room reserved for another hour so we still have plenty of time to catch up."

While Clara rambled, Scarlet waited for Corie to say something more than *Hello*. Like, why did she come here? And how much had she told Clara about their past? Something. Anything. Please. But Corie simply stood there, weaving on her heels.

"God I love this!" said Izzy. She snapped a picture of Corie. "Candids are the best, don't you think? More authentic than posed shots. Imperfect, just like life, right?" Her teeth flashed, and she stuck out a hand. "I'm Isobel Garcia, by the way. Call me Izzy."

"Nice to meet you," Corie said. Her voice shook, and Scarlet was glad. She did not want Corie Harper to be calm. At least not yet.

Izzy took a step backward trying to fit everyone in the picture. "It's a candid, Scarlet, but you are allowed to smile. Or are you still too panicked about your speech?"

Scarlet looked from Izzy to Clara then finally to Corie. "As a matter of fact," she said, "I think I am ready to say something."

When she leaned forward as if to stand, it was Corie who reached out to help. Scarlet took her hand, let herself be guided around piles of wrapping paper and boxes. As she and Corie walked together toward the cake table, Scarlet tried to name the emotions flooding her.

Love. Hate. Pain. Joy. The right words remained elusive.

What would she say to Corie if she found them?

Clara tapped a spoon against a champagne flute, and the room grew quiet. Expectant. Scarlet took in the faces of her guests one at a time, saving Corie for last. "I want to thank you all for coming," she said. Her pulse raced as she spoke. "I still can't believe you people voluntarily showed up today. I'm guessing Clara paid at least a few of you." A couple of the women laughed, and Scarlet nodded toward Clara. "I'm not kidding. She'd do just about anything for me, wouldn't you, Clare?"

Clara smiled. "Don't push it."

"Too late for that," Scarlet said. "By now most of you know that Gavin and I aren't together any more, and I'm sorry, but that's all I plan to say about that." She counted two beats of silence, the room holding its breath. "But believe me, it's for the best, and I am not alone. In fact everyone here has played a role in who I am today." Scarlet paused again, surveyed her audience. "The truth is, I've learned something from every single one of you. About what I want. About whom I can trust." Her eyes cut then to Corie. "After the accident, I thought I had lost everything. Including my mind," she said. "But Clara stuck around to remind me that my luck's not all bad." She hooked her hands below her belly. "I still have this little guy. And I've got Clara. The best friend I've ever had."

Corie took a step backward. Scarlet noticed.

The rest she'd say in private.

ॐ

As the shower came to a close, her friends approached her one last time. They said warm goodbyes, offered words of comfort, last-minute tips and well-wishes for a smooth delivery. When it was Clara's turn, she pulled up a chair and gave her friend a hug.

"I told you," Clara said.

"Told me what?"

"That this would be a good day."

"It was," Scarlet agreed. "Very good."

Still, she had one more guest to speak to. She wanted to look Corie Harper in the eye and ask her why she'd come. What had she hoped to accomplish? What did she want before she left? Then, after hearing Corie's answers, Scarlet had something to tell her too. Corie would be surprised, but Scarlet didn't care. Today was long overdue.

"Did you see where Corie went?" Her gaze traveled the room, but she saw no turquoise blouse or snow white curls.

"The bathroom, maybe?" suggested Clara. Izzy overheard and came toward them.

"I saw Corie head to the parking lot a few minutes ago," she said. "I thought she was going to her car to get the gift that goes along with the card."

"What card?" asked Scarlet.

"The one she left there."

Izzy pointed to a thick envelope propped on the loveseat. Scarlet could just make out the address scrawled in a looping, hopeful cursive. Shivers traveled up her spine. Spirits from the past. Ghosts over a grave. "Oh my God."

This wasn't a baby shower card.

And Corie Harper Slater was long gone.

Greetings Scarlet Hinden, Esq.

Allow me to begin this letter by saying that today's assignment is complete and total bullshit. Bull. To the. Shit. I wouldn't even do it if it was any teacher other than Mr. Roosevelt. I know he's trying to provide another one of his "watershed" moments of youth; a chance for us to capture our innocence and relive it in our late twenties. But instead I can't help thinking what he was like ten years ago and what he will be doing ten years from now.

I'll admit—if you held a gun to my head—that the Mozart playing in the background is mildly soothing. In fact, it would be perfect if—rather than being stuck here—I were in a rocking chair, wrapped in a hand-knitted blanket, about to be served hot tea in a china cup. But no.

I'm with two dozen ass-kissing students in a drafty AP English classroom. (As an aside, Corie hates, hates, hates when people use classical music as some sort of 'background.' She says it deserves full attention. Whatever. She's sitting behind me so I can't see her eyes, but I'm sure they're about to roll right out of her skull. The good news is, I'll get to read this to her in ten years and remind her how much she loves me.)

OK. Spooky. Mr. Roosevelt just made an announcement reminding us this assignment is worth points, and we need to take it seriously. Was he reading my mind? After he swore he wouldn't read our letters? I almost asked him how he would know whether or not we simply filled these pages with crap. But a star student with a full ride to Berkeley (thank you very much) is not supposed to ask "those types of questions." So, whatever. I'll play along in case the man's a liar.

(Insert serious face here_____.)

Future Scarlet: How does it feel to be a successful lawyer? I'm sure you breezed through your undergraduate requirements, aced the LSATs and completed law school with honors. So tell me. Is your crappy life finally awesome? (Be honest, now. You're talking to me. No one else is reading this letter, right, Mr. Roosevelt? Right? If you are reading this, I think you're really hot for a teacher. Call me sometime. We'll do dinner!)

Anyway. By now I'm sure you've found the love of your life (It's not HIM, Scarlet, no matter how much you want it to be. HE doesn't see you 'in that way,' and besides, you made a promise—but is it too much to ask that he be tall, dark and handsome?) and you and your man are both successful and happy and life is a goddamned bowl of cherries. Am I right?

Now. Listen to me, Scarlet. This is important: To ensure you remain this way—all joyous and cherry-filled—you, my dear, must NOT HAVE ANY KIDS!!!

What's that, you say?

I'll rephrase it in words you can understand:

You, Scarlet Hinden, will be a horrible mother, no matter how hard you try. I'm sorry, but it's the truth. You won't know how to be anything but awful at it. I mean, let's look at your two biggest role models:

Mama. A desperate failure.

Mrs. Harper. Just plain desperate.

Plus there's this little nugget of reality: Good things come to those who are selfish.

It's a sad motto to underline, but nevertheless.

There it is.

So please remember: After everything you've had to overcome, you can achieve anything you set your mind to, but you have to keep your eye on the prize, sister. Never lose sight of who you were and who you are. And don't forget you actually have two of the most awesome friends ever (Corie and Tuck!). No one can take that away from you. By the time you receive this letter, you will no doubt have achieved greatness.

A Nobel Prize?

The Pulitzer?

How about an Academy Award for all the acting you've done?

(Cue the Mozart for my acceptance speech. Now.)

Ahem.

I, Scarlet Hinden, would like to thank Corie Harper and Tucker Slater and my own damn self and every other person in this stupid graduating class who made me who I am today.

For better or worse.

And I can't wait to see who we'll turn out to be tomorrow. And ten years from now. Until then, let's all keep on keeping on. And maybe, just maybe, every single one of us will end up insanely happy.

(Applause. Applause. Applause.)

Scarlet Hinden Slater.
Esquire.

Spring

Corie

When Tuck and I eloped, I didn't ask my mother if I could borrow her wedding dress. She was still mourning my dad—we all were—and the moment just didn't feel right. So I sneaked into her guest room closet where she kept the veil and gloves. Then Tuck and I took off with my sad mother's dress in my dead father's car.

The Dragon Wagon.

I still miss that old green junker mostly because it was his. I loved the stiff Naugahyde leather and the smell of his Old Spice. We drove straight through to Vegas in the middle of the night, and we were wed by an Elvis impersonator whose actual name was Byron. He sang *Jailhouse Rock* before the ceremony. I knew my father would approve. I felt him smiling down on us while Tuck and I repeated our vows.

When we returned, Ma was less than thrilled that we had kept her from our wedding. She didn't care about the dress or the wagon, she was upset she hadn't been there. We told her we were afraid of the reminder that her own husband was gone. She told *us* that was something she'd never forget and seeing her daughters happy was all she had left.

Today I sit beside her on a bench at *That's Amore* where the future Mrs. Joseph Farinelli is trying on wedding dresses. Bets is behind a satin curtain with Matilda Bonasuerte, a salesgirl with a nose piercing and questionable taste in gowns. After some rustling and a few indecipherable murmurs,

Matilda pulls back the curtain, and my sister emerges from the dressing room in Choice Number One.

"Don't laugh," Bets says, peering at us over a cloud of white tulle. I think she is smiling, but it's impossible to tell. "I wanted to try something fit for a princess."

"How helpful," says Ma. "Now we can rule this one out." She squeezes my knee hard. "We can rule it out now can't we, Bethany?"

Matilda crouches to rearrange the hemline, and a sliver of orange thong peeks out from her pants. "Give it a chance. Let it sink in." She fluffs the skirt. "This is the latest trend in bridal couture. Everyone stopped pretending less is more two years ago." She looks up at Bets. "The future is all about bigger and better. Not only in your future as a married woman, but in the dress you wear when you walk down that aisle."

"See, Ma," Bets says. "Bigger is better."

"Besides," Matilda says. "It's not every day you find out the love of your life is the guy you thought you hated."

"I suppose that's true," my mother says. Her mouth lifts into in a smile.

"So how much is the dress?" I ask.

"Only three," says Matilda.

"Hundred?"

Her brows meet in the middle of her face. "Three thousand," Matilda tells me. "You won't find a bridal dress for three hundred dollars outside of a thrift store."

"I wouldn't know," I tell her. "I wore my mother's dress. For free."

"I'm sorry, Mattie." Bets reaches behind her and unzips herself in the middle of the showroom floor. "This is out of my budget. I should've told you we're trying to keep it at one."

"Thousand?" I ask.

Bets glares at me. "Don't worry, Corie. You're not paying."

"Who is?"

"I am," says Bets. "And Joey gave his blessing. He is making a grand gesture by letting me spend so much money. Isn't that romantic?"

"It is," says Ma. "Now, let me help you out of this dress

while Matilda looks for something more… *you.*" My mother leans toward the salesgirl. "In price and in silhouette?" Matilda shrugs, then disappears into the racks of gowns at the back of the store.

Ma fusses with a hook and eye latch above the tulle. "Corie, sweetie, why don't you browse through the bridesmaid's dresses. I'm sure Bethany wants you to be her matron of honor."

"Too late," Bets says. "I asked Kate Turlow, and she's totally into it."

"You did what?" My mother gasps.

"I'm kidding," says Bets. "Corie is my first choice, but I don't think she wants to spend money on a dress she'll wear only once."

"You mean until your next wedding," I tease.

"Hush up, both of you," Ma says. "Don't make me think twice about what I'm about to offer."

"Hold on," says Bets. "I'm officially hushed. What's this about an offer?"

Ma looks at us, her eyes bright. "I think your father would have loved nothing more than to see his daughters standing together at the altar. To him you were the most beautiful girls in the world, and he always dreamed of walking you down the aisle. But he never got that chance. So please. Both of you. Pick out dresses, and let them be my treat."

"Ma! That's too much," I say.

My mother nods. "But I insist."

"Done and done!" says Bets. "Maybe Joey and I can take that honeymoon to Costa Rica." She starts rambling about palm trees and sand as I glance at a display of puffy-sleeved gowns in a rainbow of taffeta.

"Ma. Would you consider paying me *not* to wear one of these?"

My mother shakes her head. "I'm sure you can find something that suits you. Maybe in pink? You're so pretty in pink."

While Ma guides Bets behind the curtain, I survey the choices in the bridesmaid's section. I know bridal attendants aren't supposed to overshadow the bride, but these dresses could have been designed by Wella. At the thought of my niece I smile, wondering what she and Cam might wear to the wedding. They both seem thrilled that their parents are finally getting married after all these years. I'm happy for them. Mostly. And maybe a little jealous.

In another rack of gowns, I come across a cornflower blue slip dress that isn't the worst thing I've ever seen.

"Now that is lovely," Ma says, coming up behind me. "It'll bring out the blue in your eyes."

"You think?" I run a finger up the spaghetti strap, test its sturdiness.

"As a matter of fact, there are a few things a mother just knows," she tells me. "For instance, I know this is your favorite color."

"Yep."

"And I know you think Bets is making a mistake." I open my mouth to protest, but Ma holds up a finger. "I also know you've been avoiding me since that day on your front porch. If you don't want to talk about it? Fine. But I did what I thought was right."

"I'm not avoiding you. I've been busy."

"Of course you have," she says. "But don't worry. I am positive that you and Tucker will get through this."

My body stiffens, but Ma is too busy wrestling the dress off its hanger to notice. She spins me around and holds the silky fabric up to my collarbone. "This could be the one," she says. "Ask Matilda for a dressing room so you can prove your mother right."

"Ma." I push her and the dress away from me gently. "You can't say something like *you'll get through this*, then tell me to put on a pretty dress. What are you so sure Tuck and I need to get through?"

She tilts her head. "You and Bets act as if I haven't been where you are. That I can't possibly understand what you're going through. But I was young once, you know. And in love. I've felt my share of insecurity. I've had my doubts. I even questioned whether or not I married the right guy."

"Be serious."

"I am," she insists. "Your father and I had plenty of

troubles over the years. We had highs, sure. But don't kid yourself. We also had lows. We just happened to make it through them until we didn't."

"He died, Ma."

"Exactly," she says.

"So you're telling me as long as Tuck and I stay alive we'll be fine? That's just weird."

"You're the English teacher," Ma clucks. "Surely you aren't that literal." She glances around and lowers her voice. "I'm saying you'll get through this rough patch. And Tucker will get through this rough patch. And maybe it'll be together."

"Or?"

She drapes the dress over my arms and gives my shoulder a squeeze. "A couple makes it through their troubles until they don't."

I shake my head. "You're supposed to help me believe in happy endings, Ma. Isn't that the law of being a parent?"

"If you must know, I think my job is the exact opposite of that. And when you have children of your own," she bends in close and adds, "notice I said *when*, not *if*—you too will help them navigate the truth."

"Which is what?"

"That there's no such thing as a happy ending, Corie. There are beginnings. And middles. Then ends. What you do with them is up to you." She puts a hand on my shoulder. "Don't be afraid to change your mind during any one of those parts. It's not too late."

"But what if the changes aren't up to me? What if something or someone else takes away my choices?"

"Oh, sweetie," she says, "there's always a choice. No matter what happens to us, we decide how to act afterward. Now... go try on this dress."

∽✌

I text Tucker in the parking lot and ask him if we can talk. When his reply is *6:00 CHS ball field*, I am unsurprised. It is the birthplace of our history, the spot where we first kissed. Those bleachers represent the moment we were brave enough to be honest with each other for the first time.

Tuck was the varsity pitcher then, and Scarlet and I never missed an inning. We sat in the stands cheering him on, the two of us, always together. Until one game in April when Scarlet's mother called her home, and I stuck around after they won to hitch a ride with Tuck. The rest of the team was already gone, but we stayed in the dugout to celebrate. On my third lukewarm beer, I confessed.

I've wanted you for-practically-ever.

He stared at me then, silent, confirming my worst fear. I'd ruined everything. Not only our friendship but my promises to Scarlet. Of course I had noticed her gazing at him. I'd seen the shine in her eyes when he laughed. Had envy caused me to make a move? Or alcohol? Maybe I'd been trying to save him. It didn't matter. I was wrong, and I begged him to forget.

Pretend this didn't happen. And please. Don't say anything to Scarlet.

Head buried in my hands, I waited for Tuck to speak, but I felt his hand under my chin, and he lifted up my face. *I want you too*, he breathed. Then he put his lips on mine. He wanted to be saved. I wasn't wrong. Tuck Slater wanted me.

♋♋

At six o'clock he parks across the street from the ball field to change out of his scrubs. Then he grabs a ball cap and heads toward the bleachers where I sit with a blanket in my lap.

"Did you have fun shopping?" Tuck straddles the bench and offers me a sympathetic smile.

"It wasn't as awful as I thought it would be. I bought a dress. Well, Ma bought it for me. And what we really did was order it because they didn't have my size."

"Your mother bought you a wedding dress?"

"Bridesmaid. As it turns out, I'm the Matron of Honor."

Tuck raises a brow. "I thought you didn't approve. And I know you don't like Joey Farinelli."

"I'm beginning to realize I'm in no position to judge," I

say. "Maybe I've been too harsh. With both of them."

"You love Bets," says Tuck. "You want her to be happy. There's nothing wrong with that. The hard part's letting her decide what her happiness looks like."

I shrug and gather the edges of the blanket around me.

Tuck nods at my lap. "Cold already?"

"You know me."

"Yes, I do." His dark eyes crinkle, and he nudges my knee.

"For better or worse," I say.

"Uh oh, Core." Beneath the brim of the hat, he blinks. "Is it that bad?"

"Is *what* bad?"

"The thing you brought me out here to talk about."

"It's not awful," I say. "I've just been reminding myself that a situation isn't always what it seems to be on the surface. You know?"

"I do," he says. "I spend my days looking at what's under people's skin. Haven't met a doctor yet who can tell what's wrong with someone by checking on his outsides."

"I wish there was an X-ray for relationships."

"Sounds serious," he says.

"I saw Scarlet!" I say. Then I take a deep breath and spit out the rest of my story before I reconsider telling Tuck.

"It was last month when you were taking that course in Arizona. I flew up to San Francisco and crashed her baby shower except I actually was invited by Clara. She's the one who's been checking in on Eleanor Hinden because Scarlet's not supposed to travel." I hesitate, hoping Tucker will react to Scarlet's name, but he seems only to be listening. "I barely said a word to her," I tell him. "I was hoping we could have a one-on-one conversation after the party, but instead she gave this speech thanking Clara for being her best friend and then she said something about not being with Gavin any more. He must be the boyfriend Mrs. Hinden told me about. So I guess Scarlet's having this baby on her own."

"That's too bad," he says.

"It is." My words tumble out now, honest and hard. "But the ridiculous part is that I was jealous of her. Like, out-of-my-mind jealous."

"You were," he says, a statement not a question.

"I am," I admit. "Still. I mean, she's pregnant, right? And she's so beautiful. And... I can't believe I'm even saying this... but it occurred to me that you might have picked Scarlet instead of me if you had known back then that I couldn't have your baby now."

"Core—"

"Let me finish," I say. "Sometimes I think we're being punished, you know? For what happened back then. For what we did or didn't do. And—" I cut myself off and swallow while Tuck's eyes laser in on mine. Like arrows except sharper and more black.

"And what?"

"And I left without even talking to Scarlet because I didn't want her to find out any of this. She's got no one. And a baby on the way. So I can't help wondering: What if she still wants you? Or worse, what if a part of you wants her?"

After a moment of silence, Tuck opens his mouth. "Am I allowed to speak?"

"There's one more thing I need to tell you first," I say. "A couple of months ago, I went a little crazy and poked through your bills and checked your phone records. I read your emails. It was terrible and snoopy, and I'm so, so sorry. I just couldn't stop myself from feeling sick every time you left the house. I didn't trust you, Tuck. But it was a mistake." I take another deep breath and gaze down at the hands folded in my lap. "The truth is, it's sometimes hard for me to believe you chose me. Even now. After all these years."

Tuck begins shaking his head.

"You don't deserve a suspicious wife," I add. "And I promise that if you forgive me, we'll get through this. We can move forward. Together."

He reaches up and tugs the brim of his hat lower on his forehead. I can't see his whole face, but it seems to me he is either laughing or really angry.

"The thing is, Corie, I saw Scarlet too."

In that instant, time slows, and my senses sharpen like knives in my gut. I smell the freshly cut grass at our feet and hear a crow flap its wings on top of the batting cage. I taste grit on my tongue. Feel slivers from the bench pierce my jeans. But I cannot look my husband in the eye.

"You saw who?"

"I saw Scarlet. Twice. The first time was at the cemetery last summer. She was home visiting her mother, and it was just a coincidence, both of us showing up there at the same time. I didn't tell you because talking about her always gets you upset."

He moves closer to me on the bench, and I wonder if he can feel the slivers too.

"You ended up with that letter of hers, and you weren't even trying to give it to her," he says. "So I got to thinking it might be an excuse to mend fences. I took it with me to San Francisco, Googled her law firm and followed her on a lunch break. We talked for maybe five minutes." He pulls his hat off and runs a hand through his hair. "I'm embarrassed to admit this, but I almost asked her if we could adopt her baby. I know it sounds insane, but the words were in my mouth, and I had to force myself not to say them out loud. So." He looks at me and laughs as if he didn't just blow up my whole world. "Who's the crazy one now?"

I nod my head, bewildered, but he goes on. "Thank God I realized it was an idiotic request. I looked like an idiot tracking her down to give her some stupid letter she wrote in high school. Why would I even do that?" He pauses, but I don't answer him because I have no voice left in me to speak. "So I put the letter back in your drawer, and I haven't seen or talked to Scarlet since."

He pauses now, eyes in a squint, waiting. "You wanted us to be honest, right? To clear the air? Say something, Core. Please."

I pull the blanket off and hand it to him. It's been my favorite for years, soft and nubby at the same time. Tuck's stepmother sent it to us from New York one Christmas, a gift from his father and her. The card said they hoped we would always be warm together.

I look at Tucker, and our eyes meet as I speak.

"Get away from me," I tell him.

And he does.

Scarlet

Scarlet sat on a bench in the waiting room, her foot tapping against the travertine. Shouldn't a psychiatrist whose clients were at greater risk of frazzled nerves have installed carpet in her reception area? Surely choosing stone of any kind was shortsighted. Scarlet chewed on her frustration, then swallowed it whole. She was the last person to judge another woman for her choices.

Tap, tap, tap.

She leaned against the wall, and her stomach rumbled as she checked her watch. After two months of avoiding Dr. Kagawa, she was thirty minutes early for this appointment. Clara had tried to convince her to return after the accident. She'd threatened and bribed to no avail. What finally drove Scarlet back to the doctor were the letters.

The one she wrote ten years ago and the one her mother wrote last week.

They smoldered in her purse now, like two hot coals of truth. She wasn't sure why she had brought them. She didn't plan to show either one to Dr. Kagawa. Why risk being asked questions she had no intention of answering? Some losses were too deep to share, even with paid professionals. She never spoke about hers with anyone. Not with Clara or Gavin. Only Corie and Tucker knew a piece of it. And Mama, of course. Mama knew it all.

Hey Baby, Eleanor's letter began.

I'm pretty sure the right words haven't been invented yet to say how sorry I am. And if they already exist, I don't know a single one of them. I should've realized right away that trying to force you to get rid of your baby was the quickest way to make sure you would keep it. You always were one to dig in your heels now, weren't you? And baby, you come by that trick honestly.

I don't expect you'll be talking to me anytime soon, so I wanted to tell you something I should've copped to a long time ago. The truth is, Sam didn't leave because of you. Sure, I blamed you when he went, like it was your fault you weren't his kid. But the truth is, I was so busy being mad at myself, some of the madness leaked out onto you. That man loved you hard. He just hated me harder. And I gave him reason to, I know.

You got a raw deal being stuck with me for a mother, and you'll have to take that up with God. Lord knows, I've got plenty to say to the Devil when I see him. As for you and me and our past, it's time for you to let go of what I wrecked between us. You can start by hugging that baby of yours extra tight when he comes. Then tell his daddy he better marry you and make you happy. You can make things right, Scarlet. You can. For all of us. I'm only sorry I couldn't fix things up myself.

Mama

"I'm not getting better," Scarlet announced midway through her session.

"OK," said the doctor. Her expression did not change.

"That's it?" asked Scarlet. "Just *OK?*"

"Yes," Dr. Kagawa said. "It is."

"But it's not OK with me."

"Then let's explore that. Why it's not OK with you."

Scarlet picked at a hangnail, tore it with her teeth. She sucked the blood from her finger, and the doctor tapped her notepad with a pen.

"Are you angry?" Dr. Kagawa asked. This was unusual for her. Typically she waited for Scarlet to name her own emotions.

"No," Scarlet said.

"All right."

"I'm not."

Dr. Kagawa peered down at her pad. "How are things going with Clara? It must be different with you two living together now."

Scarlet flushed.

Clara had flown to LA that morning and would be gone for the next forty-eight hours. She was in Scarlet's hometown now taking care of things Scarlet should be doing herself. There were papers to be signed. Insurance matters to address. And Clara was the English bulldog who could make sure Eleanor got what she needed.

On the surface, Scarlet was grateful. No, deeper than the surface. Clara was generous in the extreme. What kind of monster wouldn't feel gratitude? But a space inside Scarlet harbored frustration. She could never repay Clara's kindness, and the permanent imbalance made her feel small.

"Clara's fine," Scarlet said.

The doctor bobbed her head. "Fine."

"Yes."

"You rely on her a great deal."

Scarlet shifted in her seat. "I guess I do."

"Do you have a Plan B?"

"For what? The birth?"

"That's a good place to start. But I'm also talking about after he is born."

Scarlet frowned. "Here's where I admit I have no plan. In fact all I've done is make mistakes."

"Before we get to that, tell me what you've done right."

Scarlet shook her head.

"Nothing?" the doctor pressed.

"When I fail, I tend to go down in a blaze of glory."

"In what ways do you imagine you're failing?"

"For starters my son could have had a father. Maybe even a great one. But now—" Scarlet's voice trailed off.

"Now what?"

"It'll be just the two of us."

"Are you worried about being alone?"

"That's exactly it."

"What is?"

"I won't be alone," she said. "My son will be with me. All the time. And I don't know how to be with someone else. Not completely. Not comfortably."

"Intimacy makes you uncomfortable?"

"That's not what I said." Scarlet placed a palm on her stomach.

"Then explain what you did say."

"I don't know."

"What do you know?"

Scarlet sighed. "This baby is going to rely on me for everything. Not just physically but emotionally." She paused. "What if I totally screw this whole parenting thing up?"

"Ah. But what if you don't?" asked Dr. Kagawa.

Across Scarlet's abdomen, the baby's limbs rippled. He was so low in her pelvis, she often dreamed he'd fallen out while she slept. "See?" Scarlet dropped her eyes. "Even he knows he's doomed."

The doctor's lip curled at one edge, and Scarlet wondered what the gesture betrayed. "Children are remarkably resilient," said Dr. Kagawa. "They're quite capable of forgiving mistakes."

Scarlet nodded. "So you're saying I *am* going to screw this up."

"I'm saying you might surprise yourself. Maybe you'll be better at motherhood than you think." The doctor set down her pen. "At the end of the day, children just want to love and be loved by their parents."

"But my son will have only one parent."

The doctor leaned forward, her pen cradled inside the crack of the notebook's spine. "Isn't that precisely what you wanted?" Scarlet opened her mouth to speak, but Dr. Kagawa cut her off. "Think about my question before you answer. Really think."

For a moment, Scarlet remained quiet. Then she cleared her throat. "I broke a good man's heart. A man who, I'm pretty sure, could have loved me. I also guaranteed that my son will grow up without a dad." She splayed her hands. "Why would a sane person do either of those things on purpose?"

"Listen to what you are saying," the doctor told her. "Think for a moment. Then answer the question yourself."

Scarlet considered her response as the second-hand ticked around the orb of the cuckoo clock. Had the doctor not seen the irony of hanging something labeled "cuckoo" in her office?

"I've never heard your clock chime," Scarlet said.

The doctor nodded. "I disabled it. The noise used to startle my patients, but I can't get rid of it."

"Why not?"

"It belonged to my mother," said Dr. Kagawa. "And that was an artful digression."

"I've never thought of myself as artful. Is your mother dead?" The question sounded hollow, and Scarlet's head ached with the bluntness.

"She is," answered the doctor.

Scarlet blinked. "I'm sorry."

"She died in childbirth. I never knew her or what I might be missing."

"I'm sorry," Scarlet said again.

"Thank you," Dr. Kagawa told her. "I was raised by my father. With the help of my grandparents."

"Ah," Scarlet said. "Something else my baby isn't going to have."

"A cuckoo clock?" The doctor lifted a brow, and Scarlet smiled at the unexpected humor.

"I meant grandparents."

"What about your mother?" asked Dr. Kagawa. "Perhaps there will be room for the two of you to repair your relationship."

Scarlet brushed a finger along the edge of her purse, pictured the chicken scratch of Mama's letter. "I don't see that happening."

"Why is that?"

"Did you know my mother warned me not to have this baby? She told me flat out to have an abortion."

"How did that request make you feel?"

Scarlet grimaced. "I'm still pregnant."

Dr. Kagawa leaned forward, cupped her chin in her hand. "You like to be defiant, don't you? To do the opposite of what someone else says you should do?"

"Not intentionally. Things just turn out that way."

"Really? I think it's how you show others you are in control."

"Maybe," said Scarlet. "I never thought of it that way."

"Fair enough. So what if you stopped."

"Stopped what?"

"Go back and think about the choices you have made, times when you wanted to prove you were in control."

"Why?"

Dr. Kagawa settled back against her seat. "I want you to imagine what you might do differently."

"What's done is done." Scarlet shrugged. "I can't change the past."

"Pretend you can," said the doctor. "Play along with me."

Scarlet considered the question. There were many options. Professionally. Personally. *What would I change?* Only one answer made her pulse quicken.

"There is something," she said.

"Tell me."

It was a longshot, but Scarlet had to try. "I need to go," she said. "Right now."

"But your time isn't up yet," Dr. Kagawa said.

"Yes," said Scarlet. "It is."

§∽∾

With Clara out of town, Scarlet had the apartment to herself. There would be no searching looks, no questions to avoid. Since Corie's disappearance at the shower, Clara had been strangely quiet. More observant. Scarlet sometimes felt as if she were living under a microscope. And although Clara never pushed for answers, Scarlet could sense her friend's growing curiosity. They shared a home after all, and in a matter of weeks, a newborn would be added to the mix. Everything would change.

Everything.

Don't be silly, Clara told her. *We'll be exactly the same. Except, perhaps, there'll be a few more dirty diapers lying around.* Scarlet had smiled, relieved. At least she and her baby would have a safe place to live. And someone who cared about them. But was that enough?

Scarlet wanted more.

She shut herself in her bedroom and dragged the curtains closed. Some truths were better faced in darkness, and she realized she might be too late. That what she had done could be unforgivable. *What if the best bridge of her life had been burned beyond repair?*

A sliver of light peeked through the curtains as she reached for the phone in her purse. The contact had been deleted, but she knew the number by heart. She tapped it in, held her breath. With each ring she made a promise.

If Gavin picked up, she would never betray him again.

Corie

Meeting Clara Broxton for drinks at The Brewhaus is the second-to-last thing I want to do tonight. The first even worse thing is admitting to Ma that my husband hasn't been sleeping at home. But these days my wants and needs are mutually exclusive, and I am not going to get out of either task.

Ma called this morning to tell me my bridesmaid's dress was ready. Then she offered to pick it up so I wouldn't have to stop by *That's Amore*. She planned to drop it off at five o'clock, which means she'll be here any minute. Once she's inside the house, she'll figure out something is happening between Tuck and me. Or, more accurately, not happening.

She wouldn't question his being gone on a Friday evening. The whole family is used to his traveling, his unpredictable schedule. We've all had the pleasure of canceled plans because of delayed cases and missed flights. But these circles under my eyes suggest a different story, and Ma will take one look at me and ask about our current chapter.

I'm changing out of my work clothes when I hear her car in the driveway. She's always fifteen minutes early, and she never forgets her key.

"Knock, knock," she calls from the stairs. As she comes into my room, I'm straightening the duvet. I don't want her to see that the pillows are disturbed on only my side of the bed.

"You can't say 'knock, knock' if you're already inside."

"Sure I can. In fact, I just did."

Her smile is unusually bright. She is wearing candy pink lipstick and two lids full of frosty shadow. Her hair has been swooped into an elegant updo, and if I'm not mistaken, she is sporting false eyelashes.

"Aren't you lovely," I tell her.

"You like it?" She rotates slowly. "This is just a trial run. The girls at the salon want to do this for the wedding, but I don't know. It might be a bit too much."

"Besides the fact that you'll show up the bride? It's perfect."

"Oh stop it, Corie." My mother puts her hands on her hips and curtsies. "A lady never steals the thunder on someone else's wedding day." When she chuckles, I know she is in a good mood, and my stomach churns. I don't want my bad news to steal a piece of her joy.

"It's awfully dark in here," she says. She moves to the window and opens the blinds. I notice then that her hands are empty.

"Where's the dress?"

"I hung it in the hall closet," she says. "You can try it on if you like, but since you refused alterations, I guess it doesn't matter if it fits. It's yours. As is."

"I told you, Ma. It's a waste of money to alter a dress I'll wear only once. I can either skip the donuts or double my consumption between now and June if I have to."

Ma takes a seat on the edge of my bed. "Suit yourself."

"I think I just did."

She pats the space beside her, and I collapse there on my back. Across the ceiling a new crack spreads from the east corner to the center of the room. It took Tuck and me weeks to scrape the popcorn off when we moved in, but we didn't care. We were new homeowners and in love; newlyweds ready to take on the world. Neither of us had any idea how much the world would keep fighting back.

"You all right?" Ma asks, peering down at me. "Are you sick, sweetie?" I look at her, and she searches my face. "Oh my God. Are you pregnant?"

"Ma. No."

"I need to stop asking that, don't I?"

"Yes. You definitely do. Never again, please."

Her sunny expression darkens a shade. "That doesn't sound good."

"Because it's not." I prop myself up on an elbow. "Tuck and I had a fight, Ma. A bad one."

"I know these past few months have been rough," she says. "But I thought you two were working it out."

"I wanted to," I tell her.

"Past tense?"

When I don't answer, she sighs. "I was hoping that Bets and Joey's reuniting again would be just what you and Tucker needed to get your marriage back on track."

"It's hard to get back on track when he's not here."

"You're used to that, though."

"Not for this long." I swallow hard, and her eyes narrow.

"How long are we talking about?"

"Two weeks," I say, almost a whisper. "He's been gone two weeks, Ma."

"Oh, Corie." Her lips purse, a prune of concern.

"Please don't say anything to Bets. To anyone."

"Of course not," she says. "But where is he?"

"I don't know. There have been zero calls or texts between us. Nothing. For the first few days, I thought we were both blowing off steam. That he would schedule some overdue work trips and wait for me to beg him to come home. Then another couple of days went by, and I couldn't bring myself to be the one to break the ice. I was so angry at him. But now..." My words trail off because I'm not sure how to finish the sentence.

But now, what?

"You two are so bullheaded," my mother says. "You want what you want when you want it."

"Tuck is maybe. Not me."

Ma looks at me sideways. "Whatever you say." She chews her lip. "Do you mind if I ask what happened?"

"I don't mind, but I'm not sure it will help any of us if you know the details."

"Even so," she says. "How about I make us some tea, and we can talk things through?"

"We don't have any tea. When Bets left, she took the kettle and all the steeping bags."

"Then I'll make us a fresh pot of coffee. You still drink coffee, don't you?" I nod as she heads toward the door. "Join me in the kitchen when you're ready. I want to hear all about what's gotten into your husband."

"You're assuming it's Tucker's fault?"

"I'm sure there's blame on both ends," she says. "But you're my daughter. I'm familiar with your brand of trouble. His? I'm not so sure about."

Ma clanks around downstairs in the kitchen while I lie back on the bed, thumbs pressed to my temple. When I was thirteen and braces made my teeth sore, I used to grind the top row against the bottom, jaw clamped down tight. Taking charge helped me cope with the discomfort and made me feel I was in control. I guess a part of me still clings to this process, magnifying the hurt until I'm ready to put an end to it. I blink back tears as Ma returns with a bottle of water and two Advil.

"Take these while we wait for the coffee to brew," she says. "It'll help with that headache of yours."

"How did you know I have a headache?"

"I'm your mother," she says. "I can tell when you're in pain." Then she smiles at me.

And so I tell her everything.

ॐ

The Brewhaus is a sprawling restaurant split into two wings, one featuring a wine bar, the other an old-school coffee house. In between sits a lobby with enormous double doors featuring wrought iron handles and dungeon-style windows. Although the building was constructed only two years ago, the stone walls have been treated to look ancient. The lights are dimmed. Soft music hums. In the air, a hint of oak. Everything about the space is subdued.

While I wait at an abandoned hostess station for someone to tell me where to go, I check my cell phone again to be sure it's not on mute. No texts from Tuck. No missed calls or messages. Nothing from Clara, either. Maybe she's standing me up.

I hope she's standing me up.

I'm about to let myself off the hook and leave when a door behind me creaks open, and Clara emerges from the bar side of the building. She clacks toward me on high heels and her pin-straight bob brushes her neck.

"Corie!" My name echoes in the cave-like foyer. "I got us a spot in the bar instead of the coffee shop. Hope that's OK."

"Sure," I say, but what I think is *I have never needed a drink more in my life.* Clara leads me through the doors past a man on a stage playing an acoustic guitar. Our pub table is nestled in the back corner of the bar.

"I hope this is far enough away from the music," she says. "I want us to be able to talk."

I force a smile and take a seat on one of the high stools. On the other side of the table sits an empty wine glass. Clara has already finished at least one drink.

"Sorry if I kept you waiting," I say.

"No. You're right on time. I was early." She leans over the table. "Honestly, I needed a bit of liquid courage." At this my throat tightens, but I nod to show support. *What exactly does Clara Broxton want to talk about?*

She hands me the laminated wine list and bends her head to indicate her glass. "That was a Chardonnay. From Napa, I think. Or maybe it was Sonoma. Either way, it's buttery if you like that kind of thing."

A young waitress in a tight miniskirt approaches our table with a fresh glass of wine. "My second," Clara says. Then she shrugs. "I'm taking a taxi."

"Can I get you something?" asks the waitress. A loose braid drapes over her shoulder, and she fusses with the hem of her miniskirt. She reminds me of Greer Larson, and I suddenly feel old.

"I'll have the Rodney Strong Cab," I tell her. The girl studies my face, so I add, "Cabernet Sauvignon?" When she still doesn't move I say, "Please?"

"Do you have ID?"

"Oh!" I fumble for my wallet. "Sorry. I haven't been carded in a while."

"No problem, ma'am," she says. "I'm required to ask. I'm sure you're over twenty-one."

Ma'am. Right.

I flash her my driver's license, and her braid flips as she whirls away to fill my order. While Clara works on her wine, I shove the wallet into my purse, then balance my purse next to Clara's on a barstool between us.

After a short stretch of silence, the guitarist begins to play *Blackbird*. It's my favorite Beatles song, but the opening notes sound mournful now.

"Thanks for meeting me," Clara says.

In the background, the man sings. *Take these broken wings and learn to fly.*

"How's Mrs. Hinden?" I ask. "I assume you're in town to check on her, not to see me?"

Clara nods and takes another sip. "Eleanor is doing quite well. I was finalizing some insurance paperwork for New Horizons. Going over her will." I open my mouth, but Clara stops me. "No one's dying or anything. She just wants to be prepared."

"I guess that's good," I say. "So... has Scarlet seen her since...?"

"Not yet," says Clara. "At this stage of the pregnancy, Scar's not supposed to travel in the first place. And a visit back here could be too stressful for her." She pauses. "At least that's what Dr. Kagawa thinks. She's Scarlet's psychiatrist."

"Oh." My stomach twists, and I wonder if I am still among the demons haunting Scarlet. Did my showing up at the shower cause her pain? Has the letter made things worse for her? And what about Tuck? Did seeing him again stir up feelings from the past? I picture Scarlet sitting across from her psychiatrist sharing our betrayal. Her loss. My gain. *Oh, God.* Does her doctor know more about my husband than I do?

Clara drains her glass and sets it on a cocktail napkin. "Of course I'm not meant to discuss any of this," she says, "but after a glass of wine or two, I get chatty."

"Don't worry." My shoulders sink. "I won't say anything."

"Well, you couldn't now, could you? It's not like you and Scarlet ever talk to each other." Clara studies my face. "What's with that anyway?" she asks. "You come round to the shower with some mystery letter and then you disappear before any of us gets a chance to talk. I'm confused."

"She didn't tell you?"

"Scarlet... declined to discuss the matter," Clara says. "If you must know, I'm a bit annoyed with you both."

Before I can respond, the waitress returns to our table with my wine. I mumble a *thank you* as she sets my drink on a clean napkin, then spins away again leaving me to suffer Clara's quizzical stare.

"Whatever's gone on between you is none of my business," she says. "But I hope you know that if you tell me, I would keep it to myself." Clara glances at her empty wine glass. "I am not a gossip."

"I have no reason to doubt you," I say.

"No, you don't," she agrees. "But I want the fact well-established because what I'm about to ask may make you think otherwise."

From the stage now come these lyrics: *All your life, you were only waiting for this moment to arise.* Laughter erupts from a table across the room, and I edge closer to Clara.

"OK," I say. "What is it?"

"Can you think of anyone," she asks in a low voice, "anyone at all, who might be the father of Scarlet's baby?"

At her words, the seconds crawl, and I struggle to find my voice. "Isn't it that lawyer? Gavin?"

Clara shakes her head. "Turns out, he's not the father. When he found out, he left Scarlet and moved back to Nebraska."

Blood races through my veins. Hot lava. I am melting on the inside.

"That's why I'm asking you," she says. Her words are soft now, slurred at the edges. "I realize you two aren't close any more, but you've known Scarlet forever. Do you have any idea who the father might be? Could it be someone from her past?"

I look down, afraid I might scream.

"Corie?"

Into the light of the dark black night.

"Corie?"

My heart is a drum beat in my ears, and at first I don't realize it isn't Clara calling my name. From behind me, the voice comes again. "Corie, I think you dropped this." I turn around to find Rick Roosevelt standing next to our table holding my purse. A smile spreads across his face, and when I don't respond, he slides the strap up his arm as if he plans to walk away with my bag.

"I'll keep it if you don't want it," he says. The sound of his laughter is an echo from my past, of classes he taught when I was his student. It invokes the days when I loved Tucker Slater and the road stretched out before us, both simple and intertwined.

And now Tuck may be the father of Scarlet's baby. My husband. The man I've been unable to give a child.

Rick pulls the purse off his arm and hands it to me.

"Thanks," I manage to tell him.

"You're welcome." He attempts another smile, this time smaller, less ambitious.

"This is Clara," I say. "Clara Broxton."

He breaks our gaze to shake her hand. "Rick Roosevelt," he says. "Nice to meet you."

Clara grins at him. Her cheeks flush pink. "Join us for a drink?" she asks.

"Can't. I'm meeting someone for coffee." His eyes travel the length of the bar. "It's my first time here, and I think I ended up in the wrong wing."

"That's a matter of opinion," says Clara. "How do you two know each other?" She cuts her eyes to me, but it is Rick who answers.

"Corie was my student longer ago than I care to remember."

"Ah. So you're a teacher too?"

"I was," he says. "And I am again now."

Her head tilts.

"In between, I got a little restless and a lot frustrated with the system. I took a leave of absence, went to law school. But it wasn't the life for me." He runs a hand over his smooth scalp, and his wince is an apology. "I'm a recovering blood-sucking attorney. Hope you can forgive me."

Clara's grin returns. "As a *current* blood-sucking attorney," she says, "I salute you."

"Oh! No. I'm sorry," Rick stutters, backpedaling. "I didn't mean—"

"I know exactly what you meant. And I am not offended in the least." Clara pauses as if working out an equation. "If you were Corie's English teacher," she says, "you must know Scarlet, then. Scarlet Hinden?"

"Yes." Rick shifts his weight, continues to stammer. "Yes," he says, "of course."

"What a small world!" Clara beams. "Scarlet's my roommate! She's a blood-sucker too."

Rick squares his shoulders. "Right. At Olson Brickman in San Francisco." He takes a beat. "The last time I saw Scarlet, she was putting together a scholarship for them."

"Ah," Clara says. "So you're the lovely man who was helping her out. How wonderful!" Clara surveys the room, then leans toward Rick. "Scarlet and I both work at Olson Brickman, you know. Well, she will again, once she's back from maternity leave."

Rick looks at me, and his jaw tightens. "Scarlet's pregnant?" he asks.

So much for not gossiping, Clara.

"She is," Clara answers. She waits for Rick to shift his gaze back to her. When he does, she says, "It must be strange for you to imagine your students as all grown up."

"Strange." He nods. "Yes."

"Are you absolutely sure you can't join us?" Clara asks.

He shakes his head as if coming back to himself. "I'm sorry, ladies. I just realized I'm running late." He takes a small step backward, then adds, "Please give Scarlet my best."

"I certainly will," Clara says. "Now, go. Get on with your coffee plans, Rick Roosevelt. Or I might force you to stay with us."

"Enjoy your night," he says, and I can't make myself reply. Clara's eyes follow him as he moves through the maze of bar tables and disappears into the lobby.

She clutches her heart in a dramatic show. "Well. He's

simply gorgeous, isn't he?"

I nod.

"Did you see his face when I talked about Scarlet?"

I nod again.

"Bloody hell, that girl gets all the men, doesn't she?"

"I guess she does," I say. Then I gulp my glass of Cabernet and wish that I were dead.

Scarlet

She waited on a thin blue mat, limbs growing numb as the minutes dragged. The gymnasium filled with pairs, each man escorting his woman with a hand at her lower back. Some of the couples were smiling. Others whispered. Scarlet slumped. Around them the air crackled with anticipation. A room full of first-timers at cotillion.

From a side door two women entered and made their way toward the mat next to Scarlet. One was petite with flame-red hair and a high, protruding belly. The other was tall and angular, her dark, wiry curls wrangled into a bun. The brunette bent to whisper to her partner who lifted her face to listen. She tucked a length of red hair behind her ear, and images flooded Scarlet's memory.

A thatch of carrot-colored hair. That fair, freckled skin. The scent of him. Leather and cinnamon. His own mix of sweet and spice.

Gavin.

By now he would have seen her missed calls, would know she had tried to contact him. But she had received no response, his silence loud and clear.

Her betrayal was too big to overcome.

Scarlet checked her watch. Four minutes past seven. *Damn.* They'd be lucky to complete the course before her due date, and Clara was already late for the first class? As if registering his own protest, the baby kicked, a sharp jab in her side. Once again Scarlet cursed herself for taking so long to sign up.

Months ago Dr. Nguyen had recommended Lamaze classes, but Scarlet had balked. "Why should I pay someone else to help me practice my breathing?" she asked. "I'm planning to get an epidural."

"When it comes to babies," the doctor told her, "it's best to be prepared for any contingency. The best laid plans go oft awry."

Scarlet nodded, but in her head she thought, *No. They "Gang aft agley."*

She had studied Robert Burns in Rick Roosevelt's English class, memorizing *To a Mouse* in the original Scottish dialect. More than most she understood the fate of a "wee, sleekit, cow'rin, tim'rous beastie," knew how a creature could work and work to make his home safe, all for nothing.

Through the open doors of the auditorium Scarlet heard a horn honk. Was Clara finally arriving? Could she still be stuck in traffic? She fought the urge to text her and instead risked a peek at the women on the mat beside her. The redhead sat between the bent knees of the brunette who rested a hand on her partner's swollen belly. When the pregnant woman stretched, she caught Scarlet looking at her.

"I'm Wendy." She leaned her head back. "This is Val."

Scarlet's lips twitched. Small talk was not her strength. "I'm Scarlet," she said. Then she glanced at her watch, and the baby kicked again.

"He's late, huh?" Wendy asked. "I'm not being nosy."

"Yeah you are," said Val. "Wendy likes to adopt people. Like puppies. Not that you're a dog. But you know what I mean." Scarlet nodded but didn't respond. She knew what Val meant.

"It's just I noticed you checking the time," said Wendy. "So I figured you were waiting on someone. He's gonna be in the doghouse, right?"

"Not that I'm a dog," Scarlet said. She managed a small smile. "Actually. I am waiting for someone. She's late."

"She?" Wendy tilted her head. "Are you a couple?"

"Not that she's nosy," whispered Val. Scarlet smiled now

in earnest.

"Her name is Clara. She's a good friend. Only."

"There's nothing 'only' about a good friend," said Val.

"I suppose you're right," Scarlet agreed. "I hope she gets here soon."

The Lamaze instructor moved to the front of the gymnasium. Her long floral dress gathered below her breasts, and leather sandals poked out beneath her skirt. She was sifting through a stack of papers, and her lips moved as she counted them. When she was done, she raised her head to greet the group.

"Good evening, everyone. I'm Calliope, and you are all welcome here. Before we begin, I have a handout for each couple. An overview of the course." Calliope navigated the rows of mats, handing each couple a stapled pamphlet. Scarlet was the only one without a partner. When she received her packet, she read the title. *Expect the Unexpected.*

Of course, thought Scarlet. *There's probably no mention in here about the miracle of epidurals.*

When Calliope finished handing out her packets, she remained at the back of the room. She was standing behind everyone when she began to speak again. "I know most of you have birth plans already," she said, "but you can't predict what will happen when you go into labor." Several of the couples craned their necks, attempting to see the instructor better. Other pairs scooted their bodies around to face Calliope. "You probably thought I would stand in front of the class," she continued. "But by now you have discovered you were wrong. And my friends, I'm here to tell you you'll be wrong about plenty on this journey we call parenthood."

A few couples chuckled, and one or two moaned, but Calliope was right. The group had behaved according to expectation, following the crowd. Upon their arrival, everyone had found a mat and taken a seat on the floor. They had, all of them, faced the same way. And while they waited, they'd watched each other. Imitating. Striving. Like sheep.

Pregnant sheep.

"My point here," Calliope explained, "is to demonstrate that there are no rules when it comes to birthing babies. No rules about birthing classes for that matter. Over the next few weeks I hope we'll have the opportunity to learn a lot from each other. But the first lesson you must accept is that your children will come in their own way on their own time."

"What if we're being induced?" asked a woman behind Scarlet. Scarlet couldn't see if she had raised her hand, but the edge to her voice suggested she liked to interrupt.

Calliope smiled. "No matter how much you try to orchestrate the process, there will be variables you can't foresee," she said. "Complications. Surprises, both good and bad. You are embarking on the most exciting experience in life. Once you surrender to the things you can't control, we can work on the few things you can."

While she spoke, Calliope made her way back toward a satchel hooked on a folding chair. The couples who'd turned around now had to maneuver themselves, crablike, back into their original positions. "All right then." Calliope slipped the extra birthing packets into her bag. "Let's begin by dispelling some myths about contractions."

Again Scarlet checked her watch.

Seven-nineteen. Clara's lateness was hardly a tragedy. In light of everything her friend had done for her, this was a small disappointment. But as Scarlet waited, she found herself composing a mental mantra in her head. The names of those she trusted who had let her down before.

Mama. Corie. Tuck. Sam.

Sam.

After all these years, she sometimes forgot he had ever been in her life. Like the father she never knew, Sam had been there one day, then he was gone. She understood why he wanted to leave Mama. Forgave him for it even. But it was harder to forgive his leaving her.

At least this baby would never endure a similar loss, never see a dark crater where a father figure used to be. She'd saved her boy from this. But would her name be a part of the mantra in her own child's head someday?

Would her son count his mother among the first to break his heart?

Several hands flew up around her now. What had Calliope

asked them? Scarlet glanced at the couple beside her, hoping for a clue. Then across the room came a commotion. Clara banging her way through the doors of the gymnasium. She took a dozen noisy steps in her high heels. Then she kicked off her shoes and hurried to Scarlet's side in her bare feet.

"Traffic," she sputtered under her breath. A strand of hair was stuck to her lipstick. She tugged at the bottom of her skirt, then gave up on modesty and collapsed on the mat.

"I forgive you," Scarlet whispered.

"Did I ask for forgiveness?" Clara maneuvered closer to Scarlet. "Please tell me you don't want to sit between my legs."

Scarlet smirked. "I don't want to sit between your legs."

Calliope approached their mat. "Glad you could join us," she said. "Now. Let's find out just how pregnant we are. Raise your hand if you are in your third trimester... and keep them raised as I call out how many weeks you've got to go. Eight... seven... six... five... four..."

Scarlet raised her hand, and so it went.

༆

For the next forty minutes they practiced breathing patterns. Scarlet would pant, then hiss air out through her clenched teeth. *One, two, three, blow.* Clara timed the intervals. Again. Then again. The repetition was a comfort to Scarlet, anticipation tempered by predictability. At one point Calliope stopped everyone to remind them this was an illusion. That the rhythm created a sense of control where none existed. Still, the sense of it was good enough for Scarlet.

Good enough for now.

After class they were exiting the gym when Clara complained that she was starving. "I rushed here straight from work," she said.

Scarlet frowned. "Lying doesn't suit you."

"Fine. I met Henry for drinks."

"That's better."

"No it's not. I'd eat a placenta right now if I could."

"I hope it doesn't come to that," Scarlet said. "Let's see what we can find."

Across a grassy quad, the school cafeteria boasted a row of vending machines. Clara bought a bottle of Evian and a bag of Fritos, and they made their way to a nearby lunch table. Behind them crickets chirped in the juniper bushes, and a chill seeped through Scarlet's cotton pants. Her waistband was already stretched to maximum capacity. Would she fit into her old suits when her maternity leave was up?

At the thought of returning to Olson Brickman, Scarlet felt a tightening in her chest. Excitement. Guilt. Sadness. She had not been back there since the accident. She missed the people. She missed her work. She missed Gavin. *God, how she missed Gavin.* Above all else, she found herself dreaming of *before.* Of the days she had not appreciated when she was in them.

Clara peered at Scarlet. "You look a little green," she said.

"It's the fluorescent lights."

"Are you sure?"

Scarlet set her elbows on the table and rested her head on her upturned palms. "I'm fine."

"Is it your head? Didn't Dr. Nguyen say headaches are a sign from your body that you—"

"I said I'm fine, Clare."

"I hope you are." She ran her tongue over her teeth. "Because there's something I need to tell you. And I know this is probably a terrible time, but not telling you has been absolutely killing me."

Scarlet shrugged. "So. Tell me."

"I don't want to upset you."

"That bad, huh?" She straightened, shoring herself up for what was to come. "It can't be the worst news I've heard this year."

Clara dropped her eyes. "You know I adore you, right? And that I have only your best interests at heart."

"I do."

"And you know I want to be there for you when this baby comes. No matter how noisy he is. Or how messy or wrinkled or—"

Scarlet stopped her. "You want me to move out, don't you?"

"Of course not!"

"Because I will. I have no idea where we'll go yet, but I figured this was coming, and I've been thinking—"

"That's not it." Clara shook her head.

"Then what *is* it?" Her voice caught. Whatever it was could not be good.

"Do you trust me?"

Scarlet sighed, a gust of impatience. "Yes, Clare. I trust you. Maybe not to show up to Lamaze on time but you've more than proven yourself in the matters that count. So, please. Quit stalling."

Clara reached for Scarlet's hand. "Don't be mad, but when I was in LA, I met up with Corie Slater. And we had a long talk."

Scarlet's eyes widened. "I—"

"Let me finish."

"But—"

"No buts. You've been so secretive with me. More than usual. And I couldn't help it."

"Clara!" said Scarlet. The second syllable pitched high, and her mouth hung open.

"In a way it's your fault really," said Clara. "You won't say who the father of your baby is, and you sure as hell haven't told me the whole truth about what happened between you and Corie." Clara focused on the slope of Scarlet's mouth. "That's right, Scar. I've guessed there's more to your story. I refuse to believe you stopped speaking to that poor girl just because she decided not to go to Berkeley with you."

Clara paused, and Scarlet groaned.

"Don't worry," Clara said. "We didn't talk about the past, but I did ask her if she had any idea who knocked you up. I'm sorry. I know I shouldn't have, Scar. And it's been eating away at me ever since. But we were drinking wine and—"

"Clare!" Scarlet gasped.

The color drained from Clara's face. "Don't yell at me in the middle of a confession," she said. "I'm trying to apologize."

Scarlet sucked in her cheeks, her face suddenly hollow.

"I think my water just broke."

࿇࿇

Three hours later she lay in a labor bed squeezing Clara's hand while Dr. Nguyen placed a monitor inside her. "You're about twenty percent effaced," the doctor said. "You're also at minus one station. A solid two."

"Two babies?" Clara squawked. A fresh contraction stole Scarlet's breath.

"Two centimeters dilated," the doctor clarified.

"Is that a good thing?" asked Clara.

"It's a two," said Dr. Nguyen. "She needs to reach ten centimeters before she can push, which for a first-timer can take a while." The doctor patted Scarlet's knee. "I'm going to get you going on some Pitocin."

"What's that?" asked Clara.

"A drug to stimulate contractions." The doctor's voice was calm. Steady. Still, Scarlet trembled. "We have to deliver this baby within the next twenty-four hours."

"But he's not due for at least three weeks," said Clara.

"Yes, however the risk of infection increases once the amniotic sac has ruptured."

"Oh Jesus, Scar," said Clara. "I'm so, so sorry."

Scarlet gritted her teeth, bracing herself for the next contraction. "You've said that already," she told Clara. "About a million times."

Clara wiped her nose with a crumpled tissue. Dr. Nguyen touched her elbow. "You did not cause Scarlet's water to break. She's been at risk for premature delivery ever since the accident. Try not to worry. The baby will be fine, just a little early. The important thing is that Scarlet is here where we can keep an eye on her progress." The doctor turned her attention back to Scarlet. "To be on the safe side, I'm going to have your amniotic fluid tested for meconium. You know what that is?"

Scarlet nodded

"Are you doing all right?"

Instead of answering the doctor, Scarlet gripped Clara's arm. "Please don't leave me."

"I won't."

"Promise."

"I just did," said Clara. "I won't leave you. Ever."

Dr. Nguyen typed notes into a computer. "A nurse will be in shortly to get a fluid sample, and I'll come back later with the results. In the meantime we can get you set up with an epidural if you'd like."

"An epidural," said Scarlet. "Yes!"

"I'll call for the anesthesiologist. Until then, try to relax. You've got hours of work ahead of you." Dr. Nguyen's pager beeped, and she checked the number. "I've got to go."

"Are you sure Scarlet's safe alone here with me?" asked Clara.

"She'll be fine, and I'll be back to check on you both soon." The doctor offered them another reassuring smile, then hurried out the door leaving Scarlet and Clara alone.

"I'm sorry, Clare," Scarlet said. A tear dribbled down her cheek.

"I'm the one who should—"

"I was unfair to you first," said Scarlet. "I should've trusted you with the truth a long time ago. And when this whole ordeal is over, I promise to tell you everything. About all of it. The baby. His father. What happened with Corie. You're right. It wasn't about what she did. It's about what I did. I—" Scarlet stopped, gritted her teeth. "Oh no," she moaned. "No, no, no!"

"Are you having another contraction?"

Scarlet panted, then hissed out air.

One, two, three, blow.

The pain of labor was unlike anything she'd experienced before, deep and hard and overwhelming. Each time a new contraction hit, its vise-like pressure took her by surprise. Then, after a minute, the pain would disappear, a thief leaving nothing in his wake.

Sweat beaded across her forehead, and she puffed, puffed, puffed while Clara counted. When the latest contraction passed, Clara checked the clock above the bed.

"They're coming about five minutes apart," she said. "God, Scar. That seems fast. Is this what that Calliope lady called 'transition'?"

"She's not there quite yet," said a young nurse appearing in the doorway. She wore scrubs the color of spearmint, and she spoke with a sibilant lisp. "That's why I'm here. My name's Fiona."

"Brilliant," said Clara. "Someone who knows what she's doing."

"I'm glad you think so," Fiona said. She flashed a gap-toothed grin, then got to work. First she took a sample of amniotic fluid, then she added Pitocin to Scarlet's IV. "This will make your labor more productive," she said.

Scarlet gaped at her. "More productive than it is already?"

"Productive is a good thing. If you want to deliver your baby."

Scarlet shivered then, and Fiona bent to tuck a blanket around her feet. A necklace with a tiny gold cross swung away from the nurse's throat. Scarlet considered the paradox of working in medicine while also embracing religion. On the surface the two practices appeared disparate, but perhaps that's what real faith required: letting go of what you know to embrace what you believe. She had spent her life collecting things she *knew*. Perhaps it was time to figure out what she *believed*.

The drum of her abdomen tightened as another contraction clutched at her. Scarlet moaned as the pain peaked again, a crescendo of pure agony.

"Fiona! Where's that anesthesiologist?" asked Clara. "She needs that epidural. Immediately."

"I don't want an epidural!" Scarlet blurted out. She turned and locked eyes with Clara.

"But Scarlet, you—"

"No!"

"Didn't you say—"

"Fuck what I said!"

Clara took a step back, and even Scarlet was shocked by her words. She'd come here fully expecting to be drugged, had thought each contraction might kill her. And yet in between them, her body felt normal, or as normal as one can feel while giving birth. Pain, then no pain. A sweet, swift release. Scarlet breathed in, then out again. The contraction abated, and she became suddenly—impossibly—mellow. She felt like the strongest person in the world, capable of withstanding anything for her baby.

"All right then," Clara said. "If that's what you want."

Scarlet closed her eyes. "I think it is." From this day forward, she would be called upon to make decisions for her child. She'd have to be the strong one and in control. She needed that strength to begin now. She wanted to soak up the lows and the highs of this day. Every single detail. Then, when her son was older, she would be able to tell him she had never felt more alive than during the hours of his birth.

A cool hand touched her forehead, and Scarlet opened her eyes. "I just want to try to do this thing drug free," she told Clara. "We did take that one Lamaze class. We're practically experts."

Clara's eyes welled. "Practically."

"And I can change my mind, can't I? In a little while? If it gets too bad?"

"It's your call," said Fiona. "We still have time. Let me get this sample of fluid to the lab, and I'll monitor your contractions from the nurse's station. The baby seems to be tolerating labor. If his heart rate drops, we'll reevaluate. For now just keep doing what you're doing."

When Fiona left the room, Clara took Scarlet's hand.

"You OK?" Clara asked her.

"*OK* is not what I'd call this." She licked her lips, the skin there swollen. Her tongue felt dry like cotton. Like socks. Gavin's socks. He always left them on the floor instead of in the hamper. He never remembered to put his clothes in the...

Stop thinking about Gavin! Dammit. He is gone.

Scarlet asked Clara for a cup of ice chips, anything to distract her. The monitor registered another contraction, the Pitocin doing its work. Within seconds, the pain was an assault. Sharp and suffocating. Scarlet writhed on the bed.

"Are you absolutely sure you don't want drugs?" Clara asked her.

"Maybe not absolutely," Scarlet gasped.

Within the hour, however, it was no longer her decision.

Dear Scarlet,

Congratulations. I hear six pounds is a good size for a preemie. The C-section sounded scary, though, the cord wrapped around his neck. Did you know Clara called to tell me, or is she good at keeping secrets too? We met last month to discuss you. And the baby. And his father. She thought I'd want to hear. She was right.

I'm trying to be thrilled for you, Scarlet. I am. Thrilled. But inside a tiny voice is crying, why?

Why you? Why not me? And why do I still care?

Maybe it's because I'm afraid my husband still cares too. I know he saw you in August at the cemetery. And I know he went to find you in San Francisco in December. But I have no idea what happened either time you were together. After he told me, I asked him to leave. And he did. I wanted so badly to promise Tuck that if he was honest with me about you—once and for all—I would forgive him. But I was afraid that the whole story would make forgiveness impossible. And then I would be a liar. A liar without a baby or a husband.

So I'm asking again, Scarlet: Why you? Why not me?

And why is forgiveness so damn hard for both of us?

On second thought, I do not want to know.

Corie

Corie

On the afternoon of my sister's wedding, we wait in the leafy garden of Ma's backyard under the archway Joey built for the ceremony. The wood still smells like fresh paint, the beams laced from top to bottom with hydrangea blossoms and daisies. Ma takes pictures as my nephew and niece stroll toward the officiant, Cam with his serious ring bearer face, Wella in pink organza. She tosses flower petals to no one. I smile as they approach. There will be no tears from me. Not today.

Pachelbel's *Canon* wafts from wireless speakers disguised as rocks, and my mother lifts a hand to wipe her eyes. Before I can step over the white runner and offer her a tissue, Bets materializes in front of the sliding glass door and begins her slow procession. I settle a hand on Wella's shoulder and hazard a glance at my husband standing across the aisle.

Tucker, in his gray suit, a white handkerchief poking from his breast pocket, is almost unbearably handsome. His black hair shines. So do his eyes. He is Joey Farinelli's best man. I marvel at his ability to pretend.

Growing up I heard all the clichés about marriage being hard, a give and take forged by sacrifice and compromise. *Not every day will be champagne and roses*, Ma would say. *You have to work at it, like a job*. At the time I believed her. But after years of being a wife, I am starting to believe marriage is not about work, compromise or even champagne. Staying married is a decision. I only wish I knew what to decide.

Under the archway the officiant drones, his head a humming beehive. His name is Mr. Peterson, and he is squat with jowls like a St. Bernard. His remaining hair is slicked into a comb-over, a section of which has broken loose to flap in the breeze.

"If any man has just cause why these two should not be wed," Mr. Peterson says, "speak now, or forever hold your peace."

I glance again at Tuck who is fidgeting in black wing tips. A man of scrubs and sneakers, he's worn these dress shoes only a handful of times. He lifts his chin, and we catch each other's eye. His lips part, just a breath. My stomach flutters with the desire to touch his mouth.

Last night Ma had everyone over for a casual rehearsal dinner. She said we needed to discuss a few last-minute details, but I suspected she wanted to see if Tuck and I could be in the same room together comfortably. As it turned out, we could. Not only comfortably—but without clothes.

I blush now, remembering how I ambushed my speechless husband. I still don't know what came over me, what I hoped to accomplish. I know only that I had to be with him, couldn't stand another minute without his body against mine. Across the aisle, Tuck looks at me now, and I wonder if he will ever hold me again.

When Mr. Peterson reaches the part of the ceremony where the couple will recite their vows, Bets tells him she and Joey have written their own. My future brother-in-law pulls a crumpled piece of paper from his jacket pocket, then reads his list of promises to my sister. With wet eyes, Joey claims he'll always be there for his wife. His voice breaks, and I think, *Please mean it, Joe. Please do better.* If he can do it, maybe we all can.

When it's my sister's turn, she recites her vows from memory. Bets holds Joey's gaze, and there's a sweetness in her tone that makes me believe.

"In our days together," she says, "we haven't had much of the *for richer*, and we've certainly had our share of *for worse*. But we're in health, not in sickness. And being back with you makes me incredibly happy. You are the love of my life. The father of my children. We've had our storms, but if we hadn't seen those dark days, I don't think we'd appreciate the light like we do now."

She clears her throat. "So Mr. Farinelli, I do take you to be my man. For now and always. Rain or shine. But let's try to keep things shiny, OK? The end."

After a few more formal words, Mr. Peterson pronounces them husband and wife, and Joey swoops in to kiss my sister. Wella slips out from under me to throw her arms around her mother's waist, and Cam takes his father's hand in his. As Ma lifts her camera to capture the first official picture of the Farinelli family, Tuck moves toward me, arranging his mouth into a smile.

I drop my eyes, recalling the taste of his tongue last night. The smell of his skin. Warm and salty, like sand beside the ocean. Throughout dinner I'd been watching him, studying his face for signs. Was he tired or sad? Did he miss me? Had he wanted to come home? When he got up from the table, I heard myself making my own excuse. Then, without considering the consequences, I followed him down the hall.

"What?" he asked, turning to me. I grabbed his hand and dragged him into Ma's den.

"Shhh," I told him. "I don't want to talk." Then I peeled off my top.

It had been so long, I had to bite my lip to keep from crying out. And when Tuck moaned, I laughed until tears streamed down my face. Afterward we did not speak. I simply returned to the table, and Tuck pretended to search for a bottle of wine in the kitchen. At the end of the evening, Bets and Joey gathered the kids and their toys while Tuck offered to walk me to my car. No one mentioned the fact that we'd shown up separately. Only Ma knew the truth.

"We need to talk," he said on her front porch.

I shook my head. "Not yet."

"Tomorrow?"

"We'll see," I told him. I drove off before finding out where he had been staying. Or if he was sorry. If I was too late. If I even cared. Now, in the wake of the Farinellis' fresh promises, I feel no closer to the answers.

"Aunt Corie!" squeals Wella. She breaks free from her family to yank my wrist. "My mommy's married! Just like you and Uncle Tucker!"

"It's a wonderful day," Ma says, stepping between us. She pecks me on the cheek, then turns to Bets. "I only wish Daddy could have been here to see you like this." The sigh from her is long. "If you two had gotten married the right way in the first place…"

"Let's not start that again," says Bets. "It's time to celebrate!"

She floats over to the officiant who is fussing with his briefcase, and she hands him an envelope, which I assume contains his fee. "Can you join us at the Hyatt, Mr. Peterson? We'd love to buy you a round to say thanks for marrying us on such short notice."

He licks his thumb and pastes a flyaway strand back to his scalp. "Thanks, but I'm already late. I have a big civil war reenactment to get to."

"Civil war reenactment?" Tucker raises an eyebrow. While Mr. Peterson begins to explain, I pull Bets away.

"The Hyatt?" I ask.

"Yep," she says. "Their bar is attached to the lobby so we're allowed to bring the kids. I know it's a sad excuse for a wedding reception, but as you know, our budget's tight."

"The CHS prom is at the Hyatt tonight," I tell her. "In one of the ballrooms."

"So?" Bets snorts. "I assume your students won't be drinking in the bar."

"It's just—this dress." I tug up the low neckline. The fabric there is loose. "I guess I should have had it altered."

"Zip it, Corie. You look beautiful. Now get that husband of yours to stop talking about the Civil War, and let's go party, girl!"

వ౿ళ

It's just before five o'clock when our small caravan pulls up to the hotel. Tucker, Ma and I have taken my car, and my sister's family is behind us in a limousine. Inside, the lobby is spacious and bright with vaulted ceilings made of glass. Down one hall are several ballrooms. In the middle of the room, a marble table boasts a massive floral arrangement. Across the lobby a man with a beaked nose bends over a grand piano.

My eyes slide sideways to Ma who is standing between her two grandchildren. Cam's jaw wags as he talks to her, and his angular face, freed from the last vestiges of baby fat, looks more like his father's each day. Wella grips my mother's hand and swings her arm to her own imagined rhythm. As they approach the piano, Ma digs into the satin bag that matches her mint green dress. She pulls out a twenty dollar bill and drops it into a glass bowl. The pianist pauses in mid sway to nod at her, then presses his lips together again.

Ma reaches for Wella's hand. "How would you like to take piano lessons at my house?" she asks.

"Drums!" Wella replies. "I want to play the drums."

Together we make our way past a restaurant to the hotel's open-air bar, which is separated from the rest of the lobby by a row of tall, potted trees. Each branch boasts strands of delicate white lights, and although it is only May, I think of Christmas.

"Over here!" Bets waves at us from a pair of high tables in the corner of the bar. "If we scoot these two together, we'll all fit." Tuck moves the tables and gathers enough stools for our party of seven. Everyone takes a seat except for Joey, who is ordering champagne.

A solemn bartender in a crisp white shirt carries over a tray of flutes. From his apron he produces a can of ginger ale which he pours in two glasses for the kids. A female bartender with close-cropped hair opens a dripping bottle of Veuve Clicquot. We applaud the wet pop of the cork, and the champagne fizzes as she fills our flutes.

My mother lifts hers to begin a toast, but Joey stops her.

"If you don't mind, Laura, I'd like to go first."

"Of course, Joseph," my mother says. "By all means. Please."

He straightens his shoulders and puffs out his chest like a peacock showing off its feathers. If a man could strut while standing still, Joey Farinelli would. He surveys the group, pausing to nod at each one of us. When he turns to Bets, his smile is warm. My sister has never looked more beautiful.

"Mrs. Farinelli," he says to her, "you just made me the luckiest guy on earth."

"Back atcha, baby," she says. "Except for the *guy* part." We laugh, and Joey turns to address the rest of us.

"Seriously, though. I want to thank all of you here. Without your help, I don't think Bets and I would be here today. And for a while there, I didn't deserve her. Like I said, I'm a lucky man. Either that or I'm just stubborn." We laugh again and shift on our stools. "But somehow, I convinced Miss Bethany here to give me another chance."

"It's your last one," she says. More laughter. More shifting.

"We found our way back to each other," Joey continues, "back to our family." He puts a hand on Cam's shoulder. "If I've learned anything this past year, it's that it's never too late to wise up and realize what a good thing really looks like. So, kids? Take a lesson from me. When you know you made a mistake, own it. Then make it right again." Joey raises his glass, and we prepare to join him in the toast, but Wella interrupts.

"Daddy?"

"Yeah, sweetie?"

"I'm glad we're together."

"I am too," he says.

&⸱&

Split between five people, the first bottle goes down quickly. When Tuck offers to order the next one, I watch him cross the bar. Black hair, broad back. That slow, easy gait. Each piece of him as familiar to me as the lines across my palm. I knew only a sliver of Tuck Slater when I first fell in love with him. The good stuff people show others. The surface, not the depths. Over the years our layers chipped away, revealing cracks and flaws and hurt. After a decade of imperfection, does Tuck still want me?

Did he ever?

"Corie." Bets taps my shoulder. "Look. Your friends are here." Across the lobby Bart and Stella emerge from a pair of ballroom doors. As I wave at them, Stella spots me and grabs Bart's elbow, leading him to our table. She is radiant in a cherry-red dress that matches the boutonniere in the lapel of Bart's jacket. As they approach the wedding party, they both break into grins.

"You look fancy, ma'am," Bart tells me.

"So do you, sir," I say.

Stella pokes Bart in the arm. "This guy talked me into chaperoning prom again, but I swear this is the last time."

"Never say never," I tell her.

"No, seriously." Stella moves her hands down the front of her snug red gown. "I hate this dress, and I can barely breathe in these Spanx."

Bart leans toward me and whispers, "Thank goodness she's still got enough air in her to complain." He winks, then turns to my sister, who is perched on Joey's lap. "Congratulations to you both."

"Thanks, darlin'." Bets holds out her left hand, which now sports a tiny diamond. "You should try getting hitched someday. It's not so bad."

"I would," Bart tells her, "but all the good ones are already taken."

"Hey!" Stella protests. "I'm not married."

Bart grins at her. "I rest my case."

He excuses himself to order a couple of sodas from the bar, and Stella heads over to say hello to Cam and Wella. I watch as the three of them move to a booth in the corner where Stella shows the kids how to drip water on scrunched up straw wrappers. With serious faces they observe the crumbled paper unfold like caterpillars, inch by inch across the wooden tabletop.

"Stella is good with children," Ma says.

"I had no idea."

"People can be full of surprises."

I nod at her. *Yes, they can.*

Before long, dance music begins to throb from the

ballroom across the lobby. "Hey, Stell!" Bets calls out. "Can
you sneak us into prom?"

Stella looks up from the booth and points at Bart, who's
still talking to the bartender. "You're in luck," she tells my
sister. "He's the bouncer."

Bets hops off Joey's lap and takes her husband by the arm.
"Come on, baby. Dance with me!" When he objects, she pulls
him harder. "I went to this school. It'll be fine. Stella says so."
She extends her free hand to me. "You coming with us,
Corie?"

I shake my head.

"Ma?"

My mother laughs. "I think I'll hold down the fort here.
But the rest of you should go."

Bets skips over to me and plants a wet kiss on my cheek.
"Try to have fun," she whispers, then she and Joey and Stella
cross the bar to collect Bart. The four of them traipse together
through the lobby to the Conejo High School prom. A young
bar-back wipes our tables, and Ma joins Cam and Stella in
their booth. I scan the room for Tucker.

My husband is nowhere to be found.

ဓ∾ઌ

A half-hour later when the prom crashers return, Henry
Callaghan trails behind them overdressed in a shiny black
tuxedo. I slide off my stool and head over to greet him,
tugging up my neckline as I go.

"This is a surprise," Henry tells me. He takes my hand and
shakes it. This is the first time he's touched me, and I blush.

Where is Tuck?

"Nice tux," I say, releasing his hand.

"It's not a rental."

"Good to know." I laugh, then drop my eyes although I
have done nothing wrong. So what if Henry Callaghan has a
crush on me? He's harmless enough, and I don't return his
feelings. I let his attention buoy me, that's all.

"Corinna," he says, and I raise my head. "I've been
meaning to ask you something."

"Oh." In my throat, a stone of guilt. I don't want Henry to say something out loud he might regret.

"Have you ever thought about joining Academic Council?" he asks. "We're meeting this week to finalize next year's calendar. I would love to have you on board."

This is what he wants to bring up? Academic Council?

"We sure could use you." He rakes a hand through his licorice-stick hair. "More specifically, *I* could use you. The ones who usually volunteer for these things are crazy."

"Except for me, right?" Stella appears from behind Henry and drapes an arm over him. "I'm not eavesdropping," she says. "OK, yes I am. It's just that I am one of the crazies on Academic Council."

The skin above Henry's collar reddens. "I wasn't talking about you."

"It's all right," she tells him. "I *am* crazy. And I'm also ready to give up my position. I would absolutely love to leave you in Ms. Harper's capable hands." She pulls Henry close. "And speaking of Corie, she looks a little thirsty. You should get her a cocktail."

Henry's eyes dart to me, but I say nothing. "I'll be right back then," he says. I wait until he is out of earshot to turn to Stella.

"Was that a good idea?"

Her eyes widen with feigned innocence. "What?"

"All that innuendo. Talking about *positions* and *my capable hands*? You just sent the man off to get me a drink in the middle of my sister's wedding reception."

"So?"

"Tucker is here!"

"Is he?" Stella's eyes roam the bar. "I don't see him."

"Still."

"Listen, Corie. Bets told me Tuck hasn't been home for weeks. How come you never said anything?"

"Bets was not supposed to know that," I say. "And my mother has a big mouth."

Stella leans in close. "You know Henry Callaghan has a thing for you," she says. "Might as well take advantage of it. Let Tucker see this little *thing* in action." She elbows me.

"Nothing wrong with fanning the flames of jealousy."

"Yes," I say. "There is."

"Maybe what you and Tuck need is a little fire."

"No. We don't."

"Fine," she says, pouting. "I give up."

"Good."

"I'm gonna find Bart and head back into prom. Wanna come?"

"No thanks."

"You're right." Stella's voice is suddenly very loud. "You should stay here and juggle your many, many admirers."

She pats me on the shoulder and leaves in the direction of the ballroom. I look down at my wrist, forgetting that I didn't wear a watch today.

Hearing footsteps behind me, I turn, and there is Tuck holding a goblet of white wine.

"You've been gone a while," I say.

"I was in the parking lot on the phone with Dr. Khan. The reception in here is terrible." He glances around. "We're finally alone."

"Yes we are."

"You ready to talk?"

I shake my head. "I don't know."

"Here." He hands me the wine. "I intercepted this from that fine young assistant principal of yours. I hope he wasn't planning to get my wife drunk tonight."

"Don't worry," I say. "I can handle Henry Callaghan."

Tuck smiles. "You're not the one I was worried about."

"Right." My stomach is a hard ball of knots. "Of course I wasn't."

"Hey." His face falls. "I was joking."

I set my glass down on a nearby table. "I'm not."

"OK," he says. "I guess we're talking now."

I lift my head and look him in the eye. "It's just that you never seem to be worried about me any more." I pause to let the seriousness of my words sink in. "It's been weeks, Tuck. Not days. Weeks."

A vein pulses at the edge of his forehead. "You're the one who told me to leave, remember? On the baseball field?" His voice is low, and my face is hot.

"I thought you would beg to stay with me. That you'd fight for us. I wanted you to tell me I was wrong. That Scarlet never meant anything to you. But you couldn't get away from me fast enough. And then you stayed gone. Until last night."

His shoulders slump. "Core. I'm trying."

"If this is you trying, then—"

"Stop." Tuck takes my hand, leads me behind the row of artificial trees at the edge of the bar. The branches of the trees are looped with strands of small white lights. From a distance, the effect is lovely. Up close the trees look fake.

I hear Cam call out, "Where are Uncle Tuck and Aunt Corie going?"

Tuck looks down at me. "Huh. That's a pretty good question."

"What is?"

"Where are we going?" He shakes his head. "Damn, that was corny."

I turn away from him, blinking back tears. "I'm so mad, Tuck," I say. "Not just at you. I'm mad at everyone. Everything."

"I know. And I'm sorry."

"I don't think *sorry* is enough."

"I know that too."

My head drops, and I focus on the floor because I can't look at him. "You want me to forgive you anyway," I say.

"Yes." He places a finger under my chin to lift it. "I do." Our eyes lock. "But forget about me. What do *you* want, Core? Right now."

I'm silent. Considering the question. *What do I want?*

Tuck lowers his face and comes closer to me. He waits, but I do not stop him. He moves closer still, and when his lips graze mine, they are warm.

"What do you want?" he whispers.

"You." He tastes like champagne. He tastes like my husband. I say again, "Always you."

"I want you too, Core. I want to come home." His kiss is soft, and it steals my breath. "Please let me come home."

He slides his mouth down the base of my neck, almost

numbing my resolve. But only almost. Because something inside me stirs, and I remember what I had planned to ask him tonight. The favor that was to be my condition for his return.

I put a hand on his chest. "First you have to promise to do something for me."

"Anything," he says. "As long as I can be with you."

So I stare into the deep well of his eyes and tell him, "Yes."

Scarlet:

Thank you for letting me know about the CCC student who will be receiving the first annual scholarship offered by Olson, Brickman & Steinway. While I do not know Ian Rogers personally, he sounds from your description like a very deserving young man. I am happy to have played even a small role in supporting his future academic success.

I'm sorry I was not of greater assistance in the scholarship process, but it's clear to me now why you were reluctant to continue working together. I apologize if I gave you the wrong impression about my intentions, and I hope you believe that my offer to help you was (and is) sincere. Then and now, it comes with no strings attached.

When we saw each other last summer, I had the feeling you were unclear about your own future and allowed myself to imagine I could have a favorable impact on any new path you might choose. Of course I had no idea you were in a serious relationship at the time. Had I known, I certainly would have handled myself differently.

Please do not take this as criticism on my part. I know firsthand the need to have a Plan B when you're unsure about Plan A—even if you suspect Plan B is not a viable option. I also understand the difference between a person who is merely questioning her path and a person who is genuinely unhappy.

If you are, as you say, the former? I wish you well in whatever direction your life might take. If, however, you ever find yourself in need of a change? Well. Be in touch.

In the meantime, congratulations on the birth of your son, and I wish you the best of luck in this new role of motherhood. You deserve every happiness life can afford.

Yours respectfully,
Richard Roosevelt

Summer

Scarlet

Each June as the days grew longer, her shoulders became unbearably heavy. In the morning before getting out of bed, she already began to hunch, as if folding in on herself might erase who she was, who she had been. By nightfall, her muscles ached, and she felt hollowed to the core. The pain was a burden she carried even while she slept. She took the ghost of it into her dreams and awakened with the specter beside her in bed.

She never sought reprieve. Healing wasn't something she deserved. In the ten years of their friendship, Clara had learned nothing about the 19th of June. And although Scarlet had grown to trust Dr. Kagawa, she refused to discuss the date with her. Why entertain the possibility of someone suggesting she hadn't been at fault? Scarlet knew what she had done. She wasn't going to start forgiving herself now. Especially if letting herself off the hook meant letting her guard down with her son.

Distracted by the never-ending duties of motherhood, the nursing and changing and bathing, she would sometimes forget to be afraid. Then she would find herself rocking him in the silence, and she would remember.

God, she remembered.

Gathering the tiny boy in her arms, Scarlet would nestle him to her until just one corner of his rosebud mouth peeked out against her breast. Then she'd stare at the curl of his ear, so impossibly small and perfect.

Please, she'd bargain. *Please. Let me keep this one good thing.*

Since she'd first locked eyes with her baby, Scarlet had needed nothing but him. Stunned, empty and shocked, she'd lain there blinking in the too-bright lights. The air of the operating room was still coppery when a masked nurse held up a beautiful, mewling infant for her to see. Her child. Her son. "Your name is Gage," she whispered to him. "Gage Hinden. Welcome home."

That was four weeks ago, and from the looks she'd received since checking in at the airport, most people disapproved of her flying with a newborn. As other passengers boarded the plane, only a couple of them smiled. Most looked down with expressions that smacked of surprise, or worse, dismay.

First class with an infant? Who do you think you are? Their pursed lips alone were an accusation. She felt judged, but she didn't care. Since Gage's birth, Scarlet had felt a surge of strength unfamiliar to her. *You can do anything,* the voice coaxed her. *There is nothing—no challenge, no chore—you cannot accomplish on behalf of your son.*

She had let herself on one occasion only wonder about her own mother, whether Mama had felt mighty—invincible even—when holding her for the first time. Had Eleanor let herself slow down and marvel at what she'd created?

Scarlet suspected not.

In all her memories, Mama never could sit still. A cigarette in one hand, drumming fingers on the other. She cracked knuckles, collected ashes in a tray. Eleanor's constant restlessness made her appear unsettled by parenthood, not moved by it. Scarlet believed now that the tautness of her mother's skin had not been youth; it was fear pulling in on her. A daughter's need that sucked her dry. Being a mother had not flooded Mama with joy.

It had destroyed her.

So before Gage's birth, Scarlet steeled herself to feel indifference at best. Afterward, during the stitches and tests, the waning anesthesia, she felt only numb. She'd had to wait two hours in a postpartum room to finally hold her son. But those loose, slippery limbs ushered in a sense of purpose so sharp she felt rent apart, then sewn back together.

Scarlet knew him in that instant, believed he had always been inside her, deeper than her bones. Gage made her whole. *He must have been there when she herself had been an egg. Only half a potential life inside her own mother, who'd been inside another mother and before that another.* Scarlet's foggy mind followed the maternal thread backward until she felt connected to the first woman who had ever borne any child. Perhaps it was the drugs.

Or perhaps it was the love.

But in the month that followed, no amount of stiff-legged squalling could dull the intense bond with her baby. Each night as he wiggled in her hands, the shampoo a film of bubbles on his forehead, she found new patience pouring from her. Again and again. When she wiped his body, cheesy and ripe upon the changing table, she smiled. He was a miracle.

Too good to be true.

She began to scour the Internet, reading up on postpartum depression. She learned of mothers who dreamed of smothering their infants, of throwing their babies from the window. If these good women could imagine bashing in their babies' skulls, surely she would be overcome, or tempted to shake her son until he went limp in her arms, his body cold as a fish.

Weeks went by, and Scarlet waited, haunted by demons from her past. Would she open the screen or let the weight of her desperation break right through the glass? Each morning she awakened grateful that the darkness had yet to descend upon them. Instead, Gage became her light. The kernel of her future. Irrational. Inseparable.

He squirmed now in her arms, and Scarlet hummed softly to soothe him. When he began to fuss in earnest, she unbuttoned her blouse and fastened him to her. His blanket loosened, and a fist poked out as he grunted, rooted, latched. Then he was quiet. Warm and peaceful. Scarlet sighed. *If only she could find some peace.*

A few minutes prior to takeoff, a businessman in a pinstriped suit rushed onboard and hurried down the aisle. She felt his gaze on her when he paused to shove his bag into the overhead compartment. He slid into the row behind her, and the engines grumbled to life. Scarlet closed her eyes, and before they reached cruising altitude, she had slipped into a half-sleep.

Their flight was quick, and when a bump of turbulence startled her, she clutched at the bundle resting in her lap. Gage lay in her dream-slack arms, a blue vein pulsing in his eyelids. His temple had grown damp at the hairline. A trickle of milk dried at the corner of his lips. She drew him close as the airplane shuddered. Landing gear already.

Scarlet hated to fly, but this trip felt different. Gage was keeping her safe. There had been too much loss in her life, and fate could not be that cruel. The universe, hellbent on punishing her, wouldn't steal this last bit of life. *The world is a dark place*, she thought, *but it's not completely black.*

The seatbelt light turned off, and passengers prepared to disembark. The stranger in the pinstriped suit rose and stretched in the aisle beside her. Scarlet wondered if he was hoping to catch a glimpse of exposed breast. He opened the bin overhead, and she shifted in her seat.

"Do you need help with your bag?" he asked.

She looked up. His smile was kind.

"Your bag," he repeated. "I'd be happy to get it for you."

"It's the red duffle," she said, blushing at her own suspicions. The man shimmied her bag from the compartment, and she thanked him as he laid it at her feet.

"He's a good boy, huh?"

"He is," she said.

"You're lucky."

Scarlet nodded.

A flight attendant manned the exit as the passengers began to deplane. A minute later the captain emerged from the cockpit and stood beside the flight attendant to shake each person's hand.

"Thanks for choosing United," he said as Scarlet and Gage approached.

"You're welcome," she said. "But I didn't."

This was the airline Tuck Slater had booked.

His text said he'd be at the curb in front of the terminal, and she spotted him thirty yards up from baggage claim at the edge of a no-parking zone. He wore an old T-shirt and well-worn jeans. A pair of sunglasses rested above his forehead. He was leaning against a Ford Windstar with a crooked side view mirror and a dent in the front fender. Scarlet could hardly believe it. The man she'd once fantasized about was driving a minivan.

As she neared the van, Tuck straightened, hurrying around the side to get the door. He stood by as it slid open, an enormous mouth, yawning in slow motion. The inside of the van smelled like French fries. On the floor sat a black trash bag stuffed with empty water bottles and Coke cans. A few ketchup-stained napkins stuck out from the top.

Tuck had tried to clean up for her quickly.

He took her bag from her, and she peered farther into the van. In the center row was a small booster seat. Scarlet hefted the infant carrier on her hip. "The baby is four weeks old," she said. "You know he can't sit in something like that yet, right?"

Tuck bobbed his head, and the sunglasses dipped. "Yeah. That seat belongs to my niece, Wella. I borrowed Bets' van. I figured the truck wouldn't be a good fit for us." When Scarlet did not reply, he said, "I'll get this out of the way."

He hoisted the booster out and went around to deposit it into the back of the van while Scarlet secured the carrier into its proper rear-facing position. By the time she climbed into the captain's chair next to Gage, Tucker was in the driver's seat, hand on the ignition.

"In a hurry?" she asked.

"You tell me," he said. "It'll be after five o'clock before we get back to town. Depending on traffic."

"That's plenty of time," she told him. Scarlet had checked the website already. Visitors were welcome until six. Besides. She could use the hour to prepare herself for the first of their two stops.

Green lawns and leafy trees surrounded the sprawl of buildings. The central structure looked freshly painted, and neat hedges lined the walkway. Just inside the main entrance was an oversized easel with a white board. On it big block letters proclaimed ITALIAN NITE.

Scarlet's stomach growled. When was the last time she had eaten?

Gage cradled in her arms, she passed a bubbling fountain and made her way toward the welcome station on the other side of the lobby. There, a man with ink-black skin was squeezed into a desk chair. He wore a white lab coat and a look of concentration. His fingers flew across the computer keyboard, and when he glanced up, his smile was warm.

"Can I help you?" he asked. His voice was gentle, and the tightness in her chest began to give.

"I'm looking for Eleanor Hinden."

"Ah, Ellie. Didn't know she was expecting visitors today."

"She isn't. I mean, she doesn't know I'm here." Scarlet lifted Gage an inch. "We are here."

"Well." His teeth flashed brightly. "I'll take you to her now, then." He unfolded himself from the small chair. She guessed he was at least six foot five. "My name is Malcolm, by the way."

"I'm Scarlet, Eleanor's daughter."

Malcom addressed the baby in her arms. "And who is this?"

"This is Gage."

"Hey there, little man. Eleanor will be delighted to see you."

The word *delighted* echoed in Scarlet's head as they traveled down a long hallway. Tile floors gave way to carpet that looked well-worn but freshly vacuumed. Turning a corner, Malcolm stepped aside as a wispy-haired man shuffled their way. Plastic tubing ran from his nose to an oxygen tank trailing behind him. His skin was pale, but his eyes were clear. Scarlet guessed that, like her mother, the man was younger than he appeared.

"Where ya headed, Raymond?" Malcolm asked.

The man pumped a fist into the air. "Italian Nite!"

"Yes, sir!" Malcom grinned. "I'll be there soon."

"Wow," said Scarlet. "The food here must be good."

"Indeed, it is," Malcolm told her. "Come on, now. We're almost there."

Scarlet followed Malcolm down one more hall until he stopped at the last door on the right. "This is it," he said. "One-thirty-one. Your mother's Home Sweet Home." He pretended to high five Gage. "Nice to meet you, little man."

"You're not staying?"

Malcom shook his head. "Haven't you heard? It's Italian Nite!"

"I thought…"

"Hey, Miss Scarlet." He touched her shoulder. "I'm sure you'll do just fine." While Malcolm retreated down the hallway, she whispered, "Fine is relative." Then she held her breath and counted to thirty before knocking on her mother's door.

৩৯৵

She was sitting in an overstuffed chair, gazing out the window through a gap in her drapes. Beside her sat a tank identical to the one the man had been wheeling down the hall. The room was dimly lit and smelled of Pine-Sol. On a side table sat a vase of wilting daisies. Scarlet wondered who had brought the flowers and when. "Hi, Mama," she said.

Eleanor did not turn.

Scarlet took a small step forward. "Sorry I couldn't come sooner."

"Didn't expect you to," her mother said.

"No. I suppose you didn't."

Eleanor coughed, then turned to face her daughter.

"Are you gonna stand there all night?" she asked.

Scarlet's eyes swept the room for a place to sit. There was no coffee table or sofa, only a tiny bathroom and an unmade bed. Her mother's chair. Scarlet lowered herself onto a corner of the bed. Gage was still sleeping in her arms.

"You look good, Mama."

"I look like shit, but thanks."

"I would've called, but—" She stopped without finishing her sentence. She had no good reason for not picking up the phone. She simply had not wanted to tarnish the shine of this new happiness she'd found.

Eleanor dabbed at her lips with a tissue. "You get my letter?"

"I did, Mama. Thanks."

"I already knew that. Don't know why I asked. Your friend told me."

"Clara?"

Eleanor nodded. "She's pretty nice."

"Yes," Scarlet said. "She is."

"And Laura Harper visits every now and again. She told me you had the baby." As if on cue, Gage whimpered, and Scarlet pulled back the blanket so her mother could see her grandson.

"Here he is." She felt foolish as she said it.

Eleanor sniffed. "He doesn't look much like you."

"He looks like his father." In the murky light, Scarlet tried to make out her mother's gray face.

"Is he going to marry you?" Eleanor asked.

"No." She swallowed hard. "It's just the two of us. But we'll be just fine, Gage and I." At the mention of the baby's name, Eleanor covered her mouth with a trembling hand.

"That's why I'm here," Scarlet said. "I wanted you two to meet. Mama, this is Gage Hinden. Gage, this is your grandmother." For a long moment, the two women sat in silence while the baby cooed between them.

"Is he hungry?" asked Eleanor.

"Yes."

"I am too," her mother said.

Scarlet attempted a smile. "Italian night."

"It starts soon. Don't want to be late."

"Oh." Scarlet shrugged. A lump gathered in her throat. "I should leave you to it then." She stood, moved toward the door. She had hoped there would be more. Why didn't Mama say more?

"Wait," her mother said.

Yes, of course. I'll wait.

Eleanor sucked air through the tube in her nose then exhaled audibly through her mouth. Gage twisted in Scarlet's arms as she regarded her mother in silence. She was afraid of what Mama might say, afraid one of the three of them might start to cry.

"Before you go," Eleanor said, "I've been thinking. We should sell the house."

"What?"

"The house," Mama repeated. "I want you to sell it."

Scarlet couldn't speak.

"Should've gotten rid of it years ago. The place hasn't done either of us a damn bit of good for a while. Don't know why I was so stubborn. I've been stubborn." She paused for a breath that seemed to originate from deep inside her. When she continued, her voice was a shallow rasp. "The thing is, you have to do it for me."

"Sell the house?"

"I'm in no condition to handle something like that." Eleanor looked down at her lap. "I hate to ask."

"No," said Scarlet. "I'll do it. Of course I will."

"Laura Harper can help."

Scarlet's chin quivered. "I'd better go now. But I'll be in touch. Promise."

"That's just fine."

I'm sure you'll do fine, Miss Scarlet.

"So, goodbye, Mama." She groped for better words, but nothing came.

Eleanor faced the window. "Take care of that baby, now."

Scarlet turned and fled the room.

Halfway down the hall, her whole body began to shake, and by the time she made it back to the van, hot tears streamed down her face. Tucker took one look at her and gathered Gage into his arms. Then he strapped the baby safely in his carrier again.

❧

At their second destination Tuck rolled past the front parking lot and took a left down a road that wound through the center of the property. Expanses of grass on either side were dotted with angels, stones, crosses. Spaces marked by flags or urns. Arrangements of fresh flowers. A few solemn buildings sat atop the highest hillside as if those entombed inside might enjoy their eternity with a view.

The van came to a stop at the base of a small green rise. Scarlet couldn't see over the crest, but she knew what waited there. Jaw set, she gritted her teeth. Tucker cut the engine and turned around.

"You ready?" he asked.

"No," she said.

"Want me to come with you?"

Her stomach clenched as she thought back to a time when she would have given anything to have Tuck Slater walking beside her, taking her hand in his. But no longer.

"I need to do this by myself," she said.

"I'll stay with the baby."

Scarlet peered down at her son sleeping in the infant carrier. The baby's lips puckered as if the boy were nursing in his dreams. "His name is Gage," she told Tuck. Then she lifted her face to his.

"He's beautiful," Tuck told her.

"Yes," she said. "He is."

Climbing out of the van, she adjusted her skirt, smoothed the static from her hair. Tuck rolled down the window and offered her a box of Kleenex. "Want to take these?"

Her mouth went slack, and a breeze worked the edges of her tongue. "No," she said. "I'm all right." She pressed her fingers against her lids. She was afraid she might begin to sob again, that once she started, she'd be unable to stop.

"I'll take care of him," Tuck said.

Scarlet looked at him and nodded.

There was still important work here to be done.

Corie

I changed my clothes a dozen times before I realized there's no such thing as a perfect outfit for this type of reunion. No article on the cover of *InStyle* magazine suggesting what kind of ensemble one should piece together to meet an estranged friend you thought you might never see again. A friend who hasn't stood under the same stars with you in a decade.

Ten years ago.

Scarlet had been in love with Tucker then, although neither he nor I knew for sure. She told him on the evening of our graduation after we told her about us. At the time we had already survived our two-hour-long ceremony full of pomp and circumstance and tears. But as we hugged each other in the stadium, none of us suspected we'd barely survive what would come next.

I wore my cap and gown to dinner just like Bets did when she had graduated. We scarfed expensive filets with side salads a la carte. Dad encouraged everyone to try the bread pudding. We humored him of course. And then he made a speech during which Ma cried. After dessert I went home to change, and Tuck picked me up so we could head to Scarlet's.

Our plan was to hang out, the three of us, until Tuck and I headed back for Grad Night. Scarlet wasn't going, although Tuck and I had tried to talk her into it.

"It's our last chance to be stupid high schoolers," I said.

"We'll still be stupid at Berkeley."

If I close my eyes, I can still hear the sound of my laughter, a little too loud, a little too long. There had been no good time to break the news to her: that I'd accepted admission to UCSD instead of Cal.

She had to have known or at least suspected that Tuck and I were a couple. But she'd been careful not to let on, not to express any discontent. When he came near me, she would shrug her shoulders, keep the sarcasm to a minimum. I was pretty sure she was biding time until she and I left for school. I think Scarlet believed once Tuck and I were separated, we'd get over the thrill of each other.

In my memory always, our night begins at eight o'clock, and I am forever sitting on the bench of Tucker's truck. The engine hums as we drive across town, the air smells like leather and cologne. I have a secret. We both do. Not just the bottle of Jack Daniels that we bought with Tuck's fake ID.

I'm not sure whiskey will make this better, I say.

He says, *Whiskey makes everything better.*

On the radio a new remix of *Forever Young* plays, and Tuck's leg bounces with the beat of the music. His right hand rests on my knee, and his left grips the steering wheel. Our fingers are white at the knuckles.

We turn onto Scarlet's street, and my stomach sinks.

I want her to be furious with Tucker. Not with me.

The part of my heart that has never been generous considers pulling her aside, talking to her without Tuck around. I could let her think it was he who pursued me. Tell her he pressured me to go to school with him instead of her. Of course, these tactics are selfish, but I'm cowardly, afraid of losing my best friend. Who would I be without Scarlet Hinden?

Before I can answer the question, Tuck pulls up and parks under a sycamore tree three houses down from Scarlet's. Her street is crowded with cars, lining the curb, being restored in side yards. We ring the doorbell and hide the whiskey under my sweatshirt in case Scarlet's mom hasn't left for work.

Our evening proceeds at first like any teenage movie script. Scarlet sucks down one stiff drink after another, and on

Eleanor's turntable, spin albums, a collection of vinyl that belonged to Sam. The three of us take turns entertaining each other, telling jokes, attempting bad impressions. We stop to dance when a song moves us.

And we are often moved.

At some point Scarlet disappears into her mother's bedroom, returning with a joint pinched from her nightstand. By ten o'clock my guard is down. Tuck and I are unprepared for what comes next.

"So have you two finally screwed each other yet?" Scarlet is seated on the floor, leaning back against the couch. Her face is pale in the candlelight. "Time is running out. You might as well get it over with."

Tuck and I glance at each other, a look passing between us.

"Wait," she says. "I was kidding." Her cup tips over. "What the fuck?"

"Scarlet," I say. "Scar."

"You're together?"

Tucker stands. "It's not what you think."

Her eyes cut to me. "You lied to me. Fucking liar."

I flinch, wanting to tell her—once again—how much I adore her. I want her to know that nothing would ever change that. Not even Tuck. Certainly not Tuck.

What did he mean by *It's not what you think?*

While I consider the implication, Tuck seizes the opportunity, and in a slur of booze and weed, he tells her everything about us. I sit by silently watching her face rearrange itself into a mask of horror. *We did this to her,* I think. *What had we expected?*

The next hour remains a blur punctuated by sharp flashes of clarity. They tear at me still, these details, snagging at edges that cannot heal. Each one calls me back to what might have been had we handled things differently. If the three of us had been different people.

If we hadn't cared so much.

I see Scarlet, blinded by tears, stumbling into the hole of her backyard. Tuck follows with a glance over his shoulder. *It's OK,* he mouths to me.

My tongue is hot and desert dry. It tastes of ashes. Bitterness. Ribbons of smoke curl above a candle meant to hide the scent of our night.

On repeat is the lope of Bob Marley's *Three Little Birds*, and I'm awash with relief. Tuck Slater's little darling. My skin feels too tight. I am bigger than this.

Then comes the bell. It won't stop ringing. In my mind, it never stops.

The doorknob is cold and hard against my palm. I cup it gently, an egg in its nest. A fragile thing. I am scared to open the door, but someone is pounding.

Bam, bam, bam.

A fist against cheap wood, the fast rap of desperation. In the entryway a neighbor points while strange lights, red and blue, pulse beyond her hunching body. She wears a dirty housecoat, and I can see in her wide eyes that none of us will ever be the same.

Now, in the fading light of another June 19th, the stink of rotten flowers sinks over me. A mildewed blanket. In the distance a lawnmower buzzes, and I can't help wondering how long it takes mourners to accept the fact that lawns must be mowed when their loved ones have ceased to breathe. I remind myself this is one more reason to be glad my father isn't buried here. And in the space between my skin and bones, I struggle to believe it.

He told us once during dinner that he wanted to be cremated, as if this were the kind of thing one mentions over pot roast. He said he wanted his ashes scattered by the edge of Heron Lake where we used to feed stale bread to the ducks when the loaf turned green. I remember Ma laughing as she scolded him. "George, we're eating. Don't be morbid!" But her hand shook as she served him another helping of mashed potatoes.

After his heart attack our friends and family tried to talk her into a funeral and casket. These rituals of death, they argued, were for the living—not for those who'd passed. But Ma insisted on following his wishes. At least she made an effort. Eight years later his ashes wait in a heavy ceramic urn in the back of their closet on the floor behind his suits.

It wasn't until the first anniversary of my father's death that I felt a twinge of regret about not burying him. There is no stone for me to visit when I miss him; nowhere to talk to my dad except inside my own heart. Each time I come to the cemetery, it is in the presence of someone else's loss.

Today, the grass around me is sprinkler-wet, and a few determined blades have stuck to the tops of my leather flats. I check my feet, grateful I didn't wear heels, which would've sunk into the earth. A breeze brushes my skin, and I regret the sleeveless dress. Hoping to bridge the gap between beautiful and appropriate, I fear I've tripped headlong into vanity. As if what I'm wearing matters.

I hate myself for caring.

In the shade of an oak tree I wait, the branches above me familiar and stately. A single acorn gives up the fight and lands with a thud onto the ground. Instead of plucking a metaphor from this, I search the craggy tree trunk until I find them: three large knots resembling faces in the gnarled bark. For a decade they have watched me, silent witnesses to these visits. The edge of each knot curls up like a mouth, grinning. Curious. Accusatory.

A rope of self-loathing encircles my gut, and I glance around for somewhere to sit. Cement benches are scattered about the cemetery, but none of them are near this spot. I'm still standing as another acorn drops, a knock on my head, then a dull thunk on the grass. I finger comb my curls to dislodge any leaves, then I check my watch one more time.

Seventeen minutes past six. I could text Tuck to check on their progress, but an extra quarter-hour won't make a difference. She'll be here soon, I tell myself. Any minute now, probably. I swallow hard and admit the truth: A part of me wants to delay this meeting as long as possible.

It's as the first real shiver of the evening creeps up my spine that I finally see her coming over the hill. As she approaches, my arms fold in on themselves, wrapping around my chest. The envelope I've brought is half-concealed beneath my elbow. Scarlet's pace slows until she stops several feet away. Her hair is gathered into one dark twist, and she wears a taupe skirt with a neat white blouse. I feel foolish for wearing black.

"You look lovely," I tell her, blurting out the least important detail of the moment. My cheeks burn, but Scarlet's smooth face betrays no emotion. She tilts her head but still says nothing.

"The baby must be with Tuck," I say. When she doesn't confirm or deny this I add, "Clara told me you had a boy."

"You talked to her?"

I nod. "She told me your son is beautiful." At this, Scarlet's eyebrows pull in on each other, an unspoken question dancing on her lips. *She's wondering what Clara told me.* I take a breath, and she studies me in silence.

"I wasn't sure you'd come," I tell her. "That's why I had Tuck call you."

Scarlet looks at me, lips parted. "Oh."

My stomach drops.

Why had I felt the need to inform her that the request hadn't originated with Tuck? Was I that insecure? Or cruel? Perhaps a little of both. It's true I wanted to see her, but I figured she wouldn't take my call so instead I contacted Clara. Together we formulated a plan. On the night of Bets and Joey's wedding, I asked Tuck to get in touch with Scarlet. When he agreed, I took it as proof of just how badly he wanted to come back home. I chose not to consider other motives, like his wanting to see Scarlet and her baby. I believe in Tucker's love for me.

Trust is a decision, not a feeling.

For the first time since she made her way over the rise, Scarlet's eyes sweep the nearest headstone. I search for a reaction. A flinch. The tightening of her jaw. She takes in the name and dates. I register only the briefest pause before her chin lifts again.

"You left the shower before we could talk," she says.

"I was afraid."

"Of course you were."

"I'm sorry if I ruined your day. It was Clara's idea to surprise you and—"

Scarlet cuts me off. "Don't."

My mouth shuts, opens, shuts.

"You had an agenda, Corie. You always did. But I'm in control now. I get to decide what we are to each other."

"All right," I say. "And what is that?"

"We're nothing." Her lips are a slice across her face. "You made the choice then, but I'm sticking with it now."

I try, but I can't speak. What had I expected? Some Hollywood moment where we hug and braid each other's hair?

"I kissed him," she says. "Tuck." Her voice is a chisel cutting rock, and I almost turn and run. "He never told you?"

I shake my head. My insides twist, but I have to ask. "When?"

She glances at the headstone, then back to me. Her arms hang limply at her sides. "That night," she says. "He pushed me away. Almost immediately." She laughs now, a dark sound. "He told me he loved me, he just wasn't IN love with me. God. What a cliché."

I nod again, slowly. I feel sick with relief.

"Turns out, he'd already chosen. You and your perfect little family. I was too late, and Tuck and I were too much alike. I never stood a chance." She says this more to herself than to me, and I don't have the strength to argue.

Besides. A flicker of truth ignites. *Scarlet might be right.*

"I'm so sorry," I say.

"Are you?"

"Yes. I'll always be sorry."

My words are a whisper and mostly true. I don't admit to her that I have tried to move on, that our brains and our hearts seek self-preservation whether or not we want them to. It isn't out of selfishness but from some impulse beyond our bidding. At least that's what I tell myself when I manage to forget.

"You can apologize all you want," she says. "But it doesn't change what happened. I made a play for Tuck too. You're just the one who got him. Then you picked him over me."

"That's not fair," I say. "We wanted to be there for you."

"We."

"Yes," I say. "We tried to make things right. You're the one who severed ties." My voice grows loud, and I regret the protest. Blaming Scarlet was not my intention. At least I don't think it was. "I didn't mean—" I begin.

"Stop." Scarlet casts her eyes to the ground. "I lost a lot that night," she says, "but it was my fault, not yours. That's what I would have told you at the shower if you'd stayed."

"Scarlet."

She stiffens at the sound of her name, both hands balling into fists. "What?" The word is heavy, weighed down with pain. "What else could you possibly want from me?"

I hold the envelope out to her like a peace offering although I've never felt less peaceful. She looks up, and her face says she'd rather eat glass than accept a gift from me. Then again this is hardly a gift. It's the ramblings of a woman who, at times, felt as if no one else in the world could understand her. "Take it," I say. "Please." It sounds a little like begging. "You don't have to read them."

Her eyebrows lift. "Read?"

"Your mom showed up at Thanksgiving with your ten-year letter from Roosevelt's class. She wanted me to bring it to you then. Asked me to convince you not to have the baby."

Scarlet's cheeks drain of color, white like the stone behind us. "But you didn't."

"I've been trying to get pregnant myself," I say, "but instead I failed at everything." My ears are buzzing. My heart is a hammer in my chest. "I think a part of me believed I didn't deserve to be happy. I stopped being a good teacher, sister, daughter. Wife. I had no one else to talk to so I wrote. To you."

I shove the envelope into her hands, and she gazes at the new burden as if she has no idea how it got in there.

"I lost something that night too," I tell her. The words come in sharp staccato bursts. Scarlet's lips form a startled O, and she steps back as if to catch herself from falling.

"I'd love to hear about that, Corie. Please explain to me exactly how hard these past ten years have been. You know. For you." The evenness of the request is more chilling than if she'd screamed at me.

"I know I can't compare—"

Scarlet lifts her palm. A knife through butter. "You're

right," she says. "You can't."

"I'm sorry," I repeat.

"Don't be," chokes Scarlet. "I was the one who killed him." Her eyes grow impossibly big, full of a hurt I cannot fathom. "If I hadn't been so busy being angry at you and Tuck—"

"It was an accident," I tell her.

"I think you actually believe that," she says. "Which is why I've got nothing left to say to you." She turns away from me, her head cocked as if she's listening to a voice above us.

"Wait," I say.

Scarlet doesn't respond. Instead her body ripples, its own private earthquake. Then she trudges up the grass toward the road where my husband waits with her baby. I half expect her to toss my letters on the wet ground, but she crests the slope and disappears over the hill. She does not look back. Not once.

Under the darkening sky, I kneel where Scarlet stood. The dampness of the earth seeps through my dress. In front of me looms his stone, the birth and death dates etched in marble separated by only six years.

Eliot Gage Hinden
Beloved Son, Brother, Angel
Always in our Hearts

At first the letters blur as if plucked from an alphabet of grief. Hieroglyphics undecipherable to the masses. Then, as the details come once more into focus, I find the answer to a question I hadn't known I'd asked myself.

Yes. Of course.

I know exactly what to do.

Dear Gavin,

First things first: Please sit down to read this letter. You don't know me, but you can trust what I am saying: Your life is about to change. Forever and hopefully for the better. So find a seat, and maybe pop open a beer. Do you like beer?

OK. I'll stop stalling now. I swear.

I'm writing to you because I know Scarlet Hinden. She probably never mentioned me, but we used to be friends. Best friends. She and I found each other first, then a third person—Tucker Slater—made us a party of three, and we became inseparable.

You see, Tuck's mom died of lung cancer when he was in eighth grade. He couldn't wrap his brain around it. She didn't even smoke. After that, he had trouble embracing the bullshit that comes with high school. He went through the motions. Played baseball. He had a team and plenty of guy friends. But no one understood him the way Scarlet and I did. Mostly Scarlet, I guess. Her father took off soon after she was born, and then the man who'd been raising her disappeared when she was ten. Old enough to remember, to know what she was missing. So Scarlet was stuck thinking there was something unlovable about her. And that men leave. Plain and simple. Men leave.

Our freshman year, each student in our English class had to write a research paper, and both Scarlet and Tuck chose to study the impact of parent loss on kids. (I wanted to make this long story short, but I'm not. Please forgive me. The things I'm saying in the middle might help explain the end.)

The three of us spent a lot of time in the library, and we grew close. Tuck and Scarlet needed a lot of the same books and articles. They agreed to share websites, newspapers, textbooks. They even visited the cemetery together. I never could make myself go with them. Death was not my scene.

When his dad got remarried, Tuck hated being at home. No one wanted to be at my house since at least one of my parents was always around. So we started hanging at Scarlet's. And the rest is history. So to speak.

We made a pact to keep romance out of the picture because pairing up wouldn't be fair to whoever was left out. Plus we swore we didn't look at each other in that way. Except we did. For better or worse. When Tuck and I fell for each other, we kept it from Scarlet at first. When she found out, she was jealous of us both. The night we told her sparked the worst nightmare a person can imagine. She wouldn't stop. Scarlet couldn't stop yelling. We still don't know what happened.

Maybe the noise woke her little brother, or maybe he was sleepwalking. Eliot was in a room at the front of the house, in bed before we got there. Tuck and I didn't even know he was home, although we should have assumed it. Scarlet watched him most days after school while her mother was at work. Eleanor had taken the late shift and was across town when her son walked out the door in his pajamas.

The man who ran over Scarlet's brother said Eliot stepped out between two parked cars. The driver never had a chance to hit the brakes. Not until after. I still think about that man, what that night must have done to him. Scarlet blamed herself, of course. She blamed me too. And Tuck. Blamed her mom. Eliot's father. If only Sam had been spending the night with him. If only.

The next day, Scarlet refused to take my calls or Tuck's. We went on with our lives and got married. Then I lost my dad too. I assume Scarlet knows that, although I wasn't the one to tell her. We didn't speak for ten years. But I saw her today at Eliot's grave. For the first time since he died. And I can tell you this, Gavin: She was broken the last time I saw her, but there is strength in her now. Someone's come along to fix her. Maybe it was you. Or Clara. The baby. Or all three of you. It doesn't matter, really. She's healing, and she needs you. So here comes the part where you need to sit down: You, Gavin, are the father of Scarlet's baby.

I know she told you that you weren't, but she was trying to protect her child from being hurt. Hurt like she was. And like Tucker. Her little brother. She didn't want her baby to feel that kind of loss. Not ever. She lied, thinking she could save him from future pain. Once he was born, Scarlet made Clara promise not to tell you. So Clara told me instead, a clever loophole that let her keep her word.

I'm sharing the story now in the hopes that you'll consider forgiving Scarlet. And if you can't see fit to understand why she did what she did, at least you can be there for your own son. You can make things right. Make it right, Gavin.

For everyone.

Sincerely,
Corie Slater

Scarlet

She checked the clock, disappointed to discover it was not yet noon. Too early to eat lunch. Too late to crawl back into bed. She imagined her friends at Olson Brickman messaging each other about where to meet later for drinks, Clara leading the pack to some trendy pub serving discounted cocktails and appetizers. Loud music. Sweet perfume. The taste of beer and smoke. Someone would offer shots all around each time the Giants scored a run.

In truth the late night bar life never had been Scarlet's scene, although she used to play along for Clara's sake and then for Gavin. These days, however, happy hour meant something else to her. Naptime was the new Promised Land, and Baby Gage was hours from his next one.

Scarlet wished she'd seized the opportunity to sleep earlier when he had. She was exhausted now and hungry, in need of one more bowl of cereal. Except she'd already brushed her teeth, hadn't she? She couldn't remember now. She did know she had skipped her shower. Over a phone call, Laura Harper couldn't tell if Scarlet's hair needed washing.

Gage grinned at her from his bouncy seat. "At least one of us is glad to be awake." He had stirred for a feeding before dawn, and during his morning nap, she'd been too wired to return to bed. Thoughts of Eleanor had whirled in her head. Mama's house. Their house.

The house.

Unfortunately, Scarlet's burst of insomnia had all but faded by the time Clara appeared in the kitchen. "I'll pick up dinner after work," she'd told Scarlet, pecking her on the cheek like they were an old married couple. Clara was lovely in her new summer suit. Pink lips. Nude heels. Fresh haircut.

"I don't mind cooking tonight," Scarlet said. She tucked a stray strand of hair into her braid.

Clara smiled. "Only if you feel like it." Her heels clicked as she walked out the door.

It was then that Gage began to grunt over the monitor. So much for a silent apartment. When his squirming protests became actual cries, Scarlet scooped him from his crib. Since then she'd been entertaining her son while perusing the latest offers from two different couples. Her mother's place had been on the market for only three weeks but had already garnered more interest than Scarlet could fathom.

Why would anyone want to buy the shabby rancher, its overgrown lawn succumbing to weeds, the family room smelling of despair?

Family room. What a joke.

But Laura Harper had predicted it, that the Hinden's *less-ostentatious* neighborhood was ripe for gentrification. A house in ill repair meant lower pricing and an immediate increase in value. This, as long as whoever bought it wasn't afraid of *a little renovation.*

Since last weekend's open house, several parties had been interested in the property. And although it had not become an all-out bidding war, both offers Laura sent this morning were above asking price. Scarlet had taken her call early, phone in one hand, Gage's rattle in the other. Laura sounded positively giddy, but Scarlet had felt queasy. Blindsided. True, a decade had passed since the beginning of her nightmare, but that fact made this all the harder. The middle had dragged, and the end came in a rush of painful contact from her past.

Like Laura Harper with Conejo Realty.

"She'll do right by us," Eleanor insisted before she forced Scarlet to hire her.

"What makes you say that?"

"For one thing, she cares. I believe it. And she visits

regularly. She's just about the only one who does. Which isn't a criticism. You're busy. You've got your life. The baby."

"Gage."

"Right," she said. "You've got Gage."

"You used to hate her."

"Laura? Yes, I did. But that's a whole lotta yesterday to let go of."

"Yes," Scarlet said. "It is."

"Don't you think it's time now? For all of us?"

At this Scarlet's tongue grew thick. The one issue she and her mother had agreed upon for ten years was that the Harpers were *them*, not *us*. What would she and Mama have in common now if they loosened those tight reins of resentment?

"Laura Harper's only real mistake," said Eleanor, "was that both her kids survived. And I can't hardly blame her for it. I see that now. Am I jealous? Sure. Do I wish I had her fool luck? Damn straight. But hating her? That's wasted energy. If you ask me, our anger never did help any of us. Least of all you, Scarlet."

"I'm not angry any more," she said.

"What are you, then?"

"I'm not sure."

"Well, figure it out."

"I'm trying, Mama."

"Better hurry up. We're running out of time."

Weeks later she could still hear Eleanor's voice, shallow and brittle, like air escaping a balloon. Scarlet felt even now she could reach out and crack Mama's words wide open using only the tip of her finger. Eleanor was frail. Fading. How much longer would she last?

Scarlet ignored the answer whispering inside her.

These days it was easier not to think about how she might feel when her mother was officially gone. Not just out of contact. Gone. The day might come soon, or it could be years from now. Would Scarlet feel sadness or relief? Loose ends or closure? Her past with Mama had been so complicated it was impossible to say. What she knew presently was this: In her life, the wrong people left, and the ones who stayed weren't right for her either.

Even Clara had her limits, and Scarlet had begun to sense the tension stretching between them, a tightrope ready to snap. Lately, when Clara returned home in the evenings, she retreated to her bedroom instead of joining Scarlet on the couch. For television or wine. Simple conversation. Clara took extra showers at night, made plans with Izzy more often than she used to. Dinner, drinks and yoga filled her rare chunks of spare time.

Of course they would invite Scarlet, but did they truly want her to join them? Clara knew Scarlet couldn't arrange for a sitter on such short notice. "You mean you *won't* get a sitter," Clara clarified, and Scarlet never argued. She wasn't ready to leave Gage with anyone else. Not yet. Maybe not ever. Each time she declined Clara's offers, Scarlet imagined she heard relief dripping off her friend. Raindrops after a summer thunderstorm.

Believing she was loved was still hard work.

I'm trying, Mama.

She was.

Without a doubt Clara loved Gage. She would do anything for him. Already had. She was his *goddammed godmother* as she liked to remind everyone. But she was also young and single. She loved her men, worshipped her freedom. She wasn't cut out to be Scarlet Hinden's husband.

Gage looked at her now, blew a wet bubble with his mouth. From the back of the sofa, Scarlet snatched a ripe burp cloth to wipe the wet folds of his chin. The skin there would practically curdle in between baths if she let it. After she cleaned him, she waited for the grin that spread across his face whenever they locked eyes.

There it is. You love me. You're all I need. Almost.

She rose from the couch and plucked Gage from his bouncy seat in a maneuver that, two months ago, would have been foreign to her. Collecting an extra blanket to wrap around his feet she said, "Time for a long walk, Benji."

Clara had bestowed the nickname upon the baby after noting his resemblance to Ben Franklin. When he'd lost the dusting of strawberry fuzz from the top of his head, he had indeed looked like a balding founding father. Was Ben

Franklin ever a redhead? Clara promised she would Google it. "Either way, his hair will grow back," she told Scarlet. But she added Rogaine to their grocery list as a joke.

Smoothing a knit cap over Gage's scalp, Scarlet paused to stroke the soft spot pulsing there. He arched his back as she nestled him into his infant seat and strapped the baby carrier into the stroller. A few strands of hair had escaped from her braid, and she shoved them under the brim of a Giant's ball cap. Then she maneuvered the baby and stroller out the door and down the stairs as if she had been doing it all her life.

Outside the sun was bright, the air warm on her face. From a twist of vines came the scent of jasmine, and Scarlet smiled down at her son. "Do you see those flowers? They're jasmine. That smell means we're home." He looked at her, blinked. "Stay awake," she said. "I've got so much to show you."

She took the long loop from her neighborhood to the park. Apartment buildings. Stop signs. Street lights. Birds. Scarlet kept a running commentary describing objects on their path. Once they reached downtown, the sidewalks and intersections began to fill with people. Haggard. Pinched. Rushing. Were any of them happy?

Some, she guessed, were anxious. Or thrilled. Perhaps full of rage. How many strangers sharing this sidewalk wanted to cry or scream or laugh out loud? No one did these things. Not any of them. Most people barely made eye contact. They simply pushed past each other continuing on with their busy lives. All of them so busy.

Except Scarlet.

She picked up the pace as they passed the turn-of-the-century building that housed Dr. Kagawa's office. Scarlet hadn't been to therapy since Gage's birth. She had told the doctor over the phone she no longer had the luxury of going crazy. *It's time to grow up*, Scarlet explained. *To think about others. I'm letting shit go.*

"You can't will yourself out of depression," Dr. Kagawa warned. "The onset is sneaky. It creeps up on you."

"I'll be careful," Scarlet assured her. "I know the signs. I am aware." She promised the doctor she would return once she and Gage had settled into a routine. For now, fresh air would be her therapist. And sunshine. The best medicine.

Scarlet veered left at the next intersection, the tires of Gage's stroller bumping over cracks in the asphalt. Across the street she noted two men reading on a bench, one holding a newspaper, their heads bent close. It was the same bench where she and Tuck had sat after he ambushed her outside the doctor's office last spring. Well, *ambush* might be too strong a term. Nevertheless she'd been startled to see him.

Leaning against the wall, asking if he could speak with her.

She still questioned Tuck's intentions. Why her? Why then? So much effort expended for a conversation barely more substantive than *Hey, nice weather.* Last month she had almost asked him. Something. Anything. After the cemetery in the backseat of the minivan, she opened and shut her mouth. In the end, silence had been easier.

Some truths were better left unspoken.

ৡৰৢ

The park was short on shade when she took a seat on the low stone wall surrounding the playground. Scarlet wished she had taken the time to change into something cooler. Or at least clean. Her yoga pants were sagging, and the tank top under her sweatshirt sported spit-up stains. But then she remembered. This space was populated by children, tired mothers and nannies. She'd come almost every day for the past three weeks, and no one here dressed like Clara.

Three weeks.

Would she be back to work by the time Gage was old enough to swing and climb and dig? She shook the thought away. Why burden today with worries about tomorrow? In this moment, she could pretend her life was simple. Coming to the park was what mothers did with their children, and she would act the part even if neither of them were quite ready.

"Fake it 'til you make it. Right, Benji?" Scarlet lifted his chubby fist into the air.

"Right, Mama!" she squeaked in the made-up voice she'd adopted for him. Then she winced as she did each time she caught herself imagining Gage would call her *Mama*. Scarlet hadn't wanted to appropriate the name she used for her own mother but like Eleanor used to say: Old habits die hard. *Die hard. Ha.*

As if there were anything easy about death.

A man with two Dalmatians on a double leash jogged toward her, slowing to a stop when he reached the wall. His shorts were loose over extra-long legs and a Nike shirt stretched across his chest. After shoving his sunglasses to the top of his head, he offered each dog a treat from his pocket. Their tails wagged, two scrapes against the concrete. "Good girls," he said. "Stay." Damp hair curled around his ears, and beads of sweat gathered at his temple. As quickly as she noticed, Scarlet looked away. The man said, "Beautiful day, huh?"

She glanced over her shoulder as if he might be talking to someone else, but she was certain his greeting was for her. The other mothers and kids were by the playground, and when she met his eyes again—hazel? Brown?—they were trained on her.

"May I?" He indicated the empty space beside her, and before she could respond, the man took a seat. He smelled clean and salty and close. Scarlet found herself wondering what his skin would taste like. His lips on hers. His teeth. His body. *God.*

How long had it been since someone had held her? She couldn't remember. Perhaps forever. And yet the timeline no longer seemed to matter. Sure she missed sex, would like to have it again someday *and not just by herself*. But she would never be Clara, resorting to casual flirtations and random hook-ups. No. Not a viable choice—but neither was allowing others in only to hold them at arm's length. Both options left her feeling fragmented and cold. Which was why, over the past two months, she had decided, finally, reluctantly, that being in control on the outside didn't make her happy on the inside.

So she let go.

And for the first time in her life Scarlet stopped being desperate, at least in the sense she had been, for attention or validation. She'd always longed to be told she was special, had tested her worth with her stepfather and half-brother. With Mama. Then Corie and Tucker. Even with Clara and eventually Gavin. When they pulled one way, she pulled the other, until the tug of war reversed. But no one could fill the void. It was inside her. Inside everyone, she'd come to believe. This was a small comfort, learning to find value in herself.

Somewhere along the way Scarlet began to accept her aloneness. She was with Gage now, but his presence was no guarantee. Eventually he would leave her too. It was simply a matter of when. And that was OK. People left. That didn't mean you lost them.

Not forever.

She looked down at her son and bent to tuck his blanket around the tiny bare foot he had kicked free.

"How old?" the runner asked her.

"Two months. A little more."

She braced herself for the inevitable compliment. Most people appeared incapable of talking about her son without labeling him adorable. Not because he was, although of course Scarlet believed this to be true, but because strangers seemed obliged to fill the silence, and a baby's cuteness was their go-to observation.

This man, however, did not speak. He simply nodded. Scarlet bobbed her head at the dogs panting next to his feet and did the very thing she found to be so amusing in others.

"They're cute," she said. "Really sweet."

"Wanna trade?" His expression remained blank, not even a twitch of lip to betray the teasing. She opted to play along.

"You've got two dogs, and I have one kid. That hardly seems fair."

He shrugged. "I'm feeling generous today."

Scarlet smiled, unable to keep up the act. There was something about this stranger, the cut of his jaw, the twinkle in his eye, that put her at ease. Or perhaps she felt so comfortable because she hadn't showered and wore no make-up. This exchange would lead exactly nowhere. And nowhere was where she needed to be.

"I've seen you here before," he said, and it was Scarlet's turn to nod. "I've always wanted to say *hi*," he said. "I'm

Robert." He stuck out a hand.

"Can I call you Bobby?"

"Absolutely not."

She smiled again, and he grinned back. "This is Gage. My son."

"I figured."

"And on second thought, I think I'll keep him."

Robert tugged on the dogs' leashes. "Yeah, on second thought, I like these two mutts too. Plus, there's your husband to consider." Scarlet raised an eyebrow, and Robert shrugged. "The guy might be allergic to dogs, right? It was crazy of me to assume a trade would work." She watched his gaze drift down to her naked ring finger, but she didn't take the bait.

"You're funny," she said.

"I am funny." He tapped on the bill of her baseball cap. "I'm also a Giant's fan."

"Isn't everyone?"

"They're playing tonight," he said. "But you probably knew that already."

Scarlet shook her head. "I've been distracted."

"Maybe someday you won't be," said Robert. "Distracted, I mean."

She cut her focus to Gage who was beginning to fuss. "Maybe."

"Fair enough."

Robert pushed himself up off the wall and whistled lightly through his teeth. Then his dogs scrambled to their feet and took turns sniffing at his ankles. Robert knocked his glasses off his forehead, back onto the bridge of his nose. "See you 'round, Scarlet."

She smiled for the third time since he sat down beside her. "You know where to find me," she said.

He touched his fingers to his brow, snapping them outward in a salute. Then he resumed his jog past the park, the muscles of his calves flexing with each step. "Go Giants!" she called out after him, but he made no motion that he heard. It was only after he crossed the street and disappeared around the corner that Scarlet realized she hadn't told Robert her name.

❧

"I'm still waiting for the punch line," said Clara when Scarlet finished telling her about the encounter with the strange runner.

"Are you kidding?" Scarlet yelled into the phone. Why was Clara acting so calm? True, Clara was at work. She had to maintain decorum. But where was her *Bloody hell*? Why wasn't she afraid? This incident involved her *goddamned godson*.

"He called me by name, Clare. *See you 'round, Scarlet.* Those were his exact words. Were you even listening?"

"I heard you fine. But I want to know if Robert was hot. Was he hot?"

"Why on earth does that matter? The guy is stalking me. He said he's seen me before. He said he wanted my baby!"

"You do go round to that park pretty much every day."

"And?"

"And what? Good Lord, he was kidding, Scarlet. It's called having a sense of humor. Not that you'd remember what that's like." Scarlet gulped, stung by her words. Was that how Clara truly felt? And what was funny about a stranger knowing your name? "I'm sorry, Scar. I suppose I could muster up some fear and loathing to go along with your tale of woe. But do you know why I didn't?" Scarlet shook her head, which, of course, Clara couldn't hear. Still her friend knew her well enough to answer. "I assume you're still wearing the same brilliant sweat suit you had on when I left this morning."

"They're yoga pants."

"You can't call them yoga pants if you never go to class."

"Yes, you can!"

"No, you can't. But that's beside the point. I'm betting you unzipped your sweatshirt a little when you got to the park because it's warm and you forgot to change. In fact, you probably didn't shower or even brush your teeth today. Am I right?"

"And this is relevant because..."

"Touch your throat, Scar."

"What? Why?"

"Humor me."

Scarlet lifted her fingers to the dip between the hard bones of her clavicle. Against the skin she felt the scrollwork of the necklace Gavin had given her. A gift for her twenty-eighth birthday. Her name engraved on a twenty-four-carat gold charm.

"Oh," she said. "Oh."

"If you ever looked in the mirror, you would remember the necklace."

"I didn't forget."

"Maybe not," said Clara. "But you've been trying damn hard not to think about Gavin."

Scarlet lowered herself onto the couch and stared at her son still nestled in his stroller. The feverish pace of their walk home had lulled him back to sleep. "Sorry to bother you at work, Clare. I'm sure you're busy so I'll let you get back to it. And don't worry about picking up dinner. I'll roast a chicken or something."

"Smooth change of subject, my friend."

"What? You don't want chicken?"

"Fine," said Clara. "If you refuse to talk about Gavin, then at least tell me about Robert. Is he a prospect? I mean for you, of course. Not me. We must get you back out there someday. Benji will be leaving for college before you know it, and I plan to be living alone by then with twenty cats."

"Thanks for the warning." Scarlet laughed weakly, a wet hiccup escaping at the end.

"You all right?" asked Clara.

"I will be," said Scarlet. "No, scratch that. I am."

"I believe you." There was a pause before Clara continued. "Now, about that roast chicken."

"Too hot for July?"

"Yes. But that's not what I was going to say. A whole lot of us are going round to Cue's to watch the game at six o'clock. They've got garlic fries for God's sake. Huge baskets of them. So come on, Scarlet. Let Mrs. Adams sit with Benji. The poor old lady drools every time she sees him. And not just because she's eighty."

"Thanks, Clare, but—"

"But nothing," said Clara. "Stop being such a nervous

Nelly. What's the worst that could happen if you let the baby out of your sight for an hour or two?"

If only she knew, thought Scarlet. *The worst*. Someday soon she would tell Clara about how "the worst" can happen. That "the worst" does happen. It happened to her. Scarlet felt almost ready to revisit the full darkness of her past, to share with Clara why she always seemed so damn afraid. She would dip her toes in, let it wash over her again. But not today. Again she looked at Gage. Today was about feeling grateful. Lucky. Alive.

"Come on, Scar," urged Clara. "Say you'll think about it."

Scarlet sighed. Sometimes it really was just easier to lie. "I'll think about it."

"Everything's fine, you know."

"Of course it is. Now go back to work."

"See you at six, then! Hooray!" Clara crowed like she was Peter Pan reuniting with the Lost Boys.

"I love you, crazy girl," said Scarlet. "But you really are a nutter."

Setting her phone down on the coffee table, she slipped out of her sweatshirt and tucked the straps of her nursing bra back under her tank top. It was an ugly piece of lingerie. Industrial. Utilitarian. But it symbolized her new role, the most important of her life: Scarlet was now and always would be Gage's mother. Irrevocable. Permanent.

Her love for him was bone deep and stronger by far than death. She had never felt more powerful or more filled with purpose. She had also, admittedly, never felt more tired. Her head dropped back on the couch, and she closed her eyes for a few minutes of rest while Gage slept. But as her thoughts grew fuzzy at the edges, she heard the clomp, clomp, clomp of someone's footsteps on the stairs.

Damn Clara and her good intentions.

She'd probably taken matters into her own hands and called their landlady about babysitting. Scarlet sighed and shook her head. She didn't feel up to going out. She might be ready soon. For a lovely dinner. Some good company. Robert was attractive and clearly interested. Yes, soon she would search her heart, make room for someone new. But not quite yet. Not tonight.

Her little family still came first.

The footsteps stopped at her door. Why couldn't Clara leave well enough alone? Mrs. Adams was sweet but practically deaf. She would knock—or worse, ring the bell—and wake the sleeping baby.

No!

Scarlet flew across the room and hauled open the front door. But instead of Mrs. Adams' stooped gray head, Scarlet saw first a pair of blue jeans. Then a rumpled T-shirt giving way to a neck. A throat, lean and ropey. That angular face. Those green eyes. A thatch of gingered hair.

Gavin.

He stood on the welcome mat, one hand in his pocket, the other holding a letter. Scarlet's heart beat suddenly in her ears. "It's you," she said. "Hi."

Gavin peered down at her through a brush of sandy lashes. Were his eyes shining, or could she be imagining it? Had she fallen asleep? Maybe she was still on the couch, dreaming away next to her son.

"I figured you'd be here." His voice was dry. Hollow, even. As if he'd dug it up from someplace deep.

"I am," Scarlet said. Definitely not a dream. She stumbled backward, and Gavin reached out. Fingertips at her elbow. Steady. Firm. Warm. Hope, like a guilty thing, spread through her gut, hot and prickly, beyond her control.

"I should've called," he said.

"No, no. It's OK." Scarlet shook her head. An act of protest and surrender. "It's OK," she repeated. To him, to herself. She fought the tightness in her throat, the panic grappling for space. Then she decided.

Whatever came next, she would survive. They all would, one way or another, although survival sometimes looked an awful lot like loss.

Scarlet drew in a long breath and took Gavin by the hand. "Come inside," she said. "There's someone I'd like you to meet."

Corie

I blink like a bat emerging from its cave as six rows of fluorescent bulbs flicker above my head. Even the lights don't think I should be here. July is far too early. I wedge a rubber jamb under the door and open every window. This space hosted six weeks of algebra. The poor room needs to breathe.

Each year I beg that my class not be used for summer school, and each year my request is denied. I understand. Our campus is the biggest in the district, and there are too many students, so many courses. But damn if I didn't get the short stick this time: the filthiest teacher assigned to my pristine classroom. Now the air smells stale, like bread left too long in the back of a pantry. I swear if John Pickett let the kids eat lunch in here, I'll leave a tuna sandwich in his mailbox for revenge.

I imagine his students, bored in the back of the room, doodling on my posters from *Dante's Inferno*. I head to the far corner to check, and sure enough, someone's added a penis to Lucifer. In Sharpie. I tear down the poster and shove it in the trash. At least the can has been emptied recently. I make a mental note to thank Leon, my favorite of the custodians. Thanks to him my floors are swept free of staples, tacks, crumbs; the flotsam and jetsam of a classroom in use. Still, a thin layer of life—dirt, frustration, time—coats every surface. I run a finger along the top of my filing cabinet and inscribe my initials there.

CHS.

Corie Harper Slater.

Conejo High School.

The faculty likes to joke that I'm the school's most spirited teacher, but I'm not visiting our campus today by choice. I'm here because Greer Larson asked me to oversee her independent study program. Well, she didn't so much ask or say goodbye in person. But I did find a thick packet in my faculty mailbox with the proposed coursework she'd have to complete to graduate. Her note was short on words and politeness:

Please approve this. Greer.

A few days ago Henry Callaghan called to tell me her assignments were ready for evaluation, then he asked me to drop by CHS to pick them up. I didn't want to come, but I had to keep my word. So here I am. Chewing my lip. Doing my best.

I'm guessing without teacher guidance, Greer probably didn't understand much of the *Divine Comedy*, but it's not like floating her a passing grade will send the girl to Stanford. The girl will be lucky to manage CCC at this point. Being eighteen with a newborn can't be easy. Not when watching kids at twenty-nine is hard.

As a wedding gift to my sister, Tuck and I offered to take the kids while she and Joey honeymooned in Costa Rica. It meant more to me this time than when they lived here because I knew their stay was truly temporary. So we played Yahtzee and snuggled under blankets to read their favorite books. When Tuck didn't have cases, the four of us watched movies in the daytime. One evening I even let the kids make s'mores in our fireplace.

Life is short, I thought as their faces shone.

Burn your candles. Stoke your flames.

Later that night, after Cam and Wella went to bed, Tuck and I sat in our bathtub until the water got lukewarm. We drank champagne straight from the bottle. Soaped each other's backs. In the glow of a dozen tea lights, we made our last best promises: no more punishing ourselves or each other. For our past, our present, our future.

During those two weeks, the sailing was smooth, our days full and sunny. Cam and Wella wanted snacks and juice boxes. They needed my time and plenty of attention. Our niece and nephew helped us forget the empty spaces we hadn't yet filled. Then Stella called to tell me that Greer Larson had her baby.

It's a girl, she said. *Eight pounds. Mother and daughter are doing well.*

I fled to the bathroom, sat on the shower floor letting hot water scald my head. Cam pounded on the door, and I told him I was fine. When I emerged, Wella took one look at me and asked if I'd been crying. So I put thin slices of cucumber on my eyes and cooked Tuck's favorite dinner. Chicken parmesan with extra mozzarella. Everyone said it was delicious.

The next morning my period came, a red bloom on sheets I tossed out unwashed. Bets and Joey returned the same day, bursting with new stories and fresh starts. According to my sister, she and Joey were fighting more than ever.

"But the make-up sex is hotter since the wedding!" After the Farinellis drove off in their minivan, I wondered out loud how long their marriage would last.

"Let's hope forever," Ma said under her breath. "No one else will put up with your sister."

Since then Cam and Wella have stayed with us every Tuesday night, and Ma comes to make pancakes Wednesday mornings. It's our "new old" tradition. As for the future? I'm not quite sure. I know only that Tuck and I will stick it out. Together. We promised no more hurting each other. At least never on purpose.

∽∾

I've just finished cleaning my classroom shelves with paper towels and Windex when my cell phone buzzes inside my purse. A message from a number I don't recognize.

Gavin's here
Oh my God.
He asked me to thank you
Are you OK? I texted her.

I will be

How's it going?

I glance at the wall clock and watch the second hand trace a full circle around its face. I am only a little disappointed when Scarlet doesn't respond. She's with Gavin. I understand. They're not thinking about me. She's probably introducing the man to his son for the very first time. At the thought of it, I surrender to a shiver. Right now Scarlet's in the thick of it, being heard again, seen with fresh eyes by the father of her child. Maybe they'll rediscover their love. Maybe they won't. Either way, the thrill of uncertainty is on their side. All three of them taking baby steps, both literally and figuratively.

Don't be jealous.

I remind myself that what I have with Tuck is wonderful. There's a comfort to our familiarity. I know him well. And even better? He knows me. Tuck and I don't merely see each other. We recognize the space that stretches between us.

I glance at my *Hamlet* poster and read again his *To be or not to be* speech ending with *'Tis a consummation / Devoutly to be wished.* Sure, Shakespeare was referencing death in this scene, but for Hamlet, it's all about choice. And I choose Tuck. To live with. To love. For as long as I can. 'Til death do us part.

In the top drawer of my desk, I find the school calendar I stored there for the summer. On the third Wednesday of this month, I'd drawn a tiny yellow heart. When Ma called this morning to tell me about the offers on the Hindens' house, she pointed out the coincidence of the date. As if I might not remember. As if I'd ever forget.

It's true that each summer, without the anchor of a work schedule, I do lose track of days. I end up asking the gray-haired checker at the grocery line, and she chuckles about how time flies. *Wait until you're older,* she tells me. *You won't even know what year it is.* But I always remember the 21st of July. And I definitely recall this year. Today should have been Eliot Hinden's eighteenth birthday.

Had he lived, he'd be the same age we were the night he died.

More than eleven years have passed, and Scarlet is finally selling the place. She probably hopes to sell the ghosts that linger there too. But I can't help thinking she'll be haunted by them wherever she might go. As long as she's alive and her little brother isn't. In the end, we take our pasts with us into the future, curls of smoke after a fire. Without the fire, there would be no smoke. And without who we were, we can't be who we are.

The good news is the Hindens will make enough money from the sale to help pay for Eleanor's care and to supplement Scarlet's income until her maternity leave is up. This means Clara will get her rent, Ellie will get physical therapy, and Scarlet can make smart choices going forward rather than desperate ones.

Ma told me Scarlet wanted to move her mother to a fancier facility, but Eleanor insisted New Horizons suited her fine. Apparently she loves the nurses and something Ma called ITALIAN NITE, which involves pasta—not people from Italy. Eleanor also told my mother she thinks she won't live long enough to make a change worthwhile. When Ma asked me if she should pass this on to Scarlet, I shook my head.

"You're involved enough already. Do yourself a favor and stay out of it."

"Isn't that interesting coming from you," Ma said.

"Meaning what, exactly?"

"Just that you're the one who stuck your nose in Scarlet and Gavin's relationship. Writing him that letter, sharing facts that Scarlet wanted kept a secret." My mother frowned. "Let's hope it doesn't do more harm than good."

At this I dropped my eyes, annoyed that she'd brought it up. Annoyed that I had told her in the first place. "I wasn't being nosy," I said. "I was trying to help. Gavin deserved to know he's a father, and Scarlet deserves to be happy."

From the look on her face, Ma didn't buy my argument, and to be honest, neither did I. Helping Scarlet was my main motivation, but I'd also been hoping for redemption. I wanted to put pieces back together for once instead of tearing them apart. Was it selfish of me to write that letter? Perhaps. I don't know. I do know when I asked Clara for Gavin's address, she was supportive of my plan.

According to her, Scarlet had convinced herself Gavin was

better off without her. That he'd moved on, made a new life. *But that's rubbish,* Clara said. I agreed, and we decided. I would write to Gavin. And that's how I helped Clara Broxton keep her promise to Scarlet.

My classroom phone rings now, a shrill knife cutting the silence, and I answer when I see it's an outside line. "Hey, Core," says Tuck. "My afternoon case canceled, and I'm heading home. You almost done?"

"Almost. But it looks like Callaghan didn't put Greer's papers in my room like I asked him to. I'm going to have to stop by his office to pick them up."

"Fantastic." Tuck's sarcasm is sharp. "Good old Henry can work his magic on his home turf."

"You don't have to worry."

"I know," Tuck says, whether or not he really means it. We have chosen to believe. In each other and ourselves.

"I'm going to tell him." I hesitate, and the ensuing pause is both silent and deafening. "About next year, I mean."

"He'll try to change your mind."

"He can't," I say. "I won't."

"Try to break it to him quickly then and get yourself back home," he says. "I have something here I think you'll want."

"More than you?"

"Maybe."

"More than a leave of absence?"

"For sure." I can almost hear him smiling.

Alone in my classroom with the clock as my only witness, I smile back.

৵৵

An hour later on the drive home, I'm weighed down by five pounds of Greer Larson's essays, and yet I feel miraculously light. For the first time ever, I'm not nervous about starting a new school year. Each day I walk onto campus will move me one step closer to my goal. Of course I will miss teaching. The poetry and prose. The students. But I could do without parents and paperwork. Our English department drama. Not to mention all the awkwardness between Henry Callaghan and me.

When I told him I'd be applying for a leave of absence next June, he looked across his desk at me, eyes wide. "But why?"

"I'm going to write a novel," I told him. "It's always been my dream, and Tuck and I figure if not now, then when?"

"But Tucker doesn't support your writing."

"I never said that."

"I thought it was implied. Was I wrong?"

My cheeks flushed with the memory of that first conversation between us, of the small flirtations that followed, a slippery slope stopped just in time. It was Tuck who suggested I take a break next year to write. A gift for my thirtieth birthday, the second best one I could wish for. "As it turns out," I told Henry, "I'm the one who was wrong."

"I'll admit, I'm disappointed," he said. "I was hoping next year we could take things in a different direction."

"That's the thing," I said. "I like the direction I'm headed in now."

"Well." He stood to shake my hand. "You can't blame a guy for trying."

Yeah, I thought. *I can.*

"Thanks for holding onto Greer's work for me."

"Sure thing, Corinna."

I nod. He never really knew me.

᪥᪥

Coming in through the garage door, I find Tuck waiting in the kitchen. He's wearing blue scrubs, old cross-trainers and a grin that says something's up. I kiss him on the cheek. "I love it when your cases cancel."

"I do too," he says. "But not too many. I've got a writer to support now."

"Hey! Not until next year. And we can bank my paychecks for the next ten months to add to our savings. But if you're worried we won't have enough money, I don't have to—"

"Core," he interrupts. "I was kidding."

"Oh. I get jokes," I say. Then I poke him. "When they're

funny."

"I see. Because you're the last word on hilarious?"

"I'm the first word too."

He laughs. "That's what I get for marrying an English teacher."

"And I'm a writer, don't forget."

"Truly a multi-faceted woman," he says. Then he fixes me with a pointed look. "So. Are you ready to see if we're adding another facet to the mix?"

"What?"

Tuck steps aside to reveal a drugstore bag sitting on the counter behind him. It is white and folded neatly at the top. I suck in a breath when I realize what this is. He reaches in and pulls out a long thin box with two pink plus signs on the front.

"I got the double-pack," he tells me. "For next month. If we need it."

The box is wrapped in air-tight plastic, and I already picture myself peeling it off, tearing at the cardboard, plucking out a stick. I hear the tick, tick, tick of the clock counting down the seconds while we wait. My stomach twists, and I swallow hard. We've been here before, letting ourselves hope. I know the lemony taste of disappointment, and I've sometimes choked on Tucker's. But this time feels different. Special. Today I'm three days late.

I look at Tuck and smile.

"Either way, Core," he tells me.

"Yes," I say. "Either way."

Then I count each step as we head upstairs to find out what comes next.

Acknowledgments

The road to publication is long, and I have many people to thank. First, my parents Jim and Diane Christianson and my sister Nancy Stuart for loving me from the start; my grandparents for leading the way; the Gardner family for letting me in and sharing their name; Karen Morris, Linda Maples, and Kim Becotte for being bonus sisters; and Randy Stuart for getting the blog-ball rolling and supporting me in every way.

I'd also like to thank Cheryl Rosenberg, Charlene Ross, Kim Prince, Suzan Hyssan, Jennie Goutet and Stephanie Bernaba for critiquing early drafts; The Writing Safety Tree: Kim Prince, Charlene Ross, Rina Nehdar, Laurel Bryne and Lexi Rohner for encouraging and commiserating; my extended family, friends and bloggers too numerous to name for caring, asking, cheering; and Adria Cimino and Vicki Lesage for taking a chance.

A special thanks to Jennie Goutet for sharing Velvet Morning Press with me, nudging me to submit and clapping for me always.

I am grateful to Diane McEvoy for reading the first and last drafts, then saying *when* not *if;* Courtney Armendariz for meeting me halfway; Kerry Rider for listening; Robin Bielman for setting the bar; Suzie Cooper, Rowena Sales, Gail Carney and Jen Boudreau for laughing, crying, hoping; Jackie Soporito for believing. To infinity and beyond.

My final thank you goes to Jack and Karly for giving my life purpose and motivating me to keep going (and going and going). And to Bill. You're it for me. None of this would have happened without you.

About the Author

Julie C. Gardner is a former English teacher and lapsed marathon runner who traded in the classroom for a writing nook. Now she rarely changes out of her pajamas, and is an author of Women's Fiction. She lives in Southern California with her husband, two children and three dogs.

Letters for Scarlet is Julie's debut novel, and she really hopes you enjoyed reading it as much as she enjoyed writing it! If you did, please consider leaving a review on Amazon. Even a few sentences may help a future reader decide to pick up the book.

And be sure to check out Julie's other work:

Guest List (a prequel to *Letters for Scarlet*): Will Scarlet and Corie attend their ten-year high school reunion and face demons from their past?

Running with Pencils, a short story about a "midlife marathon"—twenty weeks of running and twenty weeks of writing.

Interested in finding out more about Julie and learning about her upcoming books? Visit her at JulieCGardner.com and follow her on Twitter @juliecgardner and Instagram @juliecgardner.

Read on for a sneak peek of *Guest List*...

Running with Pencils

A month before my fortieth birthday, under the influence of inspiration (not to mention half a pitcher of margaritas), I concocted a specific plan—one that offered an obvious starting line, a concrete ending and clearly digestible nuggets of achievement along the way. For the next five months I'd train for a race. Not just any race.

A midlife marathon.

While I convinced my forty-year-old legs they could run more than three miles at a time, I would also write a memoir chronicling tales of gladness and woe. Twenty weeks of running. Twenty weeks of writing. All I needed was a new pair of shoes, a couple of notebooks and a handful of pencils, and by springtime, I'd be ticking two big items off my bucket list: completing a marathon and a book. What could be simpler?

Get it for free! Join Julie's new release mailing list and she'll send you a free ecopy of *Running with Pencils*: http://bit.ly/runningwithpencils

Guest List

a novella

Julie C. Gardner

Corie

The email lurks in my inbox like a time bomb. I can practically hear a *tick tick tick* before the explosion, computer shards slicing my throat. Would the blood be trickly and thin or a hot river staining me red? I shut down the computer and teach my classes. Try not to think. Hope to forget. The next morning Kate Turlow's all-caps greet me again.

CONEJO HIGH SCHOOL 10-YEAR REUNION.

I don't open the message, but I can't bring myself to delete it either.

Wednesday. Thursday. Friday. One more month until summer vacation. After a few weeks the email is less a time bomb and more a cucumber that once was fresh but now has turned to mush. Green liquid molding in the crisper.

SAVE THE DATE DON'T MISS –

The subject line cuts off there, but I am certain it ends with "out."

Don't miss out.

Why is Kate Turlow coordinating our reunion, anyway? She graduated with Bets, not with our class. I suppose I shouldn't be surprised. Kate's friendly enough, but she's also an insinuator. She likes to have a thumb in every pie. For a split-second I'm tempted to reply, to explain that my life is full. Almost overly so. I want to tell her I'm not missing a thing. But Kate was around back then, and she would know.

This is not entirely true.

A piece of me exists in some other undisclosed location. Or maybe I'm the piece, and Scarlet is the whole. Either way, neither one of us is complete. Thanks to Tuck, I rarely dwell on this though. The empty space. Our looming absences. *Dwelling doesn't change anything*, he says, and he's right. Nevertheless. Kate's email sucks out my air. I feel the gap, and a breeze blows through me, the saddest whistle I can imagine.

It's been almost a decade since my high school graduation, back when I assumed I'd end up writing essays for *The New Yorker*—not teaching kids how to write them. At the rehearsal, our principal, Maryann Dresden, promised it would be a night we'd never forget. Of course Mrs. Dresden couldn't have known how true those words would be. Every morning when I see her on campus now, I wonder if she remembers. If she, too, thinks about that evening. If she blames me for the fallout.

I'll bet she felt sorry for me during my interview. How could you not hire Corie Harper? *It wasn't her fault*. That's what everyone swore ten years ago, what people still claim when the subject arises. But I labor hard to avoid such conversations. Because it was, you see.

It was our fault.

Tuck wants to go to the reunion anyway. He says it's time to put the past behind us, to level ourselves at the stares of others, to answer questions with an even smile. His grin always did spread quickly, creasing a dimple into his cheek. Sometimes I trace that dent with a fingertip, the first spot on his body I kissed. I've been memorizing his face ever since. I carry it inside me alongside the shadow of its cost.

As for Tuck, he is able to compartmentalize. To rationalize. Sympathize. All the *izes* come easy to my husband. It's one of the things I love most about him. Tuck is the opposite of all things Corie. The yin to my yang, the sunshine to my moon. Which is ironic (is it ironic?) if you picture his pitch-black hair and lashes like midnight. Tuck should be the sunny one. He holds the light, while I retain the dark. Yet I'm the one who is pale, a skinny thing, dull by comparison. To this day I marvel that the man chose me, that he dug deep enough to discover who I am, who I still want to become. Tuck Slater could have had anyone. He could have had Scarlet.

But he didn't know that then.

When I admit to Ma that Tuck and I have been tense these days, arguing more often, she tells me to *let it go*. My mother's a fan of conflict avoidance, and ever since we lost Dad, she worries about my marriage to avoid crying over hers.

It'll be fine, Corie. You'll see.

But the truth is, Ma doesn't know. It's not just the reunion. Tuck and I would be on edge regardless, both of us a little scared and a lot excited. It's a tricky combination. Our emotions come in waves. Sometimes on the drive to school, I feel the flutter in my stomach, and I wonder if I'm getting sick. Then it hits me: We are trying. *Trying*.

We are hoping. We are praying. Waiting.

The *ings* come easier to Tuck.

I haven't told my mother yet, although I won't be able to keep the secret much longer. I never could find the right scissors to cut her maternal ties. She'll be after me every day, leaving messages, texting when I don't call back. She's already relentless. I can only imagine how bad it'll get when she's wondering along with me. Screening her is cruel I suppose, especially since she's lonely. How hard is it to pick up the phone for my poor mother who's simply concerned and checking up on me? I'll tell you. It's hard. Monumentally hard.

Please don't hate me for it.

I know I'm lucky. To be alive. To feel loved and purposeful. I spend my days sharing words with young humans who aren't yet immune to the world's magic, and I end my nights in Tucker's arms on the couch watching *The Office* on Netflix. Yes. Corie Harper Slater is lucky. Luckyluckylucky. I never stop reminding myself. So when Bets says it again during our lunch together, when she tells me I simply need to relax, I take a deep breath and a bigger gulp of ice water.

She means well. She means well. She means well.

"You're right," I tell my sister. "I'm working on relaxing."

Bets frowns. "That's my point." She's sitting opposite me in a sticky booth at Chuck E. Cheese, one child squirming on either side of her. My niece and nephew were both accidents, or as my sister likes to label them, *surprises*. I'll give her the *one* surprise, sure. After that, the situation smacks of irresponsibility.

"*Working on it* is the problem," Bets says. "Just chill out. Let nature take its course."

Wella, who is almost six, drops her pizza crust on her mother's plate. "What's *itscourse*?" she asks.

"Great question." Bets takes a bite of Wella's crust, then talks while she chews. "Uncle Tuck and Aunt Corie need to find out the answer."

"Right," I say. "And we're trying." I smile at my sister while I consider dropping my glass of water in my lap. At least then I could escape to the bathroom. Escape to anywhere.

"Mark my words." Bets peels off a fresh slice of pepperoni and hands it to nine-year-old Campbell. "As soon as you stop trying? That's when it'll happen."

"But, Mom." Cam's eyes go wide. "You always say we should never give up."

"That's right, baby. But you're a kid. With grown-ups? It's a little different."

"I don't get it," he says.

"Just eat."

We are quiet then, and I stare at my untouched antipasto salad. Later, after the kids leave to play in the ball pit, Bets leans over the table. Her corn-silk hair, a few inches longer and a few shades darker than mine, dangles into the pizza. I don't tell her.

"Seriously. You shouldn't be so stressed out," she says. "How long has it been, anyway?"

"I don't know. Six months. Maybe eight."

"That's nothing," she says.

I nod.

But it's something.

Believe me.

It's something.

Find out what happens next… Pick up *Guest List* today!

Discover more from
JULIE C. GARDNER

For new releases, deals and a free ecopy
of *Running with Pencils*, sign up here:
http://bit.ly/runningwithpencils

Made in the USA
San Bernardino, CA
08 April 2016